DRINKING THE OCEAN

DRINKING THE OCEAN

SAAD OMAR KHAN

A Buckrider Book

This is a work of fiction. All characters, organizations, places and events portrayed are either products of the author's imagination or are used fictitiously.

Published by Buckrider Books
an imprint of Wolsak and Wynn Publishers
280 James Street North
Hamilton, ON L8R2L3
www.wolsakandwynn.ca

Editor for Buckrider Books: Paul Vermeersch | Editor: Aeman Ansari | Copy editor: Jen Hale
Cover design: Natalie Olsen, Kisscut Design
Cover images: David M. Schrader / Shutterstock.com and EyeEm Mobile GmbH / iStock.com
Interior design: Jennifer Rawlinson
Author photograph: Ramy Arida
Typeset in Adobe Caslon Pro and Futura PT Cond
Printed by Rapido Books, Montreal, Canada

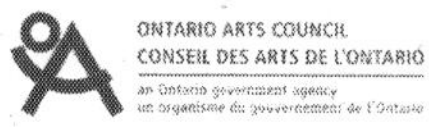

The publisher gratefully acknowledges the support of the Canada Council for the Arts and the Ontario Arts Council. We also acknowledge the financial support of the Government of Canada through the Canada Book Fund and the Government of Ontario through the Ontario Book Publishing Tax Credit and Ontario Creates.

Library and Archives Canada Cataloguing in Publication

Title: Drinking the ocean : a novel / Saad Omar Khan.
Names: Khan, Saad Omar, author.
Identifiers: Canadiana 20250158183 | ISBN 9781998408177 (softcover)
Subjects: LCGFT: Novels.
Classification: LCC PS8621.H349 D75 2025 | DDC C813/.6—dc23

For L.W.

PART 1
MURAD

Seek ye not water, seek ye thirst.
– Rumi, quoted in *Aphorisms of the Mohammedan Saints*

1

It had been seven years since Murad last saw Sofi when she appeared again, a spectre made flesh, a haunting thought turned into luminous form.

It was a Sunday, the night after his thirty-third birthday party. Murad was on the way to the subway, headed to see his friend Marco. He couldn't understand why Sofi's name looped endlessly in circular thoughts in his mind. It was the moments of transition when she entered his mind the most, imagining her life and all the permutations of what it could be now. Thinking of her was dangerous. Here, in Toronto, after they had last spoken, he made a covenant with himself, a pledge to let her float freely away from his soul. Yet now, when he let his thoughts go on unrestrained, he fantasized about meeting her, sitting down to speak and talk and connect the way he used to in those shining moments when he had first met her in London. And what would be the use of seeing her again? Would they talk over coffee, of lives continued in each other's absence, of marriage and work and God's fate? Would they speak without his wife, Samra, knowing, a thought that buoyed him with energy as much as it shamed him?

He couldn't even be certain of where she was now. Sofi was uncontainable, the possibilities where she lived innumerable – still in Toronto when they'd last met, in London where he first loved her, in myriad parts unknown. He was subdued by jealousy, thinking of the refined life he was convinced she led, the men who were her partners, the family she would have begun. Since he'd last seen her, in the years after he'd settled, found a career, made a home with his new wife, he still held her in his soul, concocting alternative versions of his life where she was always there, the singular thread that wove through his reveries.

There would be no daydreaming for the rest of the day, thought Murad before the subway stopped at St. Patrick Station. Marco would be a distraction. He was a former colleague who had worked briefly with Murad in the communications department of the bank before he left and went into business for himself. They were friends of a sort, the type of adult friendship born from shared work experiences that one feels the need to continue long after professional connections ended, an acquaintanceship solidified out of a sense of habit and familiarity. He was younger than Murad, awkward, but sincere and well-meaning. Marco reminded him of the stream of relationships that had passed through his life, the constant entropy of friends lost and gained. Coming out of the subway, crossing the wide avenue and walking the crowded streets under the merciless sun, he thought of how few friends he had, social engagements being limited by time or the pull of Samra back home. He realized how many of what counted as friends were hers, even if, out of a sense of generosity, she described them as "our" friends, friends of "our" family.

Murad walked toward Dundas Square, passing dim sum restaurants and a Japanese bakery where, even on weekends, a caterpillar-like line curved out the front door for people to buy overpriced cheesecake. He found the boutique easily, a European café where Marco wanted to meet. Marco was already seated when Murad walked in. Marco waved him over and embraced him enthusiastically when he came to the table. He had an unexpected guest: a petite, dark-haired woman, sitting in one of the café's many tan-coloured swivel chairs. "This is Laura, my fiancé," said

Marco, as she rose to shake Murad's hand. "I hope you don't mind that she tagged along." He didn't mind, of course, even if he found it strange, feeling as if Laura's presence was more purposeful than just a lack of alternative plans on her part.

They ordered French toast and eggs. Marco updated Murad on the freelance editorial business that he had started with Laura, a business partnership that had given way to a romantic one. Marco was talkative and effervescent, Laura polite, poised and quiet. He interspersed his enthusiasm for his life with questions about Samra and how Murad enjoyed married life. "Good," said Murad. "More than good, great."

Laura excused herself and left the table. Marco, briefly silent and contemplative, leaned close to Murad from his chair. "Between us, is it worth it? I mean marriage."

"I'd say it is," said Murad. "If you make the sacrifices to make it worth it."

"How can you tell?"

He thought carefully before answering. "For me, it was a way of starting over," said Murad, pausing for a moment, realizing his answer was less a response to Marco and more of a means of self-justification, a wall to keep Sofi from climbing over.

Laura returned, staring at her phone as Murad and Marco spoke. They had business to attend to, she said. They finished their meals quickly. As Marco paid for the group ("My birthday treat," he said), Murad realized how the brunch was an excuse for Marco to introduce him to Laura, almost as if seeking validation. They said goodbye outside the restaurant. Before they walked away, Marco put his hand on Murad's shoulder and turned to Laura. "I'm glad you got to meet Murad," he said. "He's one of the finest people I know." Murad smiled, genuinely touched, if slightly taken aback by the compliment.

Without aim or direction, with only a desire to walk and not to return home, Murad headed to the Square, thinking of how and why he had become so highly regarded in this friend's eyes. He remembered moments when they worked together, private conversations at lunch or after work, drinking coffee where he'd learned of Marco's life, his history of childhood stammering, bullying, loneliness, struggles at school, struggles finding work and companionship. He had the sense that Marco trusted him, an open heart available to someone who found those traits tragically rare. There was room once for connection, to be a comfort for people. His heart blossomed with the sense that Sofi would have been proud of that sense of empathy that she had seen in him all those years back. It was a thought that wounded Murad, a reminder of days when he'd wanted to share so much more than "compassion" or "empathy" with Sofi, words that wilted under the weight of his feelings for her.

Murad reached the Square. His eyes wandered from the billboards to a familiar face in the crowd across the street. He stared at her, the torch of recognition burning brighter – it was her, Sofi. Murad's eyes squinted under the sun's glare. She stood at the edge of the curb, anonymous bodies flanking her sides. A current ran through his heart as she glanced in his direction. The light changed, the rush of pedestrians started, and he stood watching as Sofi crossed the street. In the interminable seconds it took for her to stride through the congested crowd, he wondered whether he should make his presence known, whether to extend his hands to touch her, tap her on the shoulder, reignite conversations and cross lives once again.

A space opened in the crowd. Sofi came within a few feet of Murad. She took no notice of him, as if he were one more cipher in a sea of faces. Her eyes, black as the universe, were unencumbered by sunglasses. Her face seemed harried but warm and confident, small lines speaking to the force of age that only heightened her flawlessness. Beside her was a boy, a dusky-faced toddler, eyes as large as Sofi's that sparkled with the same mystery as her own.

He held a small ice cream cone in his left hand, the other hand holding Sofi's as they walked past. Murad stood still as pedestrians brushed against him, his head fixed forward without looking back to see what direction they went in. The clarity of the encounter overwhelmed him: that the child at her side was hers, the maternal Sofi he'd never known when he'd first loved her.

Daydreams had taken form. That face, her dark eyes, all brought into relief, with every step of his life leading to the present. *Don't look back*, he thought to himself. The wife of Hazrat Lut, the Prophet Lot, was destroyed for looking back at the home she'd once possessed. It was a childhood story his mother once told him that Murad pondered as he walked toward the shade of the subway's entrance in the middle of the Square. He climbed down the stairs, passing groups of children and a few worn adults grabbing the railing as they trudged up to the surface. The train waiting for him would bring him uptown where his wife waited, to the apartment where they shared a life. Into the darkness of the stairwell, before being bathed in the artificial lights of the yellow-tiled platform, he hoped he could cleanse his mind of Sofi again, even though he knew the impossibility of forgetting all he'd surrendered in the past.

◆

Time frays the edges of memory. It's one of the benefits of age, the way the years dilute the past. But Sofi didn't exist in those edges. Even as the light of the past dimmed, she was always there, shining in the centre of Murad's mind.

It was Samra who'd organized the surprise party the night before he saw Sofi. She had invited a handful of their friends: Jamal and Sarah; Omar and Neelofar; a former colleague from the bank, Althea, and her husband. Their gifts were food and dessert, and the night was spent eating and talking as a warm July breeze drifted from the windows of their apartment. They cut the cake afterward, Samra taking it from the fridge and placing it at the edge of their lone table, "Happy 33rd Birthday Murad!!" written with white frosting on a chocolate backdrop. Their friends took pictures of the evening: Samra's and Murad's arms around each other's waists, his wife feeding him a lone morsel of the first slice. He helped her clean up after the guests later in the evening, a wordless assembly line of trash gathered and plates cleaned and dried. Domestic order gave finality to the evening. The dishes given to them by Samra's phuppo, the dessert forks from the cutlery set his mother's cousin bought for the wedding – all were laid out delicately to dry on a towel next to the washbasin, displayed like a testament to the beginning of their marriage.

They went to bed quickly after Samra said her prayers. The lights went out, and she put her hand on Murad's heart as if checking for its beat. *She's become livelier*, he thought to himself. Even with people she'd known well, Samra shied away from large gatherings. She seemed pleased with the party, as if finding one more tool to be happy. She'd been sad for too long. Murad felt proud of her, proud of their marriage, even if that pride coexisted with the presence of Sofi in his life, a memory that lay in their bed like a third body.

They could never have children.

Murad assumed they would come naturally, a milestone to be reached in any marriage without effort. His first struggle, in the first months after the shaadi, was to lay the foundations for love – a type of love, he told himself, even a love that couldn't reach what he'd had with Sofi. It was the first summer they'd had with each other where her reticence had evaporated under the heat of the sun. At first, in the many walks they would take in the park, Samra would walk away from Murad, her face toward the sky, eyes closed, mouth widening in a closed smile as the light nourished her. He knew he had to give her time – these were her moments, his bride communing with the luminescent day. Eventually, he was able to enter her solitude, to become part of her world, their walking bodies coming closer together until they found comfort holding hands in public, a connection that took a long time to form.

Yet the unfulfilled next step never occurred. The hope they felt every night after they lay together diminished over time. Doctors, parents, friends, all had a multitude of explanations as to why they couldn't conceive. The help they received was meaningless, a tangle of science and folk wisdom that yielded no fruit of any sort. Friends of theirs suggested in vitro fertilization, a solution their ob-gyn discouraged given the expense, the difficulty and the uncertain chance of success.

Samra's mother was convinced someone had used jadoo, black magic, to curse her. Her solution – for her daughter to wear a taweez, an amulet containing Qur'anic verses – was met initially with scorn and frustration. It was only when the months stretched into years that Murad stumbled on Samra standing alone in their room one day, her mother's taweez over her neck, her hand clutching the amulet as if by pressing it into her hand she could break open its holy secrets. He came behind to hold her, pressing her back to his body. She was small, almost minuscule, next to his tall, thin frame. "I'm sorry," said Murad. Samra didn't respond and barely moved. He knew his words were impotent, even asinine, but he needed to say something to assuage her. For a moment, he felt a paradox – he knew that Samra felt more peace in the taweez and God than the warmth of his arms, yet he still felt close to her, a connection fully experienced as he absorbed her pain into his.

Samra's supplications became more pitiable. She wept to herself, even as Murad knew what her soul was undergoing, every barely audible whimper and dried tear blistering his heart. When she asked him to be more diligent in his prayers, to ask for God's intervention in helping them have a child, he did so, more for her sake than for any thought that things would change. Eventually, out of exhausted sadness, it was Samra who decided to abandon the cause, letting fate have its way. They resolved, without truly discussing it, that familial happiness would mean having each other rather than adding a new soul to the world.

The older generation found their capitulation to destiny unbelievable. Samra's parents – typically distant and respectful with Murad – voiced their objections to her directly through private shouting matches over the phone. Murad told his own parents of their plan not to try for children during one of his visits to their home. Abbu had retired from his bank job a few years after the wedding. It was an international bank, and he served as an executive, a position that had flung Murad, Abbu and Ammi across the world. From the Persian Gulf to East Asia and then to Canada, it plucked Abbu back from North America to work in Pakistan for the last years of his career. Canada ultimately won, largely motivated by a desire to be close to Murad and Samra and the grandchildren they had longed for.

The two houses his parents owned – one outside of Toronto and the Lahore property Abbu had inherited from his own father – had already been sold, their future lives now constrained to the functional if cramped apartment they bought just north of their son. They sat in their living room as Murad told them of their decision, his eyes staring at the floral red-and-black Afghan rug, ashamed to look at them directly. Ammi, Murad's mother, seemed surprisingly accepting. "Well, all that's written for you both," she said. It was only later that Murad realized how damaging the news had been to her. In subsequent weeks, Ammi did as she normally did, praying for the baby that could never be born, praying for a reversal of the destiny Murad and his wife had accepted. Her tendency toward sadness, which Murad hoped in her older years had abated, reappeared, manifesting itself in occasional sighs and long looks into distant visions only she could see. He often left her presence immersed in guilt, as if his failure to have children tipped the balance of her heart toward the melancholy he'd seen infect her for much of her life.

His father was less passive when Murad broke the decision. The news physically moved Abbu, his body sinking deeper into his armchair, out of hurt more than anger. The following weekend, after having lunch with his parents, Murad followed Abbu to the cramped kitchen as he carried the dishes with his increasingly arthritic hands. He ignored Murad's efforts to help him wash, preferring to roll up the sleeves of his white kameez and scrub the dishes and serving trays aggressively. After some silence Abbu asked Murad if he was feeling well. He said he was.

"Are you sure?"

"Completely."

"How are you and Samra with the decision?" Abbu asked, after some hesitation. "About the children?"

"We've accepted it."

"Did you just . . . give up?" said Abbu, as if unconvinced.

The sharpness of his tone saddened Murad. "I know this isn't what you wanted for the family."

"It isn't about what I want." His father shut off the tap. "I didn't want you to sacrifice being happy."

"We're not sacrificing our happiness," said Murad. "This is our way of trying another way of being happy."

"And this is your way?"

"It's not worth continuing on."

Abbu sighed. "And that's it? You two alone, by yourselves for the rest of your lives?"

Murad nodded. He told him they would be fine alone, together. Six years of marriage, he thought, of finding ways to bind themselves to each other and create the representation of love, if not full love itself. That alone proved that they possessed the resiliency to carry forward.

Abbu moved close to him. "I remember those days before you were married when you were at school. I remember how sad you were for reasons I could never know and how little I could do to stop it. When you told me last week how you'd given up on children I was terrified of you going back to that state again." His eyes, always strong, seemed to weaken and slink away. "I wish things were different."

Murad put his hands on Abbu's upper arms. "I don't worry about those things anymore," he said. "You shouldn't worry either." Abbu didn't smile as they embraced. His grip, so much weaker than it had been in his younger days, was still all-encompassing.

He couldn't tell whether he'd eliminated his father's concern over his mental state that day. Although Abbu never mentioned it, Murad was certain that the fear of generational extinguishment was on his mind. After some time, however, children and their absence became less of a topic to weigh his parents down. Ammi's sadness softened gradually. During every visit, her eyes looked at the world with less concern than her hopes for the afterlife. Her remaining days on this planet were for worship, prayer and recitation, insurance to protect her from the calamities of the hereafter. Visits to see her and Abbu left Murad with a sense of loss yet to be had. The pauses in their conversations, the clean emptiness of their apartment, all reminders of what would vanish when God would take them from this world.

Not all of life was tragedy and grief. Despite the disappointment felt for not having children and for breaking his parents' need for family continuity, the day he told Abbu they would be happy made Murad realize his words were not just instruments to calm his father's soul. He truly felt his words. The contented life as a couple could be made real. Hope – that thin shaft of light peering into the cave – was tangible, an object that he and Samra could grasp together.

This contentment changed at the sight of Sofi.

Murad often wondered in what ways memory consumed itself, at what age were appointments forgotten, names and faces mismatched. More confounding to him were those memories that still stained his mind. Memories like Sofi. She'd taught him about hope, of its absence and its necessity. Nine years since she'd left him in London. Seven years since he'd seen her again back in Toronto. Six years since he'd married Samra. Every day between the moment she'd walked away from him and the day of his wedding, he'd slowly accepted his capitulation to time, to the loss of her, shedding the possibility of a life in her orbit. His love for Sofi was a star collapsing, leaving an incalculable coldness in its wake, now brought back into the blazing present in one day.

Look at where she is now, he thought as he entered the elevator back at his apartment, back from seeing Marco, back from seeing her. A joke, it seemed, a cosmic farce, that all he wanted to let go, the fire of his feelings, could be spun back in his direction again to shatter the armour of the life he had built for himself.

He entered his home dazed, like a child fumbling in a dark corridor, looking for a mother's comfort from the terror of the night. Through the hallway, he saw Samra sitting on their brown armchair facing the window. She turned her head and said her salaams.

"Did you have a good time?" she asked.

Murad walked closer to Samra. He saw her tasbih in her hands. *Her piety hasn't diminished over the years*, he thought to himself. For a moment he envied that quality in her, that ability to keep her link with God solid and immutable. He had been like that once. Before Samra. Before Sofi.

"What's wrong?" she asked, jostling Murad from his silence. Her deep eyes burrowed into her husband, almost with suspicion.

"Nothing."

"Then why do you look like you're sick?" She rose from her chair and put her hand on his forehead.

Murad was touched by her gesture, her earnest concern. "It was strange seeing Marco after all this time."

Samra stepped back and continued to stare, as if searching for the past Murad had hidden from her.

"How is he?" she asked.

He summarized his time with Marco. Samra listened with full attention, the curled locks of her hair bobbing as she nodded her head. "I'm glad you both had a nice time," Samra said plainly. Beneath her reserve lay a natural sympathy and thoughtfulness for others, a quality Murad had always appreciated. But her care was limited to what she could see and witness. His inner life was an area she rarely ventured to explore. As long as they, the family of two, maintained a quiet peace, her curiosity was sated. A gentle soul, interested only in living in a gentle existence, he always thought, but passive where Sofi was restless, living a subdued energy compared to Sofi's incandescence. But how could he let Sofi shatter his new world? The marriage Murad and his wife had created – childless and resigned to a constructed happiness – proved false in comparison to what he imagined Sofi's life had become, a life kissed by fate.

"Anyway," said Samra, "the dishes are dry. I'll put them in before I say Zuhr."

"Let me do it. Go ahead and say namaz."

"Sure," said Samra. She paused before moving toward their bedroom. "Do you want to say your namaz afterward?"

She knew the futility of asking that question. Devotion was a memory to him, the lost emotion of a boy living in the soul's eternal spring. He knew of her unspoken disappointment, just as he knew she had the forbearance to accept his distance from God, in the hope he would return in due time.

"I'll think about it."

Samra said nothing more. She rubbed his arm lovingly and went into their bedroom. He went to the kitchen, the dried plates from the previous night waiting for him. From the kitchen, he had a view to the balcony window as he started to collect the dishware. The sky was clear, painted with a blueness that reached from heaven to touch the grey-brown buildings littering the city's surface. The sound of ceramic clanging against itself as Murad arranged the plates in the cupboard barely interrupted the apartment's silence. Ghosts lurked in the quiet, whispering to Murad as he asked himself all the questions that remained in his mind.

What has Sofi become?

Is she thinking of me now as I think of her again?

Am I to Sofi – like Sofi is to me – the ink in her skin that can never be removed?

2

It was only later that Murad realized how much the year he met Sofi had changed him.

He had spent New Year's Day in Lahore. The day was empty, without significance. In his room, Ammi had placed a calendar with dual Gregorian and Islamic dates, "January 2006" displayed prominently in black, with "Dhul Hijjah 1426" inscribed in bright green below. The years seemed interchangeable to Murad, an arbitrary jumble of numbers.

Spending winter in Pakistan had added to the sense of being unmoored in time. January in Lahore felt unreal, a betrayal of all Murad's childhood memories. He had often visited the city in summer, where the heat of the gardens in his grandfather's house overpowered him, where his soft body slept next to his mother in languid afternoons, the ceiling fans above them delivering a cool endless peace. Summers in Pakistan were spent away from school in the innumerable countries in which his father's bank had stationed them. When the family moved to Canada, the blistering Lahori heat still beckoned, the dried lawn of their suburban Canadian home never as green or moist as the monsoon-fed grass he remembered. The winter he was dropped to now felt dry and tasteless, only slightly warmer than the cold he'd left behind in London.

The university allowed weeks of holiday time during Christmas, and he was content to stay in London for the season. It was his parents, spending winters in Pakistan away from Toronto, who wanted him with them. Whether Ammi and Abbu simply wanted his company or if they didn't trust him to be alone by himself to stew in his own thoughts was unclear to Murad.

The morning of the new year he'd woken to face the early morning darkness, before the muezzins declared to the world how prayer was better than sleep and the chowkidars banged the gates with their bamboo staffs to remind everyone of the striking dawn. He didn't pray. Nothing pulled him toward God. He marvelled over it, how that distance between him and the Divine had grown. For miles around him were worshippers who accepted the agony of sleeplessness to wake and face that love. Thousands – but not him.

Yes, he marvelled over it – marvelled and agonized over it. What had he become now that he no longer yearned to be close to God?

He'd slept for a few hours the previous night, still exhausted, a tiredness beyond jetlag as he had already been in Lahore for a week and a half. He surveyed his room as he rose: It was small, arranged by his mother, with a bed, wooden bookshelf, television and dresser. Every object was ordered fastidiously, an arrangement made to approximate familiarity but instead felt sterile, like a guest room for visitors in transit.

He had forgotten to take his medicine before sleeping the previous night. Citalopram, twenty milligrams, half a pill before he slept. The pill performed as both an antidepressant and anti-anxiety medication. Murad sat up, turned on the side lamp and opened the dresser. The marble floor was cold against his feet. He laid out the pills on a tray in front of the dresser mirror, like an offering on an altar, with a plate, knife, glass and water bottle. Bisecting one of the pills, he swallowed one half-moon, returning the other half to the container.

Ammi and Abbu didn't know about the medication. They didn't have to. His haal, his "state," was how they referred to their son's condition in whispered conversations overheard between relatives and friends. "State" was vague, an unknowable mode of being, a barely articulate description of an impenetrable emotional situation. But how could they penetrate it when he could barely explain it to himself?

He went downstairs, passing his parents' room on the bottom floor, entering the moist chill of the open living room in front of the main door. Beneath the large, framed mirror near the entrance he lit the room's grilled gas radiator. Familiar photographs adorned the walls, collected artifacts of his family's history. The earlier photos were black-and-white and sepia portraits of men and women posing together wearing sherwanis and ghararas and karakul caps. In the dining room were framed pictures of the next generation on the sideboard in crude early colour, curated visual documents of weddings and family outings in different countries. Across the table, on the large ebony cabinet his father had purchased in the Philippines, were isolated pictures of Murad as a baby, child and teenager. There was even a photo of him in Toronto at Convocation Hall during graduation, standing unsmilingly next to his parents.

Looking at the pictures, he heard a door opening and the sound of someone walking toward the dining room. Murad knew it was his father. The house was small enough that the marble steps easily reverberated the hard slap of his heavy sandals. The noise didn't fit him. Murad always saw Abbu as unassuming and gentle, and the sound of his walking made him seem immense. Murad was still staring at his childhood photos when he felt his father embrace him from behind with his long arms.

"Happy New Year," said Abbu. "How are you feeling?"

"Thik hai, Abbu," Murad replied. "Were you awake long?"

"I woke up to pray and I've been awake ever since," he said, before letting him go. "What about you, young man? Why up so early? Not tired from last night?"

"I don't know. I actually wanted to sleep more."

"Did you pray? Did you say Fajr?"

Murad said nothing, then turned and smiled at him. His father wore a gentle grin that told him he expected no answer.

⁂

They had breakfast together. Abbu made scrambled eggs and parathas in the kitchen. Ammi kept sleeping. Abbu usually had someone to take care of their cooking needs. Rasul, their latest in-house chef, was apparently hopeless. Abbu mentioned their previous cook and all-around servant had left with his family without telling anyone, pilfering a few items before he took off down south to Multan. ("He even took that silver pocket watch I bought in Dubai!" Abbu added.) Rasul was still asleep, and rather than wake him, Abbu decided to cook for his son. His enthusiasm for food amazed Murad, although his need to make breakfast seemed to be more than parental indulgence. Since Murad had come to Pakistan, Abbu would often comment on how thin he had become, how his naturally light skin had evolved into a disturbing paleness. Murad never responded to these observations, not wanting to joke, dismiss or downplay them, wishing instead that his father would let them go and inquire no further as to what sickness truly ailed his son.

From the dining table, they could see the television in the living room. Abbu usually kept it on for background noise, set to a twenty-four-hour news channel broadcast from the Gulf. They glanced at the television from time to time while slowly tearing bits of their parathas and scooping up chunks of egg. Taliban attacks in Waziristan had prompted retaliatory measures from the army. Protests by the Muttahida Majlis-e-Amal and other religious parties closed down several major roads in Karachi. A short video clip showed a motley group of protestors with long beards carrying placards saying, in Urdu and English, "Musharraf is America's slave."

"You would think they would quit," said Abbu as he slammed

his plate on the table. “These people. Honestly, do you think they represent true Islam? I tell you, there used to be a time when people weren’t obsessed with religion the way they are now. Some said their prayers and others didn’t. That was the way it was.” He looked at Murad. “What do you think?”

“I don’t really know, Abbu,” he said, looking up from his meal. “Does it make a difference what I think? I suppose everyone’s trying to establish their own truth.”

Abbu’s face dropped slightly, looking almost hurt. It wasn’t a face Murad was used to, more pensive and preoccupied than the confident and steely countenance he associated with him.

“Can I ask you a question?” asked Abbu. “Have you been saying your prayers?”

“No,” said Murad, shaking his head.

Abbu said nothing.

“Are you disappointed in me?”

“No,” said Abbu. “Not disappointed. Saddened, for you.” Behind the table, the early morning light shone through the window’s iron grating. Abbu turned toward the glimmer as if looking for an answer to a question he was afraid to ask. Perhaps this was clue number one to explain Murad’s “state”: a slow erosion of the habit of worship, a lack of will to pray that could spiral into a larger loss of faith. Before coming to Pakistan from London, even before coming to London itself, he had felt the marrow of that faith being sucked out, not because of politics or the weight of religious oppressiveness, but more simply, the loss of majesty he’d once felt from tethering his life to God. Devotion seemed faint and without lustre. But was that really the cause of his constant sadness or the result of it? Murad was as unsure of that as his father was.

“When I asked you,” Abbu continued, “if you said Fajr and you didn’t say anything it” – he paused for a moment – “it seemed like something or someone had emptied you from the inside. The last time we were in Canada I could feel it. You were going into yourself more and more."

Murad couldn't detect any disappointment in Abbu. He wouldn't blame him if he was disappointed, anyway. When they'd first come to Canada, Abbu would take him to jummah on every Friday bank holiday. There were no masjids nearby, only ad hoc musallas in random libraries or warehouses. They were unimpressive if not ugly spaces, but there was a purity in them that Murad detected nonetheless. The other worshippers sat attentively at every sermon, their faces in silent concentration as their eyes looked downward when saying namaz. After time, with every Friday prayer, Murad saw beauty in those faces sculpted by love, a devotion he wanted to imbue in himself. He became disciplined in his rituals, waking up long before class started at dawn, even finding abandoned rooms or empty stairwells to pray in during school hours. God equalled connection, and worship was an armour against loneliness and the unbelonging he suffered. The seed it gifted blossomed into something else. After school was done, when every dusk prayer would conclude, he would stare through his room's window. In his solitude, the cold sky became clearer, every colour deepening, the world seeming different, more bountiful, as if purified by grace.

Abbu's voice changed to a louder but slightly blithe tone. "So, tell me, young man, what's wrong? Can I help you with anything?"

Murad said there wasn't anything wrong. There was nothing left to say. Abbu kept eating slowly. Murad left the room, unable to face the look his father had, the expression of silent, pursed-lip frustration one has when they feel they've failed someone.

His parents' room was next to the staircase. Murad crept past its door before going upstairs. The door was ajar. The sun beamed through half-open blinds. Ammi was half-asleep in the fetal position, wearing an old shalwar kameez. He entered the room and sat on the chair next to her bed, stretched out his arm and took her hand, which was extended almost off the mattress. City noises were audible again, sounds piercing through the window into the room: horns, motorcycles, the occasional shrieks from the crows that lurked in the back pathway.

Ammi's hand was soft and warm in the cold room; the rotating heater they usually kept on barely worked. She rustled in bed and turned to Murad. He let go of her hand and closed his eyes as he moved his face toward her. He felt the touch of his mother's fingers on his cheek. When he opened his eyes, she'd withdrawn her hand.

In the sparse light, the shadows on her face made her look wizened. Murad rose slowly when she turned her face away from him, his movements tight and drawn out. He had known since his first memory of her that Ammi lived with a personal sadness all her own. He had an inkling of what caused it, even if she never spoke of it. Nani, her mother, passing away when she was a teenager. The sense of losing her home once she married and had to leave Pakistan, her grief still shadowing her, leaving her feeling safe only in religion. This was all speculation on Murad's part. Perhaps it was something deeper than that, a darkness that infected the bloodline.

He gazed at her before he left the room, reels of memory spooling out in front of his eyes. Moments as a toddler with Ammi laughing in a dusty park in Dubai as he ran into her arms, stumbling in the patches of sand. Her kisses when he recited al-Fatiha from her personal Qur'an for the first time without error or hesitancy. Times of joy spliced with other moments seeing her hunched over kitchen counters stifling tears, or lying in bed as he'd just seen her, ignoring the day and facing away from the world. In her most extreme moments, when immobilized by the darkness within her, Abbu would lead Murad away from her room, leaving her to stave off whatever jinn was tormenting her through prayer and solitude.

He closed her door gently, climbing the stairs to his room,

thinking of how much his mother was a part of him. Had he inherited her sadness? It was a clue, one that was even more frightening for its plausibility. Faith could be won back – blood, unchangeable, could never be refined.

3

There was a tacit agreement between Murad and his parents that his visit to Pakistan would be short and quiet, which essentially meant little time was to be spent with extended family or acquaintances, and he would move as little as possible outside the home. This was an almost impossible task, especially in Lahore, but they respected his wishes for the most part. He knew they were happy to simply have him close by, and he was relatively content being homebound, reading, thinking of thesis topics to be researched when he returned to London and watching histrionic news reports of the country collapsing. The research topics that had passed through his mind – on Sunni jihadism in Pakistan, on the history of the Durand Line in creating instability in the region – were those designed to elicit topical interest in his supervisors. There was no instability in his surroundings, no apocalyptic war zone that he found himself in when in Pakistan, none that existed outside his mind at least.

One Sunday, Ammi took Murad shopping with her to Liberty Market. He didn't think about saying no. She appropriated one of the bank's drivers and told him to come along with her to get vegetables. The market was unusually busy. Despite their proximity, it took twenty minutes to enter as the traffic choked the main road off the roundabout where most of the stores were located. They finally got through the rush of vehicles and stopped alongside Variety Books, where several teenagers dressed in rough-hewn sweaters and cheap, stained jeans rushed the car, offering everything from Kashmiri chai to pomegranate juice.

The driver parked, and Murad and Ammi left the car. He followed Ammi into a passageway, one of many that snaked through the market, full of mannequins, young men selling clocks and old women combing through multicoloured fabrics at the endless row of tailors. It had rained that morning; the sky was now clear, and light draped every trinket, shawl and covered head along the narrow path.

Ammi passed right through the crowd with determination. "We need to go to the back where the vegetables are," she said. Murad followed behind her, staring blankly at the dupatta on her head.

Outside the passageway was an open-air alley. Cauldrons of boiling oil lined one side, full of dozens of frying samosas. Next to the parked motorcycles on the other side were mounds of crisp vegetables in wicker baskets. Ammi went to the first stall she saw and lazily picked up a bell pepper out of a pile. Speaking in Punjabi, she asked the seller with the large facial birthmark how fresh they were. She glanced over at Murad occasionally as she spoke to him with a look of deep consternation.

"Abbu was saying you stopped your prayers," she said, swatting away flies as she pawed at the radishes and coriander leaves.

Murad wondered how honest he should be. After a pause, he said yes.

The seller handed Ammi a bag. She placed four bell peppers inside, reached in her purse and gave him a single red-coloured note without speaking. "Why did you stop?" she asked plainly.

"Why is it important?"

He expected an angry response. Instead, his mother's eyes softened as she passed the bag of peppers for him to hold. "It is, beta," she said. "At least you thought saying your namaz was important. Abbu and I have been noticing you –"

"– withdrawing into myself."

"Yes. You're not the same since we last saw you at graduation."

"Actually, I am."

Ammi's face tightened with a hard, stony look that seemed both irritated and confused. She turned around, and Murad followed her as she started backtracking through the passageway toward the car. Standing beneath the awning that stretched across the stores in the market, they could see the driver a few yards away, bald, compact, wearing a sweater and dark slacks, smoking while leaning lazily next to the trunk. Behind him, in the grassy field in the middle of the roundabout, dozens of coloured head shawls swayed listlessly as the kaprawallahs dried them in the open air.

Ammi caught the driver's eye. He immediately dropped his cigarette as she beckoned. "You know," she said, breaking the silence, "everyone always admired the way you prayed. The family, the community. No one told you to do it. You did it by yourself, because you thought it was important."

Murad stared at the shawls, looking like fragmented rainbows staked into the ground. "It's hard," he murmured in a sharp, constricted voice. "It's hard for me to be that person anymore."

The white sedan slowly crept to the side. The driver waved away a pack of begging children tapping at the side of the car.

"It's school, isn't it? Are you just not enjoying it?" she pressed.

"It's not school. It's not anything."

She turned to look directly into Murad's eyes. "If it's nothing, why stop? You think praying isn't important now? It is. It always will be."

The driver pulled up, stepped out and opened the right rear door with the efficiency of a hotel valet. Murad and his mother entered the back seat. Moving past the car window, he glimpsed a couple walking in the green space in front of the storefronts. No more than a few metres away, he could see them clearly: young, no more than a few years older than he was, the man thin and stylish wearing jeans and a crispy white dress shirt; the woman wearing a red and white shalwar kameez and a tan shawl. She held her husband's arm gently as she stepped over a crack between the steps leading to the shops. It was a personal display of affection normally unseen in Pakistan that surprised Murad. The woman laughed, her head turning to her side, allowing Murad to see her heart-shaped face, the largeness of her eyes, the sincere doting look given to her husband. He created a story of their lives: the man, an Aitchison College graduate, probably Ivy League–educated, the woman also an international student in a foreign university who promised her parents to get engaged the second her degree was done. For a moment, the flatness of his heart spiked upward, a stirring of envy directed at the man, imagining he could one day possess what he had, the warmth of his life, the warmth of bare skin at night.

It passed through his mind quickly as the driver started the car, making their way on the short trip home without speaking. Ammi took out her tasbih and fingered each prayer bead carefully, saying alhamdulillah ("All praise is due to Allah") quietly under her breath. Traffic on M.M. Alam Road was slow. It was time for a late lunch, and cars full of families were clogging the street, moving bumper to bumper, desperately trying to get to the various new novelty Western restaurants along the road.

After they returned home, Ammi went inside, while Murad remained alone in the car for some time. The call to prayer started, turning into a blanket of white noise as every mosque in the area competed for both volume and piety. The driver came to his side after the azan was done, asking if he needed to go anywhere else.

"Do you need to go back to the office?" asked Murad.

"Yes, sir," said the driver, meekly. "Your father needs the car and I would like to pray."

He took the bag of peppers and, before leaving the car, noticed Ammi's tasbih crumpled on the seat to his side. The beads were the colour of dried blood, polished to a luminous sheen. He picked up the tasbih and brought it inside, giving the peppers to Rasul, who took them morosely to the kitchen. Before going upstairs, from outside the open door, he saw Ammi in her room saying her prayers, her hair covered, her thick limbs glued to the floor in prostration. He thought about sneaking in and placing her tasbih on her bedside table. She rose on bent knees, her hands on her thighs as she gave her supplications. Murad looked at her carefully, left the doorway and went to his room, the blood-red beads still in his hand.

4

Two days later, Murad's parents accompanied him to the airport before he left for London. Salman, the bank driver, picked them up, giving the family an open-palm salute as he opened the back doors for Abbu and Ammi. Murad sat in front, closed his eyes and tried to sleep. Throughout the ride, he heard his parents speaking of him in low voices, asking themselves if he would be all right alone. He wasn't interested in listening.

In a sleepy haze, he heard the driver say something about a security alert. Murad opened his eyes – they'd arrived at the airport. Two policemen with submachine guns were opening the trunk, while another peered underneath the car with an inspection mirror. It took no more than half a minute before Salman was on his way again. He parked the car, unloaded the bags and brought a trolley for Murad. Abbu told Salman to wait at the car. The family walked toward the red-brick airport, passing in front of the blue-uniformed security personnel allowing passengers through the gate. Before Murad entered security, Abbu gave him a hug.

"Be good," he said.

"I will."

Ammi gave her own embrace and stroked his cheek. "Be good. Really. Everything is going to turn out for the best."

"I know it will."

Abbu said nothing more. Murad stared at them for a moment

before taking his passport and ticket and turning into the line of trolleys, burning with guilt as he realized he'd just told a lie.

There was a time when flying evoked a sense of purification. They had travelled so much as a family that Murad was used to seeing flight as a way of cleansing one mode of life away in favour of another, the soul exchanging realities like an actor rolling through different roles. But if the soul is damaged, what benefit could travel bring? All countries merge into one flattened plain. And what of the cause of the damage itself? Pakistan only highlighted the many possible causes of his depression. He'd read that depression emerges in the early twenties, the college years, more than in any other time. Perhaps that was enough of a cause: the strange, blessed curse of being young when youth was at its last and most heightened stage, where the heart absorbed every emotion without armour and protection. Whatever the cause was, he felt sick of searching for a reason – it was and would be a task without end with little to be gained.

Christmas break was over. The new year was ahead, not as time to be used but as a resource too easily consumed. The flight was crowded, like every flight he had been on to and from Pakistan, full of noisy children and sullen adults drained of energy. He sat in between two rotund men in an exit row. The jet's engines droned in a subtle roar. He was relieved at first to leave, the country a reminder of a past he wanted to shed. He hoped London would be a means of escape, just as he felt in September when graduate school began. Perhaps all that was needed was a small miracle, finding a niche of his own, a job or a relationship that would give him an excuse to stay put in Britain, away from Toronto, Lahore, parents, family and community. Even his friends were becoming more distant as time passed. Desperation welled inside him. The connections he had to God and people were more tenuous. Spiritual death and the possibility of a physical death were becoming one and the same. He hadn't found that miracle or niche he needed in London yet, and he often felt gripped by the fear that failing to do so would mean going further into a lethal black hole where God, family or white pills could not support him.

The passengers beside Murad slept through most of the flight with an enviable ease. He didn't try to sleep, spending most of the voyage looking through the window on the exit door, staring at the starless sky, waiting to land.

5

Paddington Station looked more like a wartime aircraft hangar than a Tube stop. Murad exited the train from Heathrow, towing his large suitcase behind him through the sparse crowd of students and businessmen in long coats. He went outside and took a cab to the university residence in Southwark, happy the driver had taken minimal interest in speaking to him. The residence was a large brown-brick building, the university emblem affixed to the front gates, making clear its distinction from the working-class council estates surrounding it. As he fumbled inside his right pocket for his pass card, he caught the eye of the half-asleep security guard through the door window, the same thin, expressionless Nigerian guard who always took the late shift. The guard recognized him, and rose to open the door. Murad said hello as he entered, a perfunctory greeting the guard didn't return.

He walked through the vestibule and then across the inner courtyard to Block A, before taking the elevator to the fifth floor. As he unlocked the door to the flat he shared with five other fellow postgraduate students, he heard murmurs and muffled laughter from the shared kitchen. Ignoring the noises, he dragged his bags to his room in an exhausted stupor. The room was claustrophobic, the foldout bed and the functional flat-top desk within a few feet of each other. Outside the windows he saw the council estates behind the residence blending into the night, looking more like dimly lit castles than decrepit housing projects. A handful of young men stood laughing and drinking under the streetlights below, dressed in thick hoodies and camouflage gear.

Noise seeped in under the door from the hallway. Murad could hear his flatmates and other unknown voices in the kitchen laughing. He bowed his head next to the door, trying to grab snippets of the conversation, feeling a world away from the sense of joy he heard. He stopped trying to parse words out of the din of laughter and went to bed with his clothes still on.

Brief thoughts of Toronto before coming to London reeled in Murad's mind before sleep. He remembered that university counsellor he had seen for one session. Her name escaped him. He had gone in with expectations that lowered further the longer he was there. At the beginning of the meeting, while his eyes wandered to the row of fake roses that lined the windowsill overlooking a grey-brown parking lot, she asked him why he thought he was depressed.

It was a question that struck him as both asinine and circular – he'd come to her to provide that answer to him. He said nothing other than a blunt "I don't know." It was only now, in London, he could muster an answer to himself. His desk lamp was still on, creating solid streaks of light in the semidarkness, golden bars that allowed for spools of memory to flash like a film. These images were of random moments: a student walking alone along the perimeter of his elementary school's park-playground on the first day of school in Canada; a child sitting silently in the corner of a humid Lahori living room while his parents in front of him bickered over some comment an in-law had made; being invited to dinner in the second year of undergrad to the home of an older grad student and his partner, staring at every glance they made to each other, trying to suffocate the feeling of isolation with their every mutual touch.

Murad closed his eyes, lest the miscellany of random pain overwhelm him. There was more where that came from, the nebulous mass of imagery masking any moment of connection he may have felt to people, or to the world.

He knew the answer to the counsellor's question. There was no stronger explanation beyond a mass of loneliness weighing inside him for most of his life, a quiet throb pulsating louder here in London, this uncentred centre of the world.

Murad woke the next day with the frantic realization that he had class. He took the bus to his tutorial for Professor Burke's "International Relations of the Modern Middle East" course. The Thames was slate grey, blending perfectly into the colour of the sky. He arrived late to the new room in East House, an all-wood enclosure that looked more like a corporate boardroom than a place for study. A discussion on Iran's new leadership was going on. Before long, it devolved into a debate on whether the West should attack the country. The class was divided between a few American students in favour of a "calculated first strike" and the rest of the class, indignant that such a suggestion would even be considered. Those latter voices were the loudest, the most self-righteous, the shrillest. Murad defended the Americans, less out of any love for their ideology, and more out of annoyance at their detractors. Their sanctimony was a liberal, secular quality shared by many of the religious Muslims he'd met as an undergrad, full of a condescension that was both self-satisfied and slightly aggressive.

The class characterized much of his experience at the university: surrounded by egotistical intellectuals or the children of wealthy foreigners sent to an expensive London university for no other reason than status. He spent that afternoon in the library, his usual haunt. When he returned to the residence, one of his flatmates,

Kristy, had taped a note to his door: "COME OUT TONIGHT. KING EDWARD @ 7. WILL GET DRUNK EARLY."

Murad didn't want to go. He knew how the night would unfold: Kristy would overtake every conversation with random friends of hers he didn't know. Murad decided to go anyway. It was easier than finding an excuse not to.

Despite its name and outward upscale appearance, the King Edward was no different from the two other pubs near school. The décor was plain, the walls splashed white, with random student photographs of various Southeast Asian locations adorning the beams that joined the ceiling to the floor. The lights gave a bluish tint to the mixture of plastic and metals chairs, barstools and tables inside.

Murad had been surrounded by alcohol the moment he'd come to London. One Thursday in November, Philippe, a Belgian classmate from his international development class, had bought him a drink: vanilla Coke and rum. Rather than give a typical religious excuse not to drink, he accepted it readily. "It's my pleasure to make you sin," said Philippe, with the calm joy of one doing something both sneaky and magnanimous when he passed the small glass drink to Murad. Since then, he'd had drinks on two more occasions, each time with an added level of shame, every glass chipping away at his sense of self. He usually hated alcohol and felt an unspoken pride in not drinking, as if by adhering to a basic sacred law he was more spiritually disciplined than those around him, a superiority more acute when around other Muslims who drank. On the surface, he pretended to be tolerant of them, while feeling an inner sense of disdain. Since he'd come to London, he soon realized that disdain was really resentment, a subtle bitterness against those who could enjoy themselves without inhibition. He thought giving up this insignificant bit of religious doctrine, even for a moment, would be liberating, but it never was. Whenever he drank, the shame was always there, and he felt stuck in his values, a yoke that tethered him to God.

The pub was busier than expected. Murad pushed through a group of women speaking in Italian before finding Kristy at the bar with drinks in both her hands.

"You got my message?" she asked, raising her voice above the crowd.

"I did. Is everyone in the city above eighteen in here right now?" he asked.

"Just about." She looked Murad up and down. "How are you doing? You okay?"

"Just tired," he said. This was partially true – jetlag and the time difference between London and Lahore made him feel phased out of reality. He sat on the empty seat next to her. "But I didn't want to disappoint you."

"I'm going to have to disappoint you, though."

"What do you mean?"

She raised the glass in her right hand toward one of the booths on their left.

"What am I supposed to be looking at?" asked Murad. She said she was getting a drink for one of the guys she'd met on New Year's Eve. Murad said it wasn't a problem and he didn't mind being alone. It was a lie. He resigned himself to the anger and annoyance of her abandonment, taking for granted the disappointments even casual friendships provided.

"I knew you'd understand. I'm really sorry. We'll catch up soon," she said, placing her hand on Murad's shoulder. He was certain she noticed his irritation. Kristy waded through the crowd toward the booth. He caught brief glimpses of her and her companion between patrons at the bar. Her new friend was tall and dark-skinned, as well-dressed as the rest of the people there, mostly students coming from their night classes, adorned in the same chic, dark, semi-formal winter wear everyone on campus wore. It was a virtual campus uniform: a collection of soft-weave coats, scarves, leather gloves and knit sweaters. Murad quickly adopted the look, partially as a form of assimilation and partially as a means of giving himself some inner buoyancy through stylishness. He looked at Kristy and her date as if staring at a painting: her hand touching his in the faint light, the look of her piercing fascination, every basic romantic element brewing an insidious bitterness within him.

Random classmates bumped into Murad and stopped to chat. There was Abraham from Nigeria, who engaged in casual small talk before awkwardly inviting him to sit with his two friends once he noticed he was alone. Murad declined politely as Abraham and his friends made their way into the recesses of the pub to find a booth. There was Sharon, a friend of a now-distant friend from Toronto. Despite meeting a handful of times before in Canada, he remained a stranger to her. When she saw him, she came up and introduced herself before asking if they knew each other. With restrained impatience, he said they did, through a mutual friend Kevin, and that this was perhaps the fifth time they'd spoken. Either out of confusion at the brusqueness, or having a genuine need to leave, she excused herself without further discussion, turning toward a gaggle of laughing women who mirrored Sharon in almost every way, in her height, her blondness, her aloof self-confidence.

Then there was Matt, New Jersey–born, New York–raised, one of the students in the morning Middle East tutorial, the one who'd instigated the conversation on Iran. They had spoken a few times last term, most of their conversations revolving around politics and religion that had little to do with anything learned in class. He sat down on the empty stool next to Murad, ordered a drink and thanked him for taking his side during the day's debate. "I felt like you were looking out for me in class today," he said.

"Thank you," said Murad, attempting to be diplomatic, "although I was just playing devil's advocate. I can't say I agreed with everything you said." That failed to stop Matt's ingenuous friendliness and his offer to buy Murad a beer, which he said no to after a moment's temptation.

Murad caught a glimpse of Kristy sharing a kiss with her new boyfriend. Distracted, he thanked Matt again for his offer, shook his hand and headed for the door. He walked along the cobbled streets toward the library, where he sat on one of the concrete slabs laid out near the front entrance. He was upset with his behaviour at the pub, at his rudeness with Sharon, at the hurried way he'd withdrawn himself from Matt's company and his envy at Kristy's newfound romance. A gush of frigid air glided past, reminding Murad it was still winter. He sat alone, the cold of the concrete penetrating his body, humiliated by a sense of failure in his inability to connect with others so easily.

The space in front of the library was surrounded by a multitude of tables and chairs, as if put out prematurely in anticipation of spring. A handful of students stood around, even at this time of night, some smoking, some texting their friends. On Murad's left was a raised, covered platform with wooden benches where three women sat, two of them smoking and talking feverishly, the third in a red coat standing with muted patience as she nodded and smiled, absorbing every word. They spoke to each other with a lightness and ease that Murad resented, in much the same way paupers envy the rich.

The smoking women broke off from their friend in the red coat and headed into the café. The woman in the red coat waved goodbye, her body illuminated by streetlights and the buildings around them, an outline cast in crimson. She stood a few metres away from Murad, staring in his direction. He stared back, mystified. She walked toward him, allowing Murad to see her face with more clarity: tanned, brown skin; eyes dark like obsidian, looking at him with a familiar, assured look. Her hands were in her pockets, every step unwavering.

She came up to him, hovering a few feet away. "You look sad," she said.

He was at a loss for words. The woman waited, looking into his eyes as if demanding an answer.

"No," he said, plainly. "I'm not."

"Are you sure?"

He hesitated. "No."

"You didn't look happy from over there."

"That obvious?"

"Yes. That obvious."

He felt a sense of immediate, strange comfort with her. "We know each other, right?"

She brushed her hair back. "Yes, from Burke's class. I'm sorry if I'm disturbing you. It seemed like you needed company."

"No. You aren't disturbing me."

"You seem like one of those people who does fine without company."

"At times," said Murad, shifting in his seat. "Maybe I could do with some company right now."

"I guess I broke through the barrier then," she said, sitting next to him on the concrete slab, her hands still in her pockets. Her hair fell onto her forehead before being blown back by a gust of icy wind. The floodlights behind them illuminated her face, accentuating her high cheekbones.

"I guess you did," he said, smiling. "Why do I get the feeling that I know you?"

A small group of students speaking Mandarin passed in front of them like a flight of birds. "We went through this," she said. "I'm in Burke's class."

"No, I mean, I feel like I knew you from before."

Her companions, dressed in dark winter coats, emerged from the café with coffees in their hands, off to spend the rest of the night studying. The young woman got up slowly from the cold slab to join her friends.

"You didn't answer my question," he said. "Have we met before?"

She gave a warm smile that was both reassuring and evasive. She turned around and began to walk away.

"Can you at least give me your name?" Murad asked as he stood up.

She turned around again, her body facing him. "It's Sofi. We should have coffee sometime. Maybe then you can see for yourself if I really make good company or not."

"When?" he asked.

"Soon," Sofi said.

6

Burke's next lecture was Friday morning. Murad sat at the back, hearing his digressions on Palestinian nationalism, most of which revolved around a series of offhand anecdotes about his past personal relationships with various PLO politicos.

The class shuffled out the moment the lecture was over. Burke himself picked up his coat and rushed out the door with equal speed. Aside from Murad, the only student remaining was Sofi, her red coat carefully placed on the chair to her side. Her eyes were cast down as she collected her belongings, and he was briefly menaced by the thought that she had already forgotten him. She slung her handbag over her left shoulder and buttoned her coat, moving with confidence, as if she contained a strong granite centre within her. She looked up and appraised Murad. "You're looking better today," she said.

"Compared to what?" he asked, getting up from his seat, putting on his coat in the same, slow, methodical way as she had. "The other night in front of the library?"

"Yes. You know, my offer still stands."

"For coffee, you mean?"

She finished buttoning her coat and stared at him, nodding. "Or something similar."

"Coffee's fine."

"Tonight then?"

"Sure," he said, softly. "Tonight's good."

Sofi's face broke out in a wide, half-moon smile. "Good. Meet me at Notting Hill Gate. About eight."

They exchanged numbers. Murad said nothing as she left the room.

◆

Back in the residence, before Murad left to see Sofi, he received a call from Abbu in Pakistan. It was late in Lahore, he thought, close to his father's usual bedtime. Abbu and Ammi made sure to connect with him often, enough to give him space while also ensuring they could monitor their son. He never looked forward to these calls. Even if he understood a parent's need to be attentive to his condition, they always felt like intrusions into his London cocoon.

Abbu started with a few words, asking Murad how he was. He usually answered the usual script of questions with monosyllabic annoyance, but tonight was different. His father seemed tired, not the weariness of night, but a strange inner exhaustion. "What's wrong?" he asked him.

"I was worried about you. More than usual."

"Why so?"

Abbu hesitated. "What are you going to do after all this?"

Murad felt blindsided, the directness of the question arousing an irritation he tried to stifle. "Abbu, what are you asking?"

He could hear his breathing through the line. Abbu seemed more troubled than impatient or angry. "Do you know Sonny Uncle?"

"I don't."

"No, you wouldn't, you were probably too young to remember. He was one of my juniors in the bank when we first came to Canada. He mentioned his oldest son got engaged in Toronto. He was asking about you. He was wondering what you were doing, what you were studying. He also mentioned his daughter Farzana. She's doing her BBA in Chicago now. He asked me if you'd be interested in talking to her."

"I'm not," said Murad, more bluntly than intended. He vaguely remembered Sonny Uncle – a tall man, hooked nose, quiet and aloof, who assisted his father in setting up their house when they had first arrived in Toronto. He had no memory of Farzana, a ghost of the unknown past Abbu seemed to have resurrected.

"I know, beta jaan. I told him it was too early for both of you. But there will come a point after you graduate when you'll have to think about having these conversations." Abbu sighed. "And finding work. And knowing where you want to be so that when you do have these conversations people know you're a serious person."

"Don't ask me when that time is going to be, Abbu."

"I know that too. Just know there's a world after London you have to return to." He sighed. "Anyway, I don't know why this was on my mind. I'm always worry about you drifting away from me."

He had little more to say but to tell Murad to take care and have a good night. Murad felt suffocated when Abbu hung up. He knew why he'd called. This wasn't a lecture. It was the flipping of the hourglass, a signal, his father trying to bring his son back to them, and to the future they wanted for him. He regretted his curtness, his disengagement, even if he knew his father's fears were valid, that within some space inside him there was the Murad that wanted to abandon all he had known to this point, to live better, to live differently, even if that same space contained the Murad bound and tethered to the love he had for his parents.

He needed to forget the conversation. No thoughts of Abbu or Ammi, of Sonny Uncle and his son and daughter, only of Sofi, only of what thc night could bring.

Murad got off the train a few minutes before eight, expecting late-night workers and partygoers to be swarming the station. Instead, the place was empty, as if the city had been recently evacuated due to an unknown catastrophe. It was only when he arrived in the vacant space of Notting Hill Gate, observing its aged brown arches and hanging lights, that he had paused to notice a change within himself. Blankness was nowhere to be felt. Even in the drab confines of the station, the world felt reformed, the trip to see Sofi charged with possibilities he couldn't grasp.

He waited beneath the stair exits that led to the city surface until he heard the sound of the train. The station was soon populated, people streaming together like a waterfall, indivisible. Out of that crowd he saw Sofi gliding past the turnstiles in his direction. She apologized for being late.

"I wasn't waiting long," Murad reassured her. "What next?"

"I promised you coffee. There aren't many places here that sell coffee at this time, but I know one. It's a bit out of the way. It'll be easier to take a cab there than to take a bus. Interested?"

"Of course. Let's go."

♠

The night was beautiful and electric. As the cab sped through narrow streets, Sofi kept her eyes fixed on the glass pane separating Murad and her from the driver. This part of the city was unfamiliar, every building draped in multiple colours like a Caribbean flag. The taxi moved in jerking starts and stops to avoid the drunken revellers stumbling between cars.

They got off near a pub somewhere on Portobello Road. Murad hardly noticed where they were. He followed Sofi through the doors with delicacy. The lights were a warm red. Bitter smoke permeated the air. The room was narrow and confined, the bar flanked on the right by a series of booths. A band in the back played a ska version of a Joy Division song.

They sat at one of the booths in the corner. Sofi left Murad to soak in the atmosphere for a moment as she went to the bar. She returned with two drinks, placing one on the table in front of him.

"I lied," she said, taking a seat. "They don't have coffee, just Coke."

"That's fine," said Murad. "I never asked why you wanted to come here."

She shrugged her shoulders. "It seemed like an interesting place."

"Have you been here before?"

"A few times with friends," said Sofi, sipping on her drink. A heavy bass line from the band made the booth shake; at the same time Murad surveyed the bar, noticing groups of hipsters flooding in from outside.

"Tell me about yourself," she asked.

He shifted forward, taking his drink in his hand. "I rarely meet anyone who's curious about me."

Sofi stared at him thoughtfully, as if processing what she'd just heard. "When I saw you the other day," she said, eyes directed to Murad again, "you seemed like a person who didn't have much spirit left in him." The redness of the lights in the room grew deeper. Sofi wiped her dark, chocolate hair from her face. "I want to know why that is. I think the best way to know someone is to hear about their life from the beginning."

He synopsized his history to Sofi: born in Lahore, travelled around the world and wound up in Toronto by the time he was twelve.

"Do you miss it?" she asked. "Travelling, I mean."

He sighed and leaned back. "Not really, no. Once I was able to stay put in one country, I realized how displaced my childhood was. Sometimes I think my childhood would have been better off if I had been raised in one place."

"Is that why you're sad all the time?"

"I didn't realize I looked sad all the time."

"Whenever I've seen you, you've looked sad."

"That's interesting," he said, pushing his glass off to the side of the table. "Now I am really convinced I know you from someplace."

Sofi laughed. "Trust me, I don't know you from before. We do have a common connection though, besides Burke. Maybe we met each other before in Toronto at some aunty-organized davat or desi get-together back there, I don't know. I only know you from class, back from the beginning in the fall. There was something about you that was different. You seemed intelligent. Reserved. Polite. You're always talking to people, and you always seem so open. When you're with people you seem happy, and the second you're alone your face drops."

Murad shifted in his seat, not sure what to make of her observation.

"There has to be something behind that," Sofi continued. "A woman?"

He turned his head to look at the pink-haired bartender. She was serving drinks to two twentysomething men with pierced ears, both of whom were wearing a mix of leather and army camouflage. Murad never talked about relationships – rather, his one relationship, if he could call it that – with anyone. Her name was Marjan. They'd seen each other, for a time, in the last few months before Murad had finished undergrad. He didn't want to tell her about Marjan, yet Sofi's presence was warm and attentive enough to let down Murad's guard to reveal all: about how they'd met in Toronto, the classes they'd taken together, how they'd formed a relationship.

"How did it all end?" Sofi asked.

"It just ended," said Murad. "It was actually my decision for the most part. We weren't compatible. I was much more religious at that time. She was a passionate person. Worldly. We used to go out a lot, partying and clubbing, which I hated, but I did it anyway, just to be with her. Sometimes she would get me to dance, and sometimes I did, badly. Mostly I would sit back, watching her, thinking she was the most beautiful thing in the world. And I felt guilty for that."

Sofi looked puzzled. "Guilty?"

"There was a plan that was laid down for me when I was a kid. I would get good grades in school. I would be a doctor, or an engineer, something like that. I would find somebody in our community to marry, or, alternatively, have someone found for me. And then we'd have children of our own and the cycle would continue. But I didn't become a doctor or engineer. I changed my path, and I still don't think my parents are happy with that."

"So where did the guilt come in? What does that have to do with Marjan?"

He sighed. "My family's traditional. I wasn't allowed to date when I was a teenager. I had no problem with that. In fact, it wasn't something I even thought of. Then Marjan came into my life. She was from a different world. Her family were exiles from Iran, passionately secular. She was an atheist." Murad pulled his drink back toward himself and fiddled with the straw in the empty glass. "She used to tease me. I think my religiosity was funny to her. I think she saw it as something anybody with any sense would run away from. She said it didn't fit with her personality, anyway."

The temperature in the bar increased. The cover band ended their set. A new act was already performing, a stately, statuesque woman singing a soulful Roberta Flack song in a deep contralto.

"Did you love her?" she asked.

"I don't know. I may have thought I did, but we broke up."

"I know how that is," Sofi said, her voice almost inaudible. She looked toward the singer and then at the ever-increasing crowd. She remained silent, her mouth pursed. "I think I understand you now."

It wasn't that simple, Murad thought. He wanted to tell Sofi everything: how for months he'd taken antidepressants, and how, at times, he would still feel despair assault him like a black wave. He wanted to tell her that perhaps he was always like that, and that the breakup only made things worse. He wanted to speak of his mother, the sadness he feared he'd inherited, and the disconnect between himself and the God he had once loved so dearly. Sofi had put Murad at ease, and yet he felt wary of telling her everything.

"Talk to me. Whenever you want," said Sofi, breaking the wordless air around them. A waitress came to pick up their glasses. Sofi thanked her with a smile, then turned back to Murad, looking serious. "Don't be alone, and don't be a martyr."

"I'm not good at revealing myself."

"You didn't do so bad revealing yourself to me tonight. Make it a habit with me. You said you felt you knew me. Why not consider me a friend? Look, let's make a contract. The next time you're feeling depressed, let me know. Don't be stoic. Agreed?" She smiled, her temples crinkling, the sharp edges of her cheekbones rising. "Do we have a deal?"

Murad laughed and said yes. He was enthralled by Sofi's openness and warmth, yet her overtures of friendship were also mystifying. "I appreciate all this," he said. "But I also have to ask – why me?" Sofi looked at him quizzically, as if unsure of the meaning of the question. "I mean, why take such an interest in me?"

She pondered the question. "Because we share a similar sadness." Her face wore a mask of thoughtfulness and discomfort, as if wanting to unload a burden. "My brother died, over two years ago."

Murad moved back in his seat, struck by the nakedness of her disclosure, an instant flash of grief and tenderness jolting him. He said he was sorry, which he was. Sorry for her loss. Sorry for the pain. The inner ache throbbing inside him for her felt new, a signal from a past life reminding him of his capacity for openness, to feel and to desire feeling. How he wanted to, for a brief moment, extend his hand to touch some part of Sofi and scour the hurt blemishing her soul.

As if ignoring his condolences, oblivious to the silent yearning in his eyes, she continued on. "It was a car accident." Sofi stopped herself, shaking off her urge to say more. "I know what it feels like when despair takes over." They sat in the pub in silence for a few minutes longer until the end of the singer's set, as if all that needed to be said between them had been settled.

There was a world in Sofi that opened up to Murad. He wanted to continue the conversation, to explore the terrain of her life as she had with him. As if suddenly remembering a forgotten errand, she reached into her coat pocket for her phone and examined the message on her screen. "I'm so sorry," she said. "I have to go meet a few friends."

They left the pub together. Murad asked her if he could walk with her to where she needed to go.

"No need, but thank you," said Sofi, buttoning her coat to the very top. "It's just down the street." He stared at her, bereft of anything more to say, wanting to extend his time in her presence.

"How about this?" asked Murad, struck by an idea. "Let me buy you dinner next week after class. I owe you that much after tonight."

"You don't owe me anything."

"Then do it as a favour to me."

She laughed. "Fine. A favour. Just for you."

She turned around and walked up the street, her red coat almost iridescent under the glowing streetlight.

7

For the next few days, Murad spent his time as he typically did: in his room, sitting in stillness, or doing research for his final papers at the library. He began walking around outside the campus more often, taking in the city. Southwark was full of concrete underpasses, looming construction sites and new buildings, all jumbled together. Each venture outside was an excuse to hover in thought over Sofi. In only one night, she had broken down the palisades surrounding him, uplifting his heart, while also providing a window to see the wounds she kept in reserve. This glimpse into her inner life was a gateway, an opportunity to connect and to soften the shell of solitude that encased him.

The call of kinship broke that spell, if only momentarily. On Saturday, he received a call from his mother's sister, Ruqayyah Khala. Khala, the only family member he had in London, was a former schoolteacher, retired from both her job and the world. She'd been in touch infrequently since he'd stopped living with her and moved into residence in Southwark. Each time she called, it was from a familial sense of duty, partly out of sincere concern, partly out of affection for his mother. That Saturday, however, she had a more specific reason to talk to Murad: Ammi had asked her to give him something and Khala wanted him to pick it up. He didn't ask what it was, and accepted her invitation with simple acquiescence.

She told him to come the next evening for dinner at her home in New Cross. As Murad rode the double-decker southward, he noticed how uniform the houses started to look, all one deep brown melded together, allowing no room for uniqueness. They reminded him, in their conformity, of the houses in their suburban Toronto neighbourhood, without the spaciousness that Canada afforded.

The clouds darkened as Murad stepped off the bus. He crossed the street and pushed aside the low, rusted gate in front of Khala's house. She'd given him the key to the front door when he'd first lived with her, allowing him free entry to her home whenever he wanted. He climbed the staircase, a narrow series of carpeted steps steeped in the smell of dank English moisture, hearing the sounds of two children speaking Yoruba over a football match behind the door to his right. Khala rented the lower unit of her house on occasion; the turnover of renters was high. At the very least, gentrification hadn't infected this part of London. Despite the drabness, it had a vibrancy and grit that Murad found appealing.

The door, with its peeling paint, was unlocked. This was reckless and unsafe, but typical of Khala's trusting nature. The flat was only slightly wider than the stairwell and seemed brighter than the evening itself, as if whatever little illumination the city received came from within its walls. Murad walked into the kitchen and surveyed the scene: large pots spread everywhere, clothes lazily draped over a dinette table, a withered flower placed in a dirtied vase. In any other home it would seem a mess, yet nothing seemed chaotic or misplaced. The room had its own order and rhythm that he hesitated to disturb.

Instinctively, he knew she would be in the small back room typically covered with old, geometric Pakistani carpets and membrane-thin curtains that barely shut out the streetlights. The pervading silence was a sign that she was praying. When he opened the door, he saw Khala on her janamaz, facing a dusty bookshelf, wearing a dark blue shalwar kameez with a white dupatta covering her hair, her limbs prostrate on the floor. Murad stayed in the doorway, peering in with arms crossed as he bent down and leaned to the side of the frame, observing his aunt as she prayed with reverence, not wanting to disturb the delicate communion he saw inside.

♦

She hugged Murad closely after she finished her prayers. They ate together in the early nightfall in comfortable silence. Since he arrived in London in September, he noticed how different she seemed from the Khala he had known before. She was drawn into herself, much more self-contained than when Murad saw her on family visits to Pakistan or Britain. She was his mother's only sister, relatively closer in age to Ammi than to her three older brothers. His grandfather was liberal enough to let one of his daughters go to school abroad, even with his wife having passed away too soon, and making his loneliness all the more acute. He was not, however, quite so liberal as to allow her to study literature rather than medicine. She did so anyway, and disobeyed her father further by staying in London, putting her at even greater odds with him and the rest of the family.

As they ate dinner, Murad remembered an instance in Pakistan years ago when he was around ten. It was the first time he had even heard of his aunt's existence. He sat with several of his maternal cousins at Jehangir Mamu's dining table, the ceiling fan coating them with a light breeze as Mamu's oldest daughter, Nazneen, taught them all how to play rummy. Murad stole bottles of RC Cola from the kitchen for the older children with his accomplice, his youngest cousin, Haniya. When they came back to the table, Nazneen, Nazneen's cousin Hussein from her mother's side and Nazneen's sister Kiran were talking among themselves in the insular way older children do when they exclude younger children from a conversation. As Nazneen shuffled the cards, Kiran talked about the extended family, counting off the number of cousins and aunts and uncles, noting that Ruqayyah Khala was the odd one out, a childless anomaly that she found strange. Murad asked Kiran who Ruqayyah Khala was.

"You've never met her?" asked Kiran.

"How would he know who she is?" said Hussein, pouring one of the colas into a glass. "Whenever he comes to Pakistan, she's back in London. Whenever she's here, Murad's everywhere else."

"Ruqayyah Phuppo's the oldest sister among the adults," said Nazneen with authority, using the title phuppo to indicate her father's sister. Murad sat next to her. As she finished dealing the cards, she looked at him, back erect in her wooden dining chair. "She lives alone in England."

"How come she never married?" asked Haniya innocently, standing on top of her seat at the end of the table.

"Because she wanted to have lots of boyfriends," said Hussein.

"Not everyone wants to have a family," said Nazneen, almost defensively.

"She's too modern. That's what always happens to people when they live in England," said Hussein, holding his cards in his hands.

"Who told you that?" asked Kiran.

"My ammi said so," said Hussein, as if an adult reference was needed to justify his argument. "She should have been married a long time ago. She should have had a family by now. It's not right the way she lives."

"No one knows why she never married," said Nazneen, sternly. "And it's nobody's business why." She stared hard at Hussein as she took the cards she had dealt to herself in her right hand. "We're her family," she continued. "So let's stop talking about this. And don't judge her so much, Hussein."

The conversation ended there. Murad heard more of her story from cousins eventually, and even met Khala twice in Pakistan during subsequent trips back home. She hardly looked or seemed "modern" in those short, formal meetings. In those times, however, he was still weighed down with the notion that she was a bit of a pariah: too Westernized, too liberal and liberated, fundamentally too mysterious, the sister and aunt no one wanted to talk about. He was always certain, as Hussein suggested, that she had a string of men in her life – something the family went out of their way not to speak of – who shared her buoyant energy. The fact that she would turn that energy toward God at this stage in her life wasn't surprising. Murad assumed it gave her a sense of order she needed as she aged and grew to accept the increasing prospect of loneliness at life's end.

Murad often thought about the contrast between his aunt and his mother. They both embraced their faith with complete fullness, yet their paths were divergent. In a different life, could Ammi have also broken free from her father's pressures to marry? Would she have been happy to have been alone and liberated? Murad dismissed these thoughts. She had never shown an ounce of coldness to Abbu or himself. If her mother had acquiesced to his grandfather's need to settle her daughter down, she did so dutifully and without complaint, as far as he knew. In years past, he did wonder why, among all the Pakistani families he knew, he was an only child. He wondered if Ammi never really wanted children, and only through some mistake he had been born. It was only when overhearing spare conversations with his mother in bed and his father trying to console her that he heard the words "babies" and "miscarriage." Murad didn't understand the impact of what he'd heard until he was older. Still, the truth was never clear, and his mother's unspoken past, her life before he entered the world, remained nebulous. Whether this and the early death of her mother encouraged her depression and whether this fuelled her need for God's shade he could never say.

A window was open. As they ate, a quick breeze tried to snatch the dupatta from Khala's head. For dinner she made roasted chicken and potatoes, both bought fresh from a halal butcher store on Old Kent Road. She ate with her hands, removing the soft flesh from the bone with great concentration. Without raising her eyes, she asked Murad if he had prayed Maghrib, the evening prayer, before he left the residence.

"No, Khala. I didn't."

"Why not?"

The question was gentle, and he answered the only way he knew how: "I don't know."

Khala stared at her nephew as she slowly tore through the chicken's flesh. "When you were a boy, your ammi made you recite the Qur'an all the time when you visited Lahore. Your qira'at was beautiful. I used to tell your mother how good you were, and how I wanted to record your voice on tape. What happened to your recitation?"

"I haven't been keeping up with it," he said, digging into the food on his plate.

Her face was contemplative, as if pondering a mystery. Murad broke the silence by apologizing to her.

"For what, jaan?" she said, her voice calm, her green eyes sparkling.

"For not visiting more. I've been feeling guilty about it."

"There's nothing to feel guilty about."

"I've just felt like I've been ignoring you and leaving you alone here, by yourself."

"But, jaan," she said, putting a piece of chicken on his plate, "I never feel alone." She looked at Murad carefully. "Do you feel alone?"

"Sometimes."

Khala finished her meal and left him to finish his. She walked to her back room and returned with a book, an old Victorian tome with frayed, yellowing paper. "I almost forgot to give you this. Your ammi wanted me to pass this along to you," she said. She laid it next to Murad with the same tremulous reverence she gave the Qur'an. In bold letters the title read: *Aphorisms of the Mohammedan Saints.*

"For me?"

"Yes. My father gave it to me before I left for school in London years ago," she said, waving her hand on top of her head in a backward motion, as if indicating the distance between the present and the past. "I think it's the right book for you. It might make you feel less alone."

He took the book from her without looking at it and placed it in his bag.

Murad left Khala soon after – she needed to pray again before she slept. She stroked his cheek before they said their goodbyes and he descended the steps back to the streets. Their parting was almost wordless. Khala had lived as a virtual hermit for so long it often seemed like she was more comfortable with silence than with words.

When the bus arrived, Murad climbed the stairs to the top deck and found it almost completely packed, filled with South London rudeboys, chavs with hoodies and Burberry hats, old white women and a girl speaking Bangla. He pulled out the book his aunt had given him and began to read. The yellowed pages were illuminated in the artificial light, and the architecture of each letter held his attention on every page. One passage stood: *He cannot glance away without glancing back. His desire is lit again.* Murad tried to imagine what sheikh or mystic had written it. Perhaps it was someone who lived in a cave, spoke to God and felt an overwhelming force of love so powerful that the world seemed foreign, even repugnant. He understood why his aunt and his mother felt this book was important, reckoning that it held a sacred resonance with Khala since she lived in her own New Cross cave. In her devotion, he had wanted to be like her at one time. God, at this point in his life, was a distant abstraction. The only thing he could think of was Sofi – she was real, fully present in the flesh. An uncomfortable, impious thought came to his head: that Khala and his mother were lone figures in a cave in search of a force that had never existed.

As the bus careened into the late evening, Murad put his cheek against the cold plastic window and watched the rain. Thinking of Sofi, he realized that this was the first time in quite a while that he had felt anything resembling happiness.

8

Murad received an email from Sofi the next day, a message without a subject, only a sender ("Jilani, Safiyyah") and a single sentence ("call me ANYTIME if you want to talk"). He saw her again at their next class, gazing at Sofi as she listened attentively to everything Burke said. When the lecture ended and before he could speak to her, she left the classroom quickly, as if rushing to a more pressing event.

He went to the library after class and thought about her sudden disappearance. Undergrads preparing for mid-term exams and equally ambitious postgraduates doing early research for their theses littered every section of the circular, three-story library. Murad found a lone table and made an effort to do some research for his class on internal migration. When he finished working in the early evening, he felt focused and lucid, his mind free of the clouded haze that often weighed it down. He went outside and sat on the same concrete slab where he had first met Sofi. The sky's leaden greyness was darkening, and Murad found himself surrounded by small, atomized groups of students huddled together. He thought about the email she'd sent him. He had no reason to call her. He had nothing that he needed to say, no wound that needed to be tended. There was only an absence felt, a persistent emptiness without her presence.

He dialed her number. She picked up. For a brief moment, Murad hesitated to say anything.

"Sofi, it's Murad," he said, finally.

"Hi," she said, almost too casually.

"I got your message." There was silence. He fumbled for words. "I got your message, and I thought I should call."

"Is everything all right?" she asked, her voice sounding more concerned.

"No, no, everything's fine. I saw you in class and you left so quickly that I didn't get a chance to ask you about dinner. I made you a promise, and I'd feel like I'd be losing all my manners if I didn't follow through with it."

"I don't doubt you're the type who'd fail to keep a promise, Murad," said Sofi. There was amusement in her voice, the tone light, soft and comforting.

"The answer's yes then?"

She laughed. "Is it a date?"

"Two people sharing a meal. Let's leave it at that."

There was a pause on the other line. "Where and when?" she asked.

Murad looked around at the slate, anemic buildings surrounding him. "Any place that's not school."

At her suggestion, they were to meet in Covent Garden, near the station, for lunch on Saturday. Covent Garden on any given weekend was exactly what Murad had hoped the city would be when he'd first arrived in London. It truly seemed like the centre of the world, visitors and residents alike blending together with seamless fluidity. He hurried to the restaurant off Long Acre that Sofi recommended. It was a bistro, half-spilling into the street, with metal chairs and tables covered under a broad canopy. He saw Sofi to his right as he entered, sitting at a small, rounded table in front of the window. Her coat was draped over the back of her chair and she wore a thick, white, high-necked sweater. She peered outside and turned to him as he walked toward the table, without any trace of anticipation, as if waiting for someone else.

"You're late," she said, before Murad could greet her. She rubbed her hands together, her elbows on the table.

He apologized, removed his jacket and took the seat across from her. "How are you?" she asked.

"I'm fine."

"That's good," she said absently, staring back through the window. A waiter came by the table. They both ordered the soup of the day.

"I had a realization last night," said Murad.

She turned and gave him a quizzical look. "What?"

"We've been talking about me all this time and I haven't asked anything about you."

Sofi took one of the breadsticks from the container on the table and delicately broke it in two. "I said I wanted to get to know you. This has nothing to do with me."

"This shouldn't be a one-sided relationship, you know? We are getting to know each other."

Sofi nodded her head. "Maybe. I guess you're right."

"Okay," he said, leaning forward. "We started at the beginning with me. Let's start at the beginning with you. Where were you born?"

"Here, in London." She explained how her father had been a petroleum engineer, doing work with BP in Britain when she was born. He also had an accounting degree ("A genius with numbers," said Sofi). The family left for Dubai around her first birthday. She spent a few years in private British schools in the Gulf before work dried up for expatriates. They decided to immigrate to Toronto rather than go back to Pakistan or England.

Murad listened attentively, comparing her experiences to his, checking off all their commonalities: the same country of origin, the same globetrotting family history, an underlying sense of dislocation. As she spoke, the sense of familiarity he felt with her grew.

"Do you feel at home here?" he asked as a waiter came with water. "In London, I mean."

"I'm good at making myself feel at home anywhere."

"I think I'm the exact opposite of you." The waiter brought their soup, quicker than Murad had anticipated. "I try to find home in far-off places but never succeed."

"Have you tried in any place other than London?"

"I suppose not," said Murad.

Neither one of them spoke for a few moments. Murad needed to restrain the urge to ask about every aspect of her life. Outside the window, he watched men and women in dark pea coats stepping carefully across the cobblestone pavement, as if ice covered the surface. They bore a solitary elegance, sharp-featured faces peering into their phones or walking with a determined pace to destinations unknown without companions, weaving through each other like lone atoms repelling each other.

They spoke in short bursts as they ate. Murad began to feel a wariness in Sofi as she asked him questions about how his week had gone and what he had been up to since he last saw her. She seemed distant and preoccupied. Murad thought of the other night and the pain he saw in her, feeling a deep, inhibited sense of sadness at the thought of the reservoir of grief she possessed. His answers to her questions were more verbose than he was accustomed to give, almost as if he had to make up for her quiet reticence. Stories about his family seemed to interest Sofi more than any other detail of his past few days at school. He told her about his recent visit to Khala's home on the weekend. She seemed fascinated by her and her newfound religious conviction.

"She sounds like a fascinating woman," she said.

"Yes," he said, looking down at the table. "A fascinating hermit."

"Maybe she's comfortable being alone."

"You're probably right," Murad said, slumping back in his chair. "She gave me something the other day. A book, actually. It's a collection of sayings from Sufi saints, mostly bits of poetry with added commentary. It's one of those collections that was popular with educated European Orientalists, people fascinated by the culture of the East, those types of people."

Sofi leaned forward. "Do you remember any of it?"

Murad shrugged. "I just flipped through it."

"Yes, but what did you think of it? What did it make you feel?"

He thought about the question. "Conflicted," he finally said. "I think at one time a book like this would have meant something more than it does now. All these poets write about God with this overwhelming, almost self-pitying longing. I remember this one passage that goes 'anyone who has been deprived of this hurt is unfortunate, anyone is cowardly who has no pride in this pain.' At least that's what I remember from it."

"The pain you feel when you're far from God," said Sofi. She cocked her head to the left, her eyes wandering to the distance. "It's beautiful."

"I thought so too," he said, taking a sip of water from his glass, "for a moment. But the more I think about it, I feel the ridiculousness of it all."

"Why?"

"Whatever this saint meant, I'm sure he was completely sincere. But I can't take it seriously."

"What is it that puts you off? I don't understand," asked Sofi, her right elbow on the edge of the table, her head resting in her palm. The sound of dishes crashing to the floor silenced dozens of conversations in the restaurant. Someone made a joke about one of the waiters being fired.

"I'm trying to figure out why Khala gave this to me," continued Murad. "It's one of those typical things that religious relatives give you, you know, some religious tract, a book of du'as, something like that. It's weird to me that she wanted to give me a book of poetry, of all things. I read passages like that one and I think to myself that Khala wanted me to learn something about being –" Murad struggled for words.

"Empty," said Sofi, as if completing his train of thought.

"Yes," he said. "It's a funny thing when you live alone like that for so long. Some people like being alone, but I really don't think Khala is like that. I think being solitary was something she just accepted. You use religious messages like that for solace, as a confirmation that whatever pain you feel by being alone has divine justification."

"That's not what I think," said Sofi, shaking her head. "She's not justifying anything. When you stopped talking to that girl, Marjan, how did you feel?" She looked at Murad with intense focus.

"Sad. I felt as lonely as you would imagine anyone would in those circumstances."

"And you felt 'empty' too?"

"Of course." He nodded with his eyes closed, as if acknowledging the obvious.

"But you said you never blamed her. For all your sadness, whatever you want to call it."

Murad shook his head. "No, I never thought it was as simple as that."

"So what was inside this emptiness?" asked Sofi. "Even empty spaces have something. I don't know your aunt, but I don't think she's lived an empty life."

"Why?" he grunted. "Because she had God?"

"Yes."

"And I suppose any pain she feels is justified, right?"

"You're assuming she's feeling pain. Loneliness and being alone aren't the same things. Sometimes you find something valuable in being by yourself."

"Yes. Maybe there's value. Maybe you can achieve something

or do something great with it. But I don't think Khala is that type of person. What I do think is that she's someone who never could fit in anywhere. Not here, not with her family. She got tired of being alone in the world and just gave up on life. God is just an excuse for apathy."

"Is it an excuse for you?"

"I don't know," he said, exasperated by the conversation. "God's just not good enough anymore, let's leave it at that."

"Meaning what?"

"As a lonely child, He seemed enough for me. There was love there, even if I didn't realize it at the time. But the sinners had their way it seemed. The non-believers seemed fine without God. Teenagers live the life of flesh and self-indulgence, and they seemed happier for it. Happier than I was. And I wasn't sure if whatever bond I had with God wasn't self-deception, just me trying to invent a universal love to suit my needs. I still couldn't tell you if that's true or not."

Sofi looked at Murad with sympathy, her eyes soft and moist. He asked her if she wanted to take a walk in Covent Garden after receiving the bill from the waiter.

❖

The sidewalks teemed with pedestrians moving at their own pace and rhythm. Sofi walked beside Murad standing upright, her eyes looking forward as if oblivious to the world around them. He was always considered relatively tall by his family, taller than most other Pakistanis at least, yet next to Sofi, he felt almost miniscule, as if the poise with which she walked balanced out their differences in size.

"Can I ask you a question?" he asked.

"Of course," she said, raising her voice above the crowd.

"Where does 'Sofi' come from?"

She laughed. "Whenever someone asks me, I say it's just short for Safiyyah."

"Isn't it?"

"Partly. When I was a baby, my father swore I would grow up to look just like Sophia Loren. We had the same dusky features, or at least he thought so. The name just stuck."

"I think your father did you a disservice," said Murad. "Sophia can't compare."

Sofi smiled briefly at him and kept walking.

They reached Leicester Square Station almost inadvertently, the Underground's blue roundel appearing across the street like a beacon. Sofi turned to Murad and said calmly that she had to go. He was taken aback by the suddenness of her leaving. Her face looked drawn and sad, miles away from the confidence he was now accustomed to seeing.

"Yeah, sure," he said. "Okay."

"I'm sorry," she said. "I think it's best I just go."

"What's wrong?"

She looked at him wordlessly with the same bleak expression.

"You can tell me," he said, his hand unconsciously reaching out, wanting to touch her.

Sofi shook her head and bit her lower lip, as if contemplating some mistake she had just made. She turned around and merged with a group of Japanese tourists as they crossed the street, looking to both sides of the road to avoid the traffic. Sofi disappeared, the brightness of her coat vanishing into the station, occluded by the crowds. Murad stood in place, beneath theatre signs, bewildered by the sudden change in her mood. The distance he felt from Sofi pierced him, leaving him almost literally breathless. He wanted to bridge the gap between them, convinced he could uncover whatever was troubling Sofi and help her to heal, and to reciprocate the gift of healing she was giving him.

9

He was changing. It was a gradual transformation, as if his emotional life was being eroded and reformed into a new landscape. It seemed that he had lived solely on a single featureless plain, without marker or horizon. And now, he discovered an aperture, leading him into a world inflamed in red, the red of life, with all the possibilities of existence available to him.

Sofi was responsible for this. She had led him here. The deeper he travelled toward her, the more liberated he felt from himself.

Marjan was the closest comparison to Sofi that Murad had had in his life up to that point. There was something of Marjan in Sofi, a confidence and inner strength; as well as a deeper, more unknowable, quality. Vivacious and warm, Marjan could still never understand his inward moments of sadness. Sofi could do more than understand – she lived a similar sadness. It was the possibility of sharing that sadness that freed him from the boundaries of his own selfhood. The more he felt he could know her, to go beneath Sofi's veneer, the further his past and his desiccated inner world would fade.

One afternoon, Murad wandered around the grey path toward the Kingsway. The stone austerity of the buildings remained cold in the grim spring. Beneath one of the buildings, where the noise of the road could be heard and the city seemed to peer into the insular university life, he saw Sofi sitting on the steps, her legs together, leaning forward with her hands folded on her lap. Her face was stoic and worn. Winter had died out, and patches of sun broke the sky's greyness. Sofi looked upward, as if trying to peer beyond the building in front of her toward that light. Her eyes shifted down to him as he came closer. When she smiled, he felt a pulsating joy.

"The sky looks beautiful today," she said, before he could say hello.

"It does."

"What've you been up to?"

"Reading a paper. 'Statecraft in a Unipolar World.'"

"Heady stuff," she teased.

They laughed. She apologized for being aloof lately. Thoughts that she might have fallen into some private distress troubled Murad as much as the idea that the connection he had with her could break. He asked if something was wrong. She said no. Sofi looked forward at the cobbled street. "It just seems so ridiculous," she said. She turned back to Murad, her eyes black as the ocean but still luminescent. "I'm terrified of time some days."

"What do you mean?"

"Having it slip away." She clasped her hands together and placed them underneath her chin as if she needed support for further contemplation. "It's a big world that just keeps on turning."

"The world has to move."

"Does it have to move this quickly?"

Murad wanted to laugh. He noticed, instead, something in Sofi he hadn't fully realized she was capable of: angst. Her universe in that moment seemed large, complicated, but also full of untold worries and pains.

"I want to do something for you," he said.

"Like what?" she asked.

"I want to take you somewhere."

She looked at him and nodded. "Fine," she said. "Take me."

♦

They were free. The early afternoon was endless, as if the day, out of mercy, gave no sign it wanted to end. They took the Tube to Waterloo to see the London Eye. Neither one of them had been there. Murad suggested it as a way of getting away from school and imbibing the city all at once. Sofi spoke little on the way there, her general silence feeling comfortable rather than strained. In the pauses in their conversation, he studied her, careful not to let her see him lingering over each detail. She wore lipstick, a rich vermillion that almost shone in contrast to her light-brown skin, her face often deep in thought, contemplating the world around her. They walked toward the Eye when they reached Waterloo, standing out clearly from the leaden sky like a giant bicycle wheel rising out of the Thames.

They stood in line to enter one of the pods. Tourists surrounded them, a multitude of languages leaping out of their mouths as they waited in the queue.

"I love it here," said Sofi. "All these people."

"You don't get sick of the crowds?"

"I love them. In the crowd, I feel tethered to something."

Murad bought tickets for both of them. It took another queue for them to board the wheel. They were corralled in the pod with a dozen other people: a family of four, with children speaking in a middle-American lilt; a couple, who seemed newly married, speaking what sounded like Tamil; three giggling girls with Birmingham accents who looked like first-year university students; and another couple who spoke in hushed tones, clinging to each other so closely it was impossible to discern any accent beneath their cloak of intimacy.

The pod itself felt barely stable as the giant wheel started to turn. Murad stayed close to Sofi, who braced herself at the glass window, peering out with childlike wonder. Light broke again from behind the clouds as the wheel gently revolved. In quiet gasps, Sofi turned to Murad to point out the attractions: Big Ben, Parliament, Lambeth and Westminster Bridges. He had, by now, become less of a tourist and more of a temporary resident of the city, absorbing its personality, its natural cynicism, its self-absorption and aloofness. He realized, gazing as much at Sofi as at London, that she was infecting him, with her enthusiasm and with the innocence he saw in her. They shared the view together from heights that made the water shine and every building look ageless, monuments of a world worth abiding in forever.

As the wheel turned and the capsule descended, he felt Sofi tugging at the edge of his coat. "Thank you," she said.

They left the Eye and crossed the promenade next to Jubilee Gardens. Sofi had a habit of walking slightly ahead of Murad when they were together, her gait quick and almost oblivious to his presence. Eventually she slowed and they moved in unison beside the thin trees bordering the Gardens. She took her hands out of her pockets. *I could take one of those hands*, thought Murad. They were only inches away from each other. She didn't wear gloves, and with the wind bursting bitter from the river, he was struck with the notion that her hand was his to hold and his to comfort.

Toward the end of the promenade, they decided to get something to eat. They turned the corner and walked aimlessly until they found a chain store that sold sandwiches and coffee. They grabbed some food and ate at one of the small, perfectly square wooden tables near the exit. Murad was unusually talkative, gossiping about teachers and students, at least the students he had met over the school year that he found cold and self-absorbed, a trait he reckoned was typical of universities filled with the elites and the wannabe elites. He realized that he was beginning to rant. "I shouldn't be so harsh," said Murad. "There're a lot of good people here too."

"Yes, there are," said Sofi.

"I used to be able to see the good in people more," he continued. "I was more open-hearted."

"To see the good in others you have to be good yourself," said Sofi aphoristically. "But you are a good person. Today you proved it."

He asked her how so. "By wanting to make me happy," she said. "It's not that common a trait. Not as common as it should be, anyway."

Murad couldn't stop himself from smiling.

They continued to eat. It was late in the afternoon, and the coffee shop was packed, the most noticeable voices being the London patter of the women at the cash registers ("Who's next . . . Can I help you, please? . . . Fank you").

Sofi finished her sandwich. "My brother was like that. You remind me of him. He really cared about people. It came naturally to him."

A sombre tone took over her voice. Murad was flattered with the comparison to her brother. "What was his name?"

"Sikander. A strong name, my father used to say."

"I'd agree."

"He wasn't always so strong. He was sensitive. A sensitive heart like yours." Sofi's face briefly glowed in the light of a lost memory. "All gone now," she said, almost to herself.

Murad tried to think of something to comfort her. "Not everything's completely gone. God has ownership of our past, present and future, someone once said. I used to think there was something comforting in that notion, at least at the time I felt closer to him." He stopped himself from saying what he really felt, that the idea of a future determined only by an unapproachable God frightened him.

"I think there's something comforting in that too," said Sofi in a pained voice. "But it scares me to think how it all gets extinguished so quickly, for any one of us. Who's left to remember us?"

"I read a book on comparative religion once," he said. "A series of essays really. There was this one essay on the idea of divine memory. Despite all the apocalyptic gloom in the Western monotheistic tradition – constant wars, violence, God punishing his worshippers when he feels betrayed, the Final Judgment when God orders everything to be destroyed – the universe is still left with God to remember all the things of this world that were once created and alive. Maybe it's worth thinking of your brother as someone whose memory will always be protected as long as God exists."

Sofi nodded her head, her eyes dry and illuminated. "I believe that." She paused, ruminating on a thought she wanted to share. "Do you believe that?"

He wasn't sure what to say. Given the solace he was desperate to give to Sofi, Murad felt slightly uncomfortable with his true answer. "I used to. It's a powerful idea, isn't it? Being contained in some vast repository of information like a holy computer tower."

Sofi laughed. "But you don't believe in it?" she asked, her voice low and more serious.

"I don't think I do anymore."

"Why?"

Her question had an anxious curiosity to it. "For a while now, I've been taking these antidepressants. They're not that strong, but they're powerful enough to keep me afloat. They're like those safety nets you see in circuses beneath trapeze artists. It won't keep you afloat, but it'll prevent the worst from happening. I never wanted to take any medication. I assumed they were crutches, and people like me didn't need them."

"What do you mean 'people like you'?"

"Believers," he said. "I went to jummah once, when I was a teenager, on a Friday off from school. The khateeb was giving a sermon on mercy. He said that one of the worst sins you could commit was feeling despair. He also said that the reason depression was rampant in the society we lived in was because the unbelievers despaired over God's mercy, and that antidepressants were a sign of weak souls. And I believed him, until I started to feel depressed myself about the time I started university. I ignored what I was feeling, because I figured all I needed to do was to pray and that alone would protect me. It didn't, and I stopped praying. About the time I graduated, the university doctors prescribed the pills, which I only started taking about the time I came to London. After a while, as the pills kicked in, a thought occurred to me: that the pills have done more for my soul than the belief system I sincerely thought would armour me against everything I was feeling."

Sofi seemed incredulous. "But how could you say that?"

"I had been diligent about my prayers for years," said Murad with a shrug. "I prayed first out of duty, because that's what you're supposed to do, that's your ultimate obligation. I started to feel so hollow that duty started to mean less to me after a while. Love meant more, and I made sure that my acts of prayer, not just me saying my namaz, were motivated by love. I cultivated that emotion. I thought that it was a feeling that could last as long as God could last." He took another sip of water. "Which is, of course, to say I thought it could last forever."

"Doesn't it?"

"If it does, I don't feel it. No love of God, no fear of him either, no presence."

⁂

They walked outside after finishing eating, directionless, passing time as if it were a valueless commodity. Murad felt liberated talking to Sofi, having never expressed how much his deen, his faith, had weakened over the years. Shame prevented him from admitting that to anyone. Yet he felt guilty being candid. "I'm sorry," he said to Sofi.

"Why?" she asked, perplexed.

"For being too honest. You needed something more spiritual than I just gave you right now."

"No, don't be sorry. I'm glad you told me. I feel bad for you, actually. You've been surrounded by faith of some kind your whole life. Now it seems a part of your soul wants to run away. I didn't come from faith. We never paid attention to it as a family. I wasn't an atheist, but I wasn't religious in any meaningful sense. Before I came to London, things had been changing for me. I've been more attracted to the spiritual life, even if I don't fit in perfectly to the spiritual life."

Sofi walked close to him, her words sounding like whispers underneath the traffic and the grunt of buses as they alighted and spilled passengers onto the sidewalk. "There aren't many people who know this much about me," she said.

They backtracked to the university, walking back along the Kingsway in the twilight as the street filled with commuters leaving work.

As they approached the entrance of the university, Sofi said she had to meet a friend at the library. Murad said he had to go home, despite his desire not to leave her, and his inexplicable envy of whoever she was meeting. She embraced him, her arms reaching up to his neck, pulling him down toward her. His cheek touched hers. He felt her skin. Her softness. Her warmth. The seconds passed slowly.

"We'll talk soon, yeah?" said Sofi, her accent a deliberate, teasing London lilt. She took one last look at him and disappeared into the alley, the lamps hovering over her as she walked along the cobblestones toward the library, into the night and away from Murad.

Murad went back to his residence and tried to write an essay. He couldn't concentrate. He tried to write an outline for his thesis on a pad of yellow paper, but instead found himself lost in his thoughts of Sofi. He placed the pad face down on the table and went to his bed to lie down.

His phone buzzed. It was a message from Sofi, asking if he was still on campus. He wrote back, saying he wasn't. She didn't message back. He wondered if he should go back to school, if she needed him.

"I can come back," he texted her.

At first there was no reply. Then a text came in: "Yes. Please. Come back."

The bus came quickly and Murad alighted at the Kingsway near the university entrance. He texted her to ask where she was. She asked him to meet her back at the same steps they had met at earlier in the day. He walked into the university. Even with the lights from the streetlamps barely illuminating the lane, he could see Sofi clearly. She was alone, sitting on the steps of the old building, holding herself against the whistling breeze.

Murad walked up the steps and sat beside her. Sofi moved closer to him, placing her head on his shoulder and holding his arm. He lowered his head against hers. Her hair was fragrant. The presence of her body felt so still, so comfortable, next to his.

"I'm sorry for bringing you back out here," she said.

"Don't be."

"You did a lot for me today."

"I really didn't."

"I just needed to feel close to someone today."

"Tell me," he said, nearly whispering, almost pleading. "Tell me anything you want."

"I feel alone," she said.

"Do you feel alone now?"

He felt her head lifting from his shoulder. "No."

Sofi laid her head back down. They sat there, facing the street, the rush of vehicles from the Kingsway echoing through the lane. Scattered groups of huddled students walked in front of them, ignoring their presence as they stayed together, siloed from the rest of the world.

10

What Murad felt toward Sofi was more than compassion. The word itself had mostly religious connotations – God the Compassionate, God the Merciful. It was more than love – it was adoration, the need to see her with worshipful eyes. The adoration he desired wasn't the piety of a sinner longing for salvation, or the pilgrim's plea toward a God he supplicates to. With Sofi, it was temporal, physical, bound completely in this world, the only world that interested him.

The weeks moved along. Spring bloomed quickly, and exams and final theses loomed over everyone. Murad spent the weeks with Sofi in the library, texting each other in advance to make sure they would be there at the same time. Typically, they sat at the open tables on the first floor or at the computers on the second floor. They joked and took breaks outside at the coffee shop together. She introduced him to the innumerable friends and acquaintances she seemed to have made in such a short time at the university. Sofi seemed happy those days. Murad was proud to be around her. The person he was in her presence was someone with the same energy as the self he knew years ago, a personality he had shed and missed: social, warm and full of largesse to those around him.

In Murad's mind, the bond between him and Sofi had changed. Her smiles lasted longer and her eyes lingered over him with a depth and intensity he hadn't seen before. One evening, he walked with her to Holborn Station. Sofi had to see someone, she said, without giving further details. He felt like joining her – every urge in those days was to dwell in her presence as long as possible. She hugged him tightly, the fragrance of her gripping him. "I'm glad I know you," she said, touching his cheek as she paused under the long blue canopy bearing the station's name. He felt stunned by the simplicity of the statement, its directness and innocence. As she disappeared into the darkness of the Underground, Murad stood next to a newspaper stand slightly stunned, awakened by the notion that within Sofi a light had been sparked, and a solid, irreplaceable sentiment had been crystallized. Yet how could he really know, beyond the borders of their two selves, what degree her heart warmed at the thought of him? He was captivated by the chance for discovery, to explore those unknown feelings and to see whether the affection she had was a mirror of the glow radiating inside him.

The tone of the university was charged and heavy. Some students, especially the undergraduates, studied under the stress of knowing their future depended on their performance in the next few weeks. The postgraduates, for the most part, studied without those fears. There was a bland insouciance in their presence around the university. Some classmates Murad spoke to talked about life after their master's degree with a self-assurance that bordered on smugness. Kristy, whom he'd met only occasionally when they ran into each other in the shared kitchen of the flat, was insistent that her degree was only a temporary stop. "Ask any of the American students," she said one morning, overtired and underslept after days of intense studying and ecstatic partying, "and they'll say the same thing. All this is a stepping stone to law school." Some of Murad's European acquaintances were absolutely certain they were headed to the public service in their respective countries.

Everyone had a future. The students glowed with confidence because they knew, with the precision of an engineer, the blueprint they needed to follow to lead the life they wanted to live. He had no such map, no schema. He didn't seem to care that much, although he knew he probably should have, but he was too involved with Sofi. He decided that she needed to know how he felt about her and, perhaps, to validate how she felt about him.

A week before their exam together, Sofi sent him a message: a group of her friends wanted to go out. She wanted to invite him along. "We all needed a break," the text said. The club in Covent Garden where they were to meet was called The Dinner Party. The university's student council had managed to book a Tuesday night, just for students of the school. He was excited when he received the invitation, thinking of it as an opportunity. He could tell her then, perhaps, in some solitary corner of the club. *The night would be mine*, he thought. It would be ours. As if from nothing, like a conjuror, Murad created hope, the first genuine hope in recent memory.

Tuesday came. Murad burned inside, his soul combustible, energized. He spent an inordinate amount of time thinking of what to wear, how to look. He ironed a white shirt and a pair of trousers carefully, every crease pressed with detail and attention. He regarded himself carefully in the mirror before leaving the residence, ensuring that the volume of his hair was adequate, that his face was evenly and cleanly shaved. Despite the lack of sun since he'd returned to London, his normally pale skin showed some colour. Life was coming back to him. The pills were running out, and he considered abandoning them – they'd had their time with him anyway, as had every prayer he'd said to shield himself from darkness. Sofi had already given him fire, and he burned inside.

He took the bus to the Aldwych and walked to Covent Garden.

Dark streets turned into well-lit avenues. He saw the sign for the club and entered. Lights silhouetted the crowd spread out across the middle of the dance floor. Encircling the room were booths, and a collection of haphazardly placed tables and chairs. He crossed the floor, aimlessly passing through the dancers toward the perimeter, peering around, looking for Sofi.

Almost frantic by her absence, he felt a hand grab his forearm. Murad turned around; Sofi's face beamed underneath the dim lights. She hugged him, her arms wrapped around his neck with enthusiasm. "Let me introduce you to some people," she said, shouting in his ear. She led him to their table. There was a round of handshaking and introductions: Gareth, Marceline, Gudrun and Ian. He strained to say something clever or smart to Sofi, but before he could, she sneaked past Gudrun and sat next to Ian.

Murad took a place next to Gareth, stifling his disappointment, conscious not to let it show. He had seen, at one time or another, most of these people talking or generally milling around Sofi. Ian was the only cipher. His face was unfamiliar. Murad was drawn to his foreignness. There was no denying his handsomeness. His jaw was sharp, angular. His eyes had a penetrating blueness, like a clear marble, with pale skin, at least in the light of the club. Murad sat at the edge of the semicircular seat, on the border of conversations he could barely hear. Everyone spoke to each other of relationships, of trips to Europe, of the proposed smoking ban in British pubs, of bars they'd frequented and the quality of wine to be had in different cities. There was no room for him to engage with anyone, no opportunity to contribute to any discussion the group was having. As if noticing his silence, Gareth turned to him. "Can I get you a drink, mate?" he asked.

Murad hesitated for a moment, contemplating whether he should actually say yes. He declined politely.

"It's a club, mate. It's actually illegal to be in here without one. City rules," said Gareth.

"Well, I think I'm going to be a bit of an outlaw tonight."

Gareth looked at him with his head cocked. "Don't tell me you don't drink."

"I don't." A lie, but a lie he needed to maintain.

"Are you a Muslim?"

"I am, actually," said Murad with more directness than he intended, as Gareth's question had made him unconsciously defensive.

A quizzical, hesitant look came over his face. "Interesting," he said.

"How so?"

"You're the first Muslim I've met who doesn't drink."

"Am I that unusual?"

"Most of my Muslim friends are pretty secular. Are you religious?"

It struck Murad that he didn't really know how to answer that question. "I suppose I am," he said.

"Well, my friend, I myself am an atheist," said Gareth with a good-natured cheekiness that masked a deeper pride and earnestness.

"I see."

"I think it's funny when anyone in this day and age denies themselves all the good things in life because some thousand-year-old text says they should."

"Don't you think some people obey these thousand-year-old texts because they feel there's some value in following them?"

"Like what?" asked Gareth, amused but also genuinely puzzled.

"Suppose the prohibition on alcohol prevents self-harm."

"So religion exists to act as our nanny?"

"That's one way of looking at it. Then again, maybe some people obey religious dogma for other reasons."

"Such as?"

"Love."

"Of God?"

"Yes."

"People still believe in that?" asked Gareth. "I'm sorry, I shouldn't have said that," he added, placing his hand on Murad's shoulder. He was sincere in his apology. Murad felt it and told him not to worry. He was used to these conversations, and had the feeling Gareth was experienced in having had similar ones in the past too.

Murad's attention was focused on Ian and Sofi anyway. They sat inches away from each other. In the red light, she seemed happy, happier than he had seen her before. Her smile was a permanent fixture on her face; the resting thoughtfulness he was so used to seeing wasn't there. Her laughter sounded deeper, fuller. The space between Sofi and Ian diminished as the minutes trudged on. Almost as a reflex, after an unheard joke was told, she put her hand over Ian's on the table and laughed. He grasped her hand quickly, and Murad stared at their fingers coupling together, the centre of his chest constricting.

The heavy bass of the music pulsated slowly, as if coming from the heart of an enormous unknown organism. There was a beauty in the sound – the chopped blend of the heavy drums, an orchestral background underlying the caressing female voice. The music transported Murad away from what he saw, what he was beginning to realize. He wanted the music to soothe him like a soporific drug into a new day, far away from the night, so that it would seem like the memory of an unknown man.

He rose from the table and hesitated briefly – stupidly perhaps – to look at Sofi. He wanted her to say something, as if she owed him some indication that she knew she had hurt him and wanted to heal his pain. She carried on talking to Ian. Murad turned, saying no goodbyes to her or anyone else.

He made his way out to the front of the club, passing through the dance floor and the dense forest of dancers, through a narrow hall where young men in blazers texted fervently with both hands, where couples embraced and kissed each other with delicate closeness. He was welcomed into the street by a gust of wind and an unusual quiet, as if entering a knot in time where the world had abruptly stopped. He felt a nudge at his right shoulder. A group of four Asian teenagers passed him, one of whom looked back at him, unapologetic, his face stony and overconfident. Murad stood his ground to stare back. The energy within him ignited, his sadness turning into a combustible rage. The group looked back at him, the despairing warrior, with a confused glare, as if his stillness was less an invitation to fight and more the presence of an anomaly they had best move away from.

They moved on. Murad's mind was desolate, a desert. He shook off his inarticulate anger. Few thoughts were left to him, only movement, a robotic need to find a bus or a cab or some way home. He walked, at first not heeding the signs for a bus stop or surveying the street for a free black cab. He was drawn magnetically east toward the university and found himself near a familiar bus stop at Russell Square. He stood waiting until it arrived, possibly the last bus of the night. The driver sat wearily, barely acknowledging him as he tapped his Oyster card on the reader.

Murad sat down and looked out at the passing streets of London as if gazing at them for the first time, an immense loneliness overwhelming him with an electric clarity.

11

Despite waking early, Murad didn't leave his bed until noon.

His soul was a series of reactions that enervated his body, leaving his limbs leaden and useless. Rage and piercing agony fought each other within him in a war without a victor, leaving only a shocking vacuum. The emptiness was absolute, as if he were pushed back in time before he knew Sofi, before the invitation to love had been presented to him.

He counted the days until his last exam. The sun shone in from the window, patches of yellowed light making geometric shapes on his desk as he lay in bed. The day was illuminated, yet he cloistered himself like an anchorite avoiding a plagued and damaged world.

Sofi texted him. She asked why he had left so abruptly last night. The tone was more inquisitive than worried, upsetting Murad even more. He wanted an apology, an aching concern from her, even if he knew how absurd that expectation was. Ultimately, an understanding of his pain wasn't what he wanted. What he wanted was her and for the closeness Ian possessed with Sofi, all that could never be his to have.

Murad spent more than twenty-four hours in a stupor, too numb for tears. His actions were minimal, only going out of the room to the kitchenette for food once that night. He did no schoolwork. He checked his email and ignored the calls he knew were most likely coming from either Ammi or Abbu.

Everything was lost. The map that Murad had built in his mind crumbled in his hand. The pathway that had led him away from the life he knew, toward Sofi, toward joy, was gone. He tried to fight against his acrid bitterness, the contempt for all that remained. What she introduced – a future he could control, where happiness seemed immutable – receded away from him in the wake of the previous night, leaving only the debris of the life he'd had before he'd met her. The loneliness. The gales of discontent gliding over the perennial sea of unhappiness.

The next day it rained, a downpour that had become gentler through the late morning. He understood that a part of him was broken and needed mending. He made a decision to continue taking his pills: he had to stop feeling this way. Life was hateful, but he accepted its pain as if it were a duty.

He started to study again at his desk. He received no more messages from Sofi; he wouldn't have responded even if any had come. The library was off-limits, cursed. His mind worked on short-term goals: eating, sleeping, going through his notes, writing practice essays.

The days passed until the exam for Burke's class. It was held in the early afternoon. Murad deliberately arrived five minutes early so he wouldn't have to speak to anyone. The passageways of the new campus building were a pristine white; every door was made of glass. Some of the other classmates huddled around the closed door of the exam room. He positioned himself down the hallway, away from the crowd, giving a polite and crisp hello to anyone greeting him.

The proctors marshalled everyone inside the room; he didn't see Sofi until everyone had taken their seats. She sat two rows ahead of him on his right. She didn't turn around to acknowledge him. Murad spent the next three hours scribbling in his exam workbook, his eyes drawn to her dark hair in the spare moments when he needed to look away from his own words. He stared at her body, meditating on every curve before closing his eyes and realizing that, even in the silence of the room, even with the physical distance between them, he was still absorbed by her. He opened his eyes and finished the rest of the exam, resolving to stop looking at her. When the time was up, he stayed in his seat until the proctors collected the booklets. The moment they gave everyone the signal to leave, Murad collected his bag at the front of the room and left the building, leaving Sofi behind as if she were already a distant memory.

A day after the exam, Sofi sent a text. The message appeared in soft digitized letters written in all-caps: "IS ANYTHING WRONG?" Murad read the message in the late morning, frying a pair of barely palatable eggs he'd bought from the Sainsbury's closest to the residence. He sat down at the kitchen table, staring at his mobile, barely acknowledging his food, unsure whether to answer her. There is a power in passivity, he thought. In not responding, he was saving face. He realized quickly how silly that was: only he could see his own humiliation and embarrassment. He texted her back: "We should talk."

They met in the afternoon. The temperature had dropped, despite the anemic late spring sun. He waited for her in the Italian café on Aldwych, taking a table toward the back overlooking the rest of the café. She came in ten minutes after he arrived. He didn't get up; she hugged him as he remained seated. The look on her face was friendly, yet tentative and wary. She sat down and asked how he was doing. He said "okay" and kept silent. Murad expected her to say something about the exam or some other bit of small talk. Instead, her face had the look of someone already prepared to face an emotional battle.

"How long have you and Ian been seeing each other?" he asked.

There was no way to avoid asking the question.

Sofi's eyes were wide. "Since the beginning of the year." There was a clattering sound of plates being shuffled onto a tray behind them. Murad felt a strange sensation, the feeling of self-consumption, as if he were to implode. "Why do you want to know?" she asked, her voice soft, more compassionate than angry.

"Did you have any idea how I felt about you?" he asked, trying to suppress his bitterness.

Sofi brushed a solitary tear from her right eye with her finger and stared at the table.

"Maybe I thought I did for a moment, but I ignored that. It didn't seem possible."

"Me loving you didn't seem possible?"

Sofi looked back at him. "When I looked at you, I saw only a friend. And a brother. And that was special enough to me. Maybe I was blinded to everything else because that's what I needed and wanted. I couldn't see you as anything else because of that."

"You never bothered mentioning Ian to me."

"I didn't even think about it. It just never occurred to me to talk about him before we met up that night when we were out at the club."

For the first time since Sofi came in, he exhaled.

"I'm sorry, Murad," she said.

He knew she truly was.

"Say something," said Sofi. She feigned a smile. "You can say anything to me."

"Would it make any difference?"

"It might make you feel better," said Sofi, with less conviction than she probably wanted to convey.

He stopped himself from saying any more. What he really wanted to say was this: That he didn't want her compassion, her empathy, her affection or goodwill. What he wanted was what he thought she had been developing for him: to be loved by her alone, totally and completely. Anything else meant nothing.

Without saying a word, Sofi seemed to understand. Tears created a film over her eyes.

"I can't give you what you want," she said.

"I know."

There was no room for awkwardness, as it seemed they had already stated their positions, both feeling their emotions uprooted. Sofi sat in her chair with her legs crossed, her face ponderous. She broke the silence and asked Murad if he wanted to take a walk outside. Without hesitation he said yes.

It looked like rain, the clouds pushing their way into the sky where the sun had been earlier. He walked with her out into the blurring noise of the city as if in a lucid dream. There was no logical reason for him to follow her, led like a lamb under the care of a shepherd across Aldwych to the Indian High Commission and Bush House. They entered Somerset House on the Strand. Murad had never been there before. The courtyard was massive, the buildings classically styled, the entire quadrangle resembling an Italian piazza. He slowed down to absorb the grandiosity of the square. Sofi walked a few steps ahead of him and stopped herself. When Murad caught up, her arms were crossed in front of her, her bag swinging low from the crook of her forearm. "It's really beautiful here," she said.

"It is."

"I need open spaces," she said. She looked down at the ground. "What happens to us now?"

"I don't know," he said. "I actually have no idea."

"Can you see me just as a friend?" she asked.

"Looking at you the way I do right now?"

Sofi turned around and looked at Murad. "I think I know the answer." The clouds bloomed darker, and the afternoon mimicked the dusk. "You couldn't even if you wanted to."

His mouth was dry. "You don't know that."

She shook her head. "It was my fault."

"For what?"

She didn't say.

"I haven't thought about us. What would happen to us, I mean." Murad realized he said "us" as if they were a couple.

"I think I need to stay away." Before he could respond, she continued. "It's not for me," she said. A cool wind rushed into the square. Sofi reached out and grabbed the edge of his jacket as if stopping him from being blown away by the breeze.

"If it's not for you, then who's it for?" he asked with unconscious anger.

"I don't want you to get hurt."

"I can't be hurt any more than I already am."

"And I'll just make it worse."

They stood staring at each other. The square was empty except for a few old women sitting at the metal tables to their left. Sofi's face was sad yet determined; her breathing was heavy. With a final sigh, she let go of Murad's jacket. Without a goodbye, without an embrace or a touch, she turned her back on him and left Somerset House.

12

Murad abandoned the summer.

He worked on his thesis throughout the season. It was due in September. The title of the paper was "The influence of the Colonial Office on the theory and practice of international relations in pre-war Britain," a topic chosen solely because it gave him an excuse to do primary research far from the university. He spent most days in an almost hour-long trek to the Public Records Office in Kew. When not sifting through policy documents written more than half a century ago and jotting down notes, he spent his spare moments on the benches outside Kew Gardens. Cricketers played on the grounds near the garden, their white clothes gleaming in the faint sun, the grass they played on clipped and moist. He observed, and only wanted to observe. Their movements had a grace to them, with quick sprints and rounded movements of arms as the bowlers hurled their balls toward the batsmen. It was beautiful, a beauty witnessed but unfelt. The ice around his heart crystallized daily. The distance between Murad and the world expanded until existence seemed like a play, every person around him an actor.

He made it a point not to go near the university. On occasion, classmates invited him out. He seldom accepted. School work was his excuse to avoid excessive socialization. If they met near school, he declined. Otherwise, he tried to accompany them to whatever restaurant or pub they wanted to frequent, soaking in camaraderie that had little substance and a shelf life that would most likely expire the moment their theses were handed in.

Sofi remained a distraction. He pushed her image out of his head, only to have the image roll back into his mind again, a futile effort, like taking part in a war in which he had no hope of victory.

By the time Murad finished and submitted his thesis, the first shudder of fall had arrived. The temperature dropped. Unkind winds rushed along the surface of the university's cobblestone streets. He had two weeks before he had to vacate the residence. He would move in with Khala in the days before he left for Toronto. Kristy was moving to an apartment. She had enough money to get her by for two months ("And even then, just barely in this fucking expensive city," she said). She hoped to find a job, get an extension visa for at least a few months as a recent graduate. Murad was tempted to do the same. The thought of escape still lingered in his mind. It was, after all, one of his original motivations for coming to London. He dropped the idea; it was clear the city was a place he needed to escape from now as well.

Murad slowly packed his belongings as the days went by, jettisoning the unneeded scraps of his postgraduate life. He couldn't throw Sofi out; he had no mementoes of her, only acid memories. The thought both saddened and embittered him, the idea that he had to leave at a loss. He longed for an ending, some sense that this time had meaning and the emotions that Sofi had kindled carried weight.

It was seven days before he left London and three days before he left the residence. He had to speak to Sofi one last time before leaving. That evening, as the day entered twilight, Murad called her. He stood in his increasingly bare room and waited as the phone rang, wondering if she had blocked his call somehow, or if she still had his number stored in her mobile. He wondered if he occupied any space in her heart, while knowing that even if he did, it could never match the nature and power of how she occupied his.

She picked up. "Murad," she said, almost as if she were expecting him.

He couldn't even say hello. "I wasn't sure you'd pick up."

A pause. "Of course I would."

His throat constricted.

"How have you been?" asked Sofi. Her voice was soft, tender, yet guarded.

"I've been –" he stopped himself. "I've been fine."

"Are you sure?"

"I'm sure," he said. "I'm leaving in a few days."

"From the residence?"

"From London."

"I see."

"I just thought I should tell you. I wasn't sure if I should call you."

"No, it's okay," said Sofi, punctuating her sentence with a sigh.

"I want to see you before I leave," said Murad, blurting it out before Sofi could say more. "I know you thought we shouldn't see each other again –"

"Murad –"

"But I need," he continued, "just to say goodbye. We may never see each other again."

Another pause. "Where can I meet you?"

Before Murad could answer, she told him to wait. "Let me come to you."

♦

Sofi said she would come to Borough Tube Station, close to Murad's residence. By the time he walked up Great Dover Street, the sun had almost set, the deep-blue sky colouring the trees and the housing estates in a languid hue. The station was empty by the time he arrived. He waited close to the station agent, who was absorbed in counting coins in his transparent booth. The elevator behind the turnstiles opened sporadically, each time with only a handful of passengers riding up from the lower-level platforms. He watched the elevator closely, his heart racing at the thought of Sofi's arrival. Questions erupted in his mind: *Should I have left without seeing her? What will I say once she arrives? Should I say that I understand how she feels about me, and that I am sorry if I have, in any way, hurt her? Would that mean anything?*

Murad tried to steel himself against the power he knew she still had over him. The elevator continued to open, each batch of travellers spilling out looking wearier than the last. He walked the short length of the entrance, occasionally peering out on to Borough High Street to see if, through some impossible fluke, he had missed her.

When she didn't show up, he tried texting and calling. She didn't answer. Fissures broke open within him, and he was suffocated with the fear that he would never see Sofi again. He had spent so many weeks inoculated from all feelings that the riptide of his emotions threatened to drown him – the hope for connection, the suffocating dejection, all flooding his veins, amplifying the hastened speed of his pacing inside the station.

The sky's dark blue turned an inky black. Three drunken men brushed past Murad, followed by a pair of laughing women in heels. He glanced at the clock on his mobile. It was nearly ten. Murad abandoned the thought of calling her again. He turned his back on the station and crossed to Great Dover Street, his fear churning into cold bitterness with every step.

Murad left for Khala's house a few days later, carting two large suitcases on the number 21 double-decker toward New Cross. He remarked to himself how quickly London changed colour the farther south one travelled from the Thames. The grey world of stone near the university gave way to a brown world of row houses and diminished expectations. He never realized how much he wanted to be a part of that world, the world of privilege, satisfaction and interconnectedness. Riding the bus, he thought of Sofi and how she had brought him out of the pettiness of that want. Most of his sadness was based in thwarted desire, and Sofi had created a new longing in him. She lived in a world where graciousness seemed natural, a grace that was now lost, a fragrance perfuming rooms Murad could never enter.

You knew me, he said to her, the ghost of Sofi that appeared only when he closed his eyes, hearing the pneumatic sighs of the bus as it lumbered southward. *As much as I knew myself. You pulled me into the sun. Your darkness smashing into mine, bursting together to create light. Nothing else mattered. What I thought I needed – to feel bound to this world, to others, to be free of the past – was all meaningless when you set ashore on my island. What have you taken from me, when you recede from me now?*

The sight of Sofi in his mind extinguished when the bus reached New Cross. Dragging his bags behind him after alighting the bus, Murad saw Khala waiting in anticipation at the front door, her head covered, making her beaming, soft face stand out all the more. He was hit instantly by the awareness of another existence beyond Sofi and the university, one that tore at him with its cutting ambivalence.

He ate dinner with Khala that night. She was inquisitive, asking the usual questions family members would often ask, about classes and job prospects, all questions Murad answered with no more than two or three syllables. Her eyes, clear and unwavering, looked at him delicately, as if sizing him up for an even greater line of inquiry.

"Did you read anything from that book I gave you?" she asked finally.

"I haven't had the time, Khala. I'm sorry."

"There's a lot of wisdom in that, jaano. You should read it."

He said he would. "Are your neighbours ever noisy?" asked Murad, mostly out of a need to avoid further questions.

"Sometimes," she said. "But I actually like the noise. They're Nigerians, you know. I talked to one of them, one of the women. Have you seen her?"

"No, I haven't."

"She's such a fine person," said Khala with enthusiasm. "When she first came, I actually thought she was quite mean." She laughed to herself. "She never used to smile, never used to say hello. I knocked on her door once, just to give her some food. She seemed so happy I'd come. She told me her name was Mercy. I think she's quite religious. It was Sunday and she said she'd just come back from church. I told her, 'For us, Mercy is one of the names of God, so you have a holy name.' She laughed at that and said it was true." Khala stared straight ahead, her face in a gentle, reflective reverie. "Such a fine person," she whispered, tearing a bit of naan with her right hand.

Murad realized he had misunderstood his aunt. He had seen her as a fundamentally closed person, alone save for the love of God. Regarding her now, the luminescence of her face, the guilelessness of her words, he realized there was nothing insular about her. God had not shut her off from the world; she did not live in an urban hermitage. Perhaps the opposite was true: God had given her an expanded heart that would otherwise not have existed inside her.

Before he slept, Murad received a call from Pakistan. He'd already been in touch with his parents in the days leading up to his leaving the residence, mostly on sundry chores to be done once he arrived in Canada. He knew this call was different – it must have been around the time for Fajr in Lahore. It was Ammi's number. They said their salaams. Murad asked her why she hadn't gone back to sleep after praying.

"I was thinking of you," she said. Her voice was hoarse, exhausted, yet unexpectedly tender.

He didn't know what to say. "I'll take care of things when I get back to Toronto."

"I wasn't worried about that. I wanted to make sure you say your du'a before you boarded the plane," she said. "Do you know that du'a?"

"I don't remember it, Ammi," said Murad. He was embarrassed to admit it.

"Let's say it together. You'll remember if we say it together."

He hesitated. He didn't want to. There was an insistence in his mother's voice, a strange protective pleading. He followed her line, every word, and from the Arabic the translation came back to him: "Oh God, we ask you on this journey for goodness and piety and for works that are pleasing to you. Oh God, lighten this journey for us and make its distance easy. Oh God, you are our companion on the road and the one in whose care we leave our family."

Beneath the veneer of his numbness, Murad's heart throbbed. He hardly felt like a believer. He didn't want to be. He wanted to be a castaway marooned on his own island. For a moment, his mother brought him out of his exile, not toward the sacred but toward the self he longed to retreat from, the boy who spoke to God, who recited those mellifluous verses of the Holy Book on his mother's lap, who was certain he belonged somewhere in the universe.

"Call us when you reach home, jaano," said Ammi. "I love you."

She paused, perhaps expecting him to repeat those words. He felt a crack in his heart, a wound opening. "I'll call," said Murad. "I'll make sure to call."

He heard his mother sigh. They said their salaams before ending the call.

She wanted him to recite this du'a to remind him there was still a portion of love in the world for him, he thought. Even as the du'a failed to bring him closer to God and anesthetize his hurt, he was reminded of a world and a past he had tried to escape, a world so different from where he found himself now.

From his backpack, he took out the book Khala had gifted him. He flipped to a random page and read a snippet of a poem:

My heart thirsts
I long for only a drop
The caravan's jug is not enough, since
I seek the Ocean.

He ached with the thought of Sofi when he read that. This is what he needed, the ocean, not the drop; intense love, not abstracted divine love, but real love, the light that shines underneath dark lashes and eyes the colour of space.

Murad made a personal pact: he would leave a part of himself in London, like a limb recently amputated and no longer of value. He would not try to forget Sofi, as forgetfulness had no use. Instead, he resolved to treat the experience as soldiers treat a lost war: with complete acceptance and acknowledgement of defeat.

He peered out through the blinds over his makeshift bed. Sirens blared and police cars rushed through the roads while the buses ran and young men laughed and huddled next to each other in front of corner stores. In no time at all, he would be across the ocean, another life would begin, and the moments experienced in this city would fade out, like smoke billowing into the night sky.

PART 2
SOFI

In all the eye discovered – only God I saw.
Like a candle I was melting in his fire:
Amidst the flames out-flashing – only God I saw.
– Baba Kuhi of Shiraz, quoted in *Aphorisms of the Mohammedan Saints*

1

Out of the darkness, Sofi's eyes felt forced open by an unknown master. Pushed through an all-white hallway, muffled voices of nurses and doctors murmuring from unseen corridors, she moved through twisting passageways toward an abandoned gurney. On top of the gurney was a coffin, a light-coloured pine; the closer she came, the more she saw how shoddily it was made, a piece of crude furniture, made by amateurs, its seams showing, gaps between the sides and the stops visible, and, although she could smell nothing, she sensed there was death inside. She noticed a dark and viscous liquid oozing from the gaps, like thick syrup. The fluid dropped to the light-blue hospital tile, pooling near her feet.

She would always wake up the moment the blood reached her toes.

2

A thick wind hit them as they drove down Yonge Street with the windows down. As the redness in the late summer sky faded into a deep blue, Sofi gazed at the road. She and her friends were packed tightly into the car, no space between them. The wind caressed her face and she closed her eyes with delight, feeling like she was on the cusp of a grand moment.

They were all in the car: Lily, Andrew, Carlton. Andrew was driving a Pontiac Sunfire his father had bought him when he was in high school, the same high school he'd attended with Lily and Sofi. Sofi felt someone rubbing her arm. "You awake?" asked Lily, her high-pitched voice barely audible amidst the roar of the street and the cackle of laughter inside the car.

Sofi opened her eyes and nodded silently, the wind having granted her an instant sense of peace.

"Good," said Lily. "You won't want to sleep after tonight."

She knew this was her way of being comforting. Sofi needed this night. She needed people around her. Lily and she were friends, but not best friends – Sofi never felt she had close friends in high school – but their relationship was warm. When they had met up accidentally the first week of university, they were distant at first, and then became closer. Lily was a stable presence in the anonymity of university life. Lily and her boyfriend, Andrew, became constant companions in Sofi's life between classes. Carlton was a friend of Andrew's whom she had just met that night. He was amiable and sociable enough, but Sofi found his flirtations tiresome. A constant stream of talk dwelt on his scholastic accomplishments; his absorption in his cell phone, she thought, was a way to show off the pinnacles of his popularity. She tolerated him; he was convivial company, and, after this past year, she needed to be happy. She convinced herself she would put the past behind her for the night, and aim for joy, warmth and life.

They wound their way through side streets Sofi was unfamiliar with and found parking in a paid lot near the club. The bouncers checked their identification and let them pass without speaking. They passed through the corridor into the barely lit main room, signs with "Coming soon! Fall 2004 – Battle of the DJs" lining the passageways. There was a dance floor in the middle, throbbing lights, and a cardiac pump of beats emanating from unknown speakers circulating in the air. Lily and Sofi found space to sit on a couch surrounded by a few chairs on the second floor overlooking the dance floor, while Carlton and Andrew went to see if there was space on the patio.

"Apparently, this place has cheap martinis," said Lily as they sat down.

"I could use one," said Sofi.

"Is this spot okay?" asked Lily. Her look was maternal and warm under the dim lights. "I can text Andrew to see if he's found space outside."

"We're lucky we found this," said Sofi. She lifted herself and looked over the crowd. Her eyes returned to Lily. "This is great. Honestly it is. I needed this."

"I know," said Lily. She reached out and held Sofi's hand. "We both needed this."

Andrew and Carlton came back holding martini glasses in each hand. "Bad news is, we don't have any other place to sit," said Carlton. He dropped down on the chair next to the couch, placing the drink in his right hand on the table in front of Sofi. "Good news is, these really are cheap martinis."

Andrew laughed and gave Lily a glass. Lily smiled at Sofi and rolled her eyes. She saw the dance floor and felt envious of the crowd, wanting to join them. Andrew and Lily spoke of school, their stresses, their ambitions ("I need to up my GPA next year"; "I'm going to take six months off after I graduate just to study for the LSAT"). Sofi found it endearing that they spoke to her with such candour. She welcomed their trust in her, and, at the same time, found it tiresome, their sincerity and earnestness about their ambitions seemed paltry and trivial, their stresses so superficial. Beneath their concerns, she was certain they had no real fears; their confidence and assuredness told her that everything would be fine, and their destiny together – graduation, law school, master's degree, marriage, children – was charted with such cartographical precision that the doubts they vocalized seemed disingenuous. It was as if they were emphasizing to Sofi that they too had problems of their own.

She had little to contribute to Lily and Andrew's conversation, and she found herself staring at Carlton more often than she would have liked. He was lost in his cell phone, contemplating the messages he was composing with solitary intensity beneath ironically cool nerd-glasses. He had given up on his earlier flirtation, the casual grabbiness, the intellectual preening. Sofi was more than content with his change of attitude. Three men appeared behind his soft single chair, looming over him with almost threatening stillness. Carlton stood up and turned around, giving each figure a masculine, fraternal hug, followed by an exaggerated, high-pitched "What's up" with each embrace.

Sofi, Andrew and Lily stared at them. "Aren't you going to introduce us?" Lily said over the staccato beat from downstairs.

Carlton remained standing, his arm crooked, a finger tapping his lip in a faux-pensive stare. He pointed each one out. "In order of handsomeness, that's Liam, the one behind him is Robin and the tall crown prince behind Robin is Ravi."

"We're not here to stay, we just wanted to say hi to this guy," said Liam, slapping Carlton on the back. He was broad-shouldered, short, stocky, like a rugby player who had stopped growing prematurely. "We'll be on our way."

Carlton insisted they stay. Lily and Andrew encouraged them too. They made room on their already-narrow seats, Liam and Ravi clinging to the oversized armrests of Carlton's chair; Robin squeezing in next to Sofi, who shifted to make room for him.

Carlton's friends talked among themselves. Sofi listened to Lily and Andrew but felt adrift. She continued to smile, laughing at their jokes. She felt the warmth of Robin's body next to hers, and an occasional burst of hot breath as he laughed at Carlton's inane humour. This disturbed her less than the feeling of being observed. Every now and then she turned toward Robin. The first time she did it, his eyes turned downward with chaste suddenness. At other times, his gaze was steady and unwavering, and he met her stern look with one that was equally assertive.

As the evening wore on, Robin had barely spoken to Sofi. Finally, when there was a lull in their respective, divided conversations, he turned to her and asked her what she was studying.

"Economics."

"Sounds like fun."

"It isn't. I hate it."

"So you take it because . . ."

"I take it because I have to, and because I need a job."

Robin's smile was closed, as if he were restraining a laugh. "Seems like a fair reason for studying something you don't like."

A pause and a smile. Sofi could see Robin's teeth briefly illuminated under the lamp over the table. She felt embarrassed when he stared at her, his smile calm, his eyes oscillating between a lapis blue and an unknowable darkness.

"How do you know Carlton?" she asked, wanting to break the silence.

"School," he said tersely, picking up his drink.

"Studying to be a lawyer too?"

He stared at his glass before drinking. "I don't know as yet," he said, raising his glass. "Most likely. That, or going into teaching."

"In what?"

"Political science," he said with a sigh.

"These are boring questions," said Sofi.

Robin shook his head. "Not at all."

"They are, and I'm boring you. They're the type of questions your mother's friends ask you."

He placed his drink on the table and waved his hands, as if dismissing her last statement. "I'm not bored."

Robin's smile was bright; the creases on his forehead and around his mouth belied his age, making him look older, less boyish than Sofi had thought him at first.

"Well, you're boring me," said Sofi, placing her hand on Robin's shoulder, her mouth inches away from his ear. "There's a way you can stop boring me, though."

Sofi leaned back, her hand still on his shoulder. He moved forward. "How can I do that?"

"Dance with me."

The others stayed where they were, fixed to their seats, talking but unmoving, looking almost like a tableau. Sofi and Robin descended the stairs to the dance floor and wove their way through the other dancers, Sofi in front, Robin trailing behind. They danced together tightly, the music rhythmic, percussive, every blunt beat accentuated with a different flashing colour. Robin was a better dancer than she expected. There was ease in his movements, and an ease in hers when she was with him, limbs in time with the syncopated music. After unmeasured minutes, the flashing lights stopped changing, settling on a red hue that covered their faces.

The music seemed slower to Sofi, the web of the other dancers on the floor corralling them together, a miasmic heat rising in the air, enlivening them.

They grew tired; at one point Sofi, laughingly, buried her head in Robin's chest and they walked away from the dance floor, forging a path back to the sofas where Liam, Ravi and Carlton laughed among themselves, and Lily and Andrew argued under the quilt of noise.

"How did you get him to dance?" asked Lily, as Robin and Sofi took their seats again.

"She's been trying to get me to dance for the past fifteen minutes," said Andrew. "It hasn't been working, and I don't know if it's because she's 'been wanting to dance forever,' as she put it, or because her usual bossiness has stopped working on me."

They all laughed, Lily included, who tried to convince her friends that she wasn't as bossy as her boyfriend had said she was. Sofi felt tipsy, her intoxication partially a result of the martini, and partially because of a curious energy building inside her. She couldn't stop looking at Robin. She studied his face: long, with a broad forehead, his jaw square in its construction, straight, thin nose with straight, thin eyebrows over deeply sunken blue eyes. Her defences weakened, increasingly aware that she was beginning to share the attraction she knew he had for her.

◆

It was getting late and an unwanted exhaustion hit Sofi, even though she wished the night would continue. Everyone left together. Robin mentioned he was going to go to another club with Carlton.

Robin and Sofi trailed behind the rest of the group. Sofi saw Lily looking behind her with a raised eyebrow. Sofi mouthed "stop staring" silently back at her. Lily moved ahead, pushing Andrew forward, giving Robin and Sofi space.

"Can I ask you a question?" Sofi said.

He turned his face. "Anything," he replied. The wind stopped blowing. They were near the lot where they had parked.

"Why were you staring at me?" she said.

His face frozen in embarrassment. "I didn't realize I was staring."

"Yes, you were," said Sofi. "I didn't mind, though."

They stood on the corner across from the parking lot. The lights were dim on the street, and the rest of the group had already crossed, leaving Sofi and Robin alone beside a flickering crosswalk signal. He stared at her silently for a moment.

"I want to see you again," he said.

"I want to see you again too," she replied, without hesitation.

A voice from across the street called out to Robin, asking if he was coming.

They quietly exchanged numbers before crossing the street together to join their respective friends. Robin waved at Sofi as Carlton put his hand on his right shoulder, playfully dragging his friend away to a rumbling, dark-coloured Camry. Sofi, Lily and Andrew entered Andrew's Pontiac and drove off. Sofi peered through the rear-view window, looking for any trace of Robin. All she saw was motion and flashes of light from the surrounding cars in the early morning of the city.

❧

Andrew and Lily dropped Sofi near Sheppard Avenue. Persian and Korean restaurants lined the streets and spired apartments interspersed with half-completed construction sites in the background. Cars rolled by; sundry pedestrians walked laughingly and possibly drunkenly on the sidewalks, ignoring Sofi as she turned the corner onto the side street that led to her apartment.

She hated living at home. She was given complete freedom to do as she liked, but going back filled her with dread, her memories a tinnitus hum that was ever-present, overpowering. She knew her mother was asleep, so she took off her heels as she entered and tiptoed around the living room, weaving through the randomly arranged furniture in the dark. She went to her room, turned on the small lamp on her bedside table, bare except for a picture of her brother, Sikander.

That night she had a dream, one that she promptly forgot the moment she woke up. She remembered nothing – all that remained was the glow of a feeling. Everything in her world was correct, all was in alignment. She felt an unfamiliar sensation of peace, and, as she woke from the fog of sleep, she was grateful for the presence of the feeling, thinking of the dream's provenance.

She went to the kitchen dressed in a bathrobe. Mama was there, peering out of the glass frame door that opened to their balcony, the late morning sun shining in, the refracted light glimmering on their glass table. She said hello to Sofi without turning and asked her what time she had come home the previous night.

"Late."

"Who were you with?"

"Andrew and Lily," said Sofi, sitting down at the glass table.

Mama turned, arms folded. She wore an old, deep-blue shalwar kameez. Without asking Sofi what she wanted, she brought out a jar of jam and several pieces of slightly burned toast on a plate. The toast was cold and had been made long before Sofi had woken up. Mama joined her at the table and placed plates silently in front of both of them. Sofi picked up a piece of toast and slathered it with jam.

It was Sofi who broke the silence: "I met someone."

"Who?" asked Mama, biting into her toast, her thin fingers holding each side of the bread. Her face was impassive, calm, on the precipice of coldness.

"His name is Robin," said Sofi quietly. She told her mother about Robin, about dancing, a short, clear account of the night, recited like a child describing her school day, with Mama nodding at every brief detail. There were, of course, some details she did not want to reveal: how calm she'd felt, how for the first time in recent memory she'd felt hopeful.

"Do you like him?" Mama asked, finishing her toast. For the first time that morning, Sofi saw her mother look straight at her with undistracted black eyes.

"I don't know."

Mama got up, taking her plate in hand. "You like him. I know it," she said, giving Sofi a kiss on the forehead on the way to the kitchen.

Across the countertop between the table and the kitchen, Sofi watched Mama washing her plate. She noticed what looked like a smile on her face, an expression so foreign Sofi had forgotten her mother was even capable of smiling.

3

Sofi wasn't always told she was beautiful. The first time she heard that anyone found her attractive was when she was a teenager, fourteen, just after her family had moved to Canada. A friend of Mama's from Punjab College, Faiza Auntie, was visiting from Lahore, staying with another mutual friend of theirs. She had popped in for an impromptu visit, dressing in a way that was garishly youthful, a woman in her late forties attempting to pass for someone in her twenties: tight jeans, makeup and sunglasses. Sofi passed judgment the moment she saw her come through the door: Faiza Auntie was pretentious, fake, amoral and most likely selfish and mean-spirited. The fact that her mother had asked Sofi to stay and serve tea on the family's silver dolly that early summer afternoon made Sofi's distaste for Faiza Auntie turn into a very real resentment.

This changed as the conversation between the two old friends went on. Sofi sat on a side chair, her legs crossed demurely, unspeaking. She looked at them with curiosity, noting the warmth with which they spoke to each other about their lives spent abroad, about the lives of others, a flow of gossip punctuated by laughs and touched with genuine affection. Sofi was rapt by the way the two women before her were in communion. Her presence, mostly silent as it was, felt less like that of an observer and more of a participant in the rituals of an adult world she had never previously been privy to.

There was a pause in the conversation. Ammi and even the effervescent Faiza Auntie seemed tired, staring at the ground, perhaps knowing they had depleted every bit of nostalgia they could muster. Ammi turned to Sofi, and told Auntie how Sofi was going to enter grade nine the next week.

"Mashallah, that's wonderful. And how pretty you look!"

"Faiza, stop it," said Ammi.

"No honestly, she's a beauty," said Auntie, her voice changing from a low street-Punjabi to a higher-pitched, clipped English. "Give her two weeks in that school and every boy will be after her."

Sofi thanked her politely, briefly nodding in her direction. Her mother tried to change the subject back to gossip, joking that any more talk like this would almost certainly lead to a glance from the evil eye.

Sofi would remember that moment occasionally. It was not the only time someone had thought of her as beautiful – it was, however, the first time it had seemed sincere. There was an enthusiasm in Faiza Auntie's voice that enlivened her, as if her extroverted compliments were pronouncements that had to be delivered. That night, before she went to bed, Sofi gazed into the mirror, turning her head to each side, trying to validate Auntie's claim. The rigid lines of her cheekbones stood sharp under the overexposed bathroom light, no visible blemishes on her brown skin, yet she still didn't see it.

When she entered high school, however, her self-perception changed. Gradually she understood what Auntie meant. She heard the boys speak about her behind her back, commenting on the shape of her from behind when she was with her friends. Her reactions to those comments came in stages: first disbelief, as boys had either ignored or derided her looks most of her life, then muted disapproval at what she took to be early teenage sexism. Soon she realized that this was more than just crassness or unregulated hormones. Her body shape was changing rapidly, her hips filling in, her curves emerging, and with it a sense of pride in her body.

She began to wear skimpier clothes. One day, one of her friends, a hijabi from Egypt named Saima, lectured her, telling her she shouldn't be wearing tight jeans. After school Sofi told her mother what Saima had said.

"Never mind what Saima thinks," said Mama angrily. "She should mind her business."

"Saima said it's shameful if I wear tight clothes," said Sofi. "Maybe she's right."

"She's not. She can wear whatever she wants, and you wear whatever you want. Saima's saying you can't, because she believes God looks down upon anyone who actually likes to look pretty."

Sofi felt overjoyed by her mother's words and was happy for her support. Her mother's support extended to boys as well. Sofi had many friends who were boys in high school. Boyfriends too, although these relationships lacked a certain intimacy. She let two of them kiss her: the first, a tall, gangly white boy named Duncan, who bestowed on her a rather sloppy and exceedingly moist kiss that excited and repelled her at the same time; the second, a stocky, big-biceped and rather vain Filipino boy named Ricky, who gave her a kiss that was forceful, slightly intimidating and more off-putting than Duncan's inept but innocent planting of lips.

By the time Sofi was seventeen, she expected more from these encounters. She had a plan for how she wanted her romantic life to unfold: kissed in high school, virginity lost in early undergrad, engagement shortly afterward, followed by marriage. Through her friends, she gained a reputation for aloofness among the young men at school – which she thought was unfair. It was, she later surmised, a consequence of the shyness that she still retained from her childhood. Before graduation she made a decision: she would live for the future, her life one of complete openness – openness of opinion, openness in her embrace of people – every day of her life like an hourglass constantly filled, with no room for emptiness.

She had this in mind when she thought of Robin. With him, she sensed an opportunity to fulfill her romantic fantasies and drive the spikes home on the track that led to an idealized way of life.

♠

Classes started a few days after Sofi's night out. She received emails and texts from Robin, pleading, begging for her to come out. She purposefully ignored some of his messages, others she responded to, giving half-hearted hints that she *may* be interested in grabbing lunch, she *may* be interested in going out with his friends. It was her way of testing his resolve, as well as her own, to determine how strong an imprint she had left in his mind.

Mornings were cool and dark that September, but the afternoons were still warm, the concrete buildings of the university absorbing the heat of the sun, the pavement sparkling as Sofi walked between classes. After her second macroeconomics class, less than two weeks after she'd first met Robin, she received a clipped email from him while she was at the library: "Saturday. Want to take you out. Free? Robin. P.S. You can say you're busy, I'll still write you again for the next weekend, and the weekend after that, and the weekend after that."

The simplicity, the straightforwardness of the email made her smile. Her response was equally direct: "You convinced me. Saturday night. You pick a place and time. Sofi." She wanted to add her own postscript, a witty line that would tell him, with no playful coyness, how much she was looking forward to seeing the *real* him and not a facsimile stored in her imagination. Sofi sent off the message, deciding against adding anything.

She left the library and sat down on a bench, just beyond the building's revolving doors. She had forgotten the location of the tutorial to her introductory global affairs class for her political science minor, and she scrambled to locate the sheet in her notebook where she had meticulously written down her entire schedule – the Luddite in her did not trust email calendars, PDAs or cell phones to remember these quotidian details. In her desperate, impatient fumbling, she neglected to notice someone on the same bench: a girl wearing a white hijab, leaning over a cell phone in her right hand, the mocha-brown skin of her face alternating between stern focus as her thumb danced on her phone's keypad and a neutral, placid expression, her dark eyes thoughtful when she looked up, staring blankly into an unknown space.

Sofi couldn't stop looking at her. Faces always fascinated her. When she was younger, she would stare at people, memorizing every feature, and draw them rather crudely in a blank notebook. She felt like doing that to the hijabi, to etch out her features that stood out from under her covered hair, the slight curve of her nose, the thin eyebrows beneath the rim of her headscarf. There was something else that attracted Sofi to her, a wisp of familiarity that had drawn her in. The hijabi glanced briefly at her, likely realizing someone was staring at her, and Sofi felt embarrassed. She quickly placed her cell phone in her white handbag, but before she moved away from the bench, Sofi placed her hand delicately on her forearm.

"Sorry for staring," said Sofi, her hand still touching her arm. The hijabi's face was smiling but guarded, her eyes slightly narrow, as if assessing an unfamiliar situation. Sofi continued to stare at her as she was awakened by a past memory. "Jamila Khala," she said slowly, testing for certitude. "Are you her daughter?"

"My mother," the hijabi said, her voice full of a light, singsong confusion. Her head shook briefly, her eyes widening as if jolted by a current of recognition. "You're Shenaz Khala's daughter."

They laughed simultaneously, hugged and gazed at each other. "I guess that means we're cousins then," said Sofi.

◆

Her name was Fatima. They decided to spend the hour catching up in front of Robarts Library, on a garden-style bench that had been pushed into a corner near the entrance of the building. A fire of curiosity raged inside Sofi, a warm desire to know all about her. Jamila Khala was her mother's younger sister. She had emigrated to Canada from Pakistan with her husband, whom Sofi remembered calling "Jimmy Uncle," a moniker she also remembered as being odd if not ludicrous at the time. Her memories of Jamila Khala, Jimmy Uncle and Fatima were hazy; her mother barely spoke of her sister due to a falling-out after Sofi's parents had divorced. Sofi had asked Mama about Jamila Khala once, a few years after the divorce when Mama had first started working her new job at a bank, as to why they no longer spent any time with the family. Her mother lit a cigarette, contemplated the question and looked back at Sofi, coldly. "Your khala seems to think she knows what's right for everyone," said Mama. Sofi decided to let the beast of that breakup lie undisturbed, the divorce still fresh in her mind.

"It's all coming back to me," said Sofi. "It's like I blocked those days out of my memory."

"Do you remember you used to live with us when you first came to Toronto?"

"We did?"

"Yeah," said Fatima, with incredulity. "Ammi said you came from the Middle East, and I kind of expected you to have your head wrapped in a veil." They both laughed together. "This was before I started wearing this, of course," said Fatima, rubbing the top of her cloth-covered head. She stared at Sofi. "Your accent's changed. I remember you sounded more British."

Sofi shrugged her shoulders slightly. "I really took to Canada." She turned away from Fatima briefly, looking up toward the blue sky in contemplation. "It's so stupid that we had to meet like this," she continued laughingly. She turned back to Fatima. "I never really understood what happened between Khala and my mother."

Fatima's expression changed, her face heavier, her mouth pursed. "I think, with Ammi," she said, the speed of her words slowing, "your mother wasn't happy with the way her life was going, and she was trying her best to help her." Fatima stopped talking and raised her hands slightly. "That's what I think."

Sofi had an idea what Fatima was trying to say, and familial diplomacy did not stop her from recognizing the parts of her past that were broken. She wasn't angry at Fatima; if anything, it signalled a warmth in her cousin that made her comfortable.

"I know what you mean," said Sofi. "Mama has a temper."

Runaway thoughts collided in Sofi's head: her parents' divorce, overheard conversations between Babba and Mama about a woman in their new North York apartment, more overheard calls between Khala and Mama, her mother insisting that her sister mind her own business and stop judging, a solitary conversation with Babba on her bed, explaining to her that her parents were not going to live with each other anymore in his clipped, Anglicized accent, his moist eyes looking at her as he explained how much he loved her and how she wasn't to cry or complain about what was going on. She wanted to hold her father then, but she was caught, a prisoner of her resentment.

"How is Khala anyway?" said Fatima.

"She's as good as ever, I suppose."

"I wanted to see her," said Fatima with hesitation, "at the funeral."

Sofi's face dropped. She had forgotten so much of that day, so many faces, so many emotions, and she now realized she had forgotten that Jamila Khala was there too. She had quarantined that time in her life behind whatever mental barriers she could muster, aware how the rest of her soul could be infected. She now remembered Khala being at her brother Sikander's funeral, a blue dupatta covering her hair. Sofi couldn't remember if Khala said anything to her, although she could remember a brief, awkward embrace between her aunt and her mother, both faces stern and holding back tears.

Sofi turned toward her cousin. "I wanted to be there," said Fatima, her voice soft, mournful, hesitant. "At the janazah, I mean. I was out of the country, and Ammi said it was okay if she went for the family anyway."

"It's all right," said Sofi, her abruptness a way of changing the subject, and lessening Fatima's contrition.

An early autumn breeze hit Sofi. The blanket of light above them had vanished as clouds covered the sky. They sat silently together on the bench as students streamed past them, then sat up simultaneously, knowing they had classes to go to.

"This doesn't have to be the only time we meet," said Fatima. "You know, just because our mothers don't talk doesn't mean we shouldn't."

"I know," said Sofi softly. "We should see each other again soon." Her voice was calm and just barely audible over the laughter of a group of female friends rushing together into the library.

They hugged after exchanging numbers and waved as they said goodbye. Sofi walked down the street to class, her route lined with what looked like first-year students, their faces beaming as if they were excited to be real adults, with every inkling that university would be another version of high school, but with more opportunities, more friends, more freedom and more stimulation – a long road with no tolls and endless forks, a life Sofi was certain was also her own.

4

Friday mornings, Sofi had an appointment with her university therapist. She debated going to see someone for months, until over the summer Lily convinced her that she might as well give it a try. Sofi was skeptical. "What am I going to get from it?" she asked abruptly.

"Insight," said Lily. "Control."

"Control," repeated Sofi. She never spoke to Lily with any bit of impatience or disdain, and she felt horrible doing so, even if she had difficulty controlling her anger at the suggestion.

Lily took no notice of her irritability. "You get to talk to someone who doesn't owe anything to you, and you don't owe anything to them about –" Lily stopped herself from mentioning her brother. Sofi wanted to retort, wanted to lacerate her with her rage on the futility of finding relief in anything, but her friend's basic kindness and a lack of a logical excuse made her stop herself. She promised Lily she would see what it was like, even if both of them knew it was a half-hearted pledge.

The thought of seeing a private professional outside the university system wasn't possible. Therapy was expensive, a drain on her limited funds. This was her second visit to the school therapist since she'd started seeing her over the summer break; some vague university rule dictated that she was eligible for no more than three. The therapist was a casually dressed middle-aged woman with short, cropped hair, named Carol. The first time Sofi saw her felt underwhelming, a one-hour intake meeting where she was asked to summarize her life, itemizing each wound in her personal history – including Sikander's passing. She initially questioned the value of continuing after she left Carol's office but decided to continue anyway in the hope of finding some future edification from the experience.

At the start of the second session, Carol greeted Sofi with a curt friendliness and became more reserved the instant Sofi sat down in her small, studious office. Just as she had at their last appointment, she walked around the room, closing the door with deliberate slowness, fiddled with her blinds in a way that did little to change the amount of sunlight in the office, and placed a glass of water on the table next to Sofi's chair. Sofi assumed these small rituals were her way of allowing her clients time to feel at ease.

Carol finally sat down, crossed legs, leaned forward with her hands clasped in her lap and asked Sofi how she was feeling.

After a perfunctory "fine," Sofi began recounting her week: studying, the time spent starting an internship at Queen's Park doing policy research supporting MPPs at the Legislature and even briefly mentioning Robin, admitting that she had met "a boy." Sofi held back her deeper feelings, her hope that he was a chance for a clear break from the past, the possibility of change, of love.

Carol smiled, unclasped her hands and sat back. "It seems," she said, her words measured, "that things are better than the last time we spoke."

"I guess they are," said Sofi, looking down at her own hands, rubbing them nervously together. She remembered her first session, when she could barely look at Carol, when she could scarcely describe her brother's end to her. "Maybe."

"It's not an easy process," said Carol. "For things to get better, for you to accept things. It's natural for the bad feelings to linger with you."

"How long am I supposed to have things that 'linger' with me?" asked Sofi, as if looking for a concrete measurement.

"That's not something anybody can determine."

"Can I determine it?"

"I believe you can." Carol pushed herself forward again. "I've had clients who've actually set deadlines for themselves after a trauma – six months, twelve months, after the incident."

"Does that work?"

"For some it does."

Sofi didn't believe her and shifted in her seat. Carol remained still, waiting for her to speak. Sofi felt cornered.

"I wanted to come here," said Sofi, "and tell you that everything was all right now."

"But it's not," said Carol, completing her thought.

"I met someone the other day. My cousin. I hadn't seen her in years."

"That must have been nice."

"We used to live with her and my aunt and my uncle. The family grew apart." Sofi stopped herself. "Anyway, it's a long story. I was so happy to see her again. It really felt like I have a member of the family back in my life. We got to talking and she mentioned Sikander."

"What did she say about him?"

"She just apologized for not coming to the funeral."

"What did you say?"

"Nothing. I just said I understood."

"Would you have wanted her to come to the funeral?"

"No, it's not that," said Sofi, her voice strained, exasperated. "I have a recurring dream. Every time it happens, I see my brother's coffin. When I get closer to it, it oozes blood, like his body wasn't dead, like someone just scooped it up after the accident and placed it between planks of wood."

Sofi shook her head. Her face froze as she tried to hold back her tears.

"What do you think that has to do with your cousin?" Carol continued. "Were you angry that she mentioned him? Perhaps you resent her –"

"No, I don't resent her," Sofi interrupted. "I accepted that my brother was gone a long time ago. I still keep his photo next to my bed. I always turn it down when my mother comes in the room. I think of him as gone, but I never think of him as dead. The moment she talked about the funeral, I shut it from my mind. Then at night it all comes back."

"What comes back?"

"Death." Sofi brushed a tear from her cheek. "And it's telling me that, no matter how far I run toward someone to care for, to love, someone in this world who can take me away from death, that person will end up underground too."

"That's part of the fight everyone has to face," said Carol, her voice echoing in the room. Sofi heard the faint sounds of keyboards and ringing phones outside the door.

"Yes, all of us," said Sofi. "My brother tried to fight that fight, and he lost. He just lost quicker than most people. And I'm left fighting life alone. Without him."

5

Sofi considered not seeing Robin, cancelling the date and taking some time for herself. She thought better of it. Since her brother's death, she had noticed different parts of her personality coming out: the angry Sofi; the maudlin, self-pitying Sofi; the escapist Sofi. She pledged to herself that tonight would be the "stone Sofi," with iron in her heart, stoic, immune to hurt.

She took the subway to meet him. There was a stream of people coming in and out of the train, like a vessel being emptied and refilled constantly, each set of new occupants louder, younger, hanging on the overhead bars, jamming themselves next to her, their bodies facing every direction but hers. Sofi felt alone as the train hurtled through concrete and metal veins. She needed to fight against herself and the tendency to go deep within her own mind since Sikander had passed away. Perhaps Robin was a guide to a new place, a vehicle to a higher ground, away from death, from sadness, toward warmth, toward flesh.

It was Robin who suggested a sushi restaurant, not far from the university. Sofi was less interested in food that night than in simply being out. She had assignments due – some completed, others in their nascent stages – but she wanted to give herself a break. Robin insisted on meeting her outside the subway exit. "I'm trying to be a gentleman," he explained to Sofi as they walked to the restaurant. Every word he said was spoken softly, the movement of his mouth settling into a comfortable, sincere smile.

The restaurant was new and sterile in its cleanliness. The tables were as square, polished and unadorned as the chopsticks and ceramic soy sauce containers that lay upon them. The narrow entrance was blocked by an effortlessly friendly greeter, who whisked them to a back booth within seconds of their arrival.

Tiny candles on the table illuminated Robin's face as he talked. They started with typical chit-chat: being back in class, new courses taken, desired courses full for registration. There was a reserve in Robin that Sofi picked up on, and she asked him about himself as a way to make him feel more at ease. Robin took it as an opportunity to reveal his entire life to her: his parents, very political academics who taught in Guelph; his interest in politics, law and human rights. His words came out at a telegraphic pace. Sofi sat attentively, her forearms crossed on the table, right hand coming up occasionally to support her chin. The garrulous types were usually her least favourite; she used to equate talkativeness with self-absorption. But Robin was different. His voice and the speed of his words revealed a childlike enthusiasm beneath a cerebral veneer, seeming to Sofi that he had someone to share his thoughts with for the first time in his life.

Robin continued talking and caught himself in mid-sentence. "I haven't even bothered to ask about you," he said, embarrassed. He asked Sofi first about her accent, and she told her story: about growing up in the UK and the Middle East, about going to a mishmash of American and British schools before coming to Canada.

"Your parents are Pakistani, right?" asked Robin.

"Well, yes. I'm a Pakistani too."

His hands raised briefly from the table, a placating motion, acknowledging a mistake had been made, a point had been conceded. "You're right, of course. The country's fascinating to me."

Sofi giggled and cocked her head. "Fascinating?"

"I mean, what's going in the world right now. I was talking

about this with my father. He was saying that we should expect the next ten or twenty years to be centred on four countries: Iran, Pakistan, India and Afghanistan." Robin stopped talking. Ridges formed around his mouth, his lips slightly elongated, as if suppressing that default smile Sofi was beginning to become accustomed to, most likely embarrassed by his own pedantry.

"I haven't been back in years," said Sofi. A waitress came by, and they ordered their food. Robin asked her with elaborate politeness if she wanted a drink. Sofi declined. When the waitress left, Robin maintained an attentive pose and Sofi continued her life story. "It's so strange," she said. "People like asking me questions about Pakistan or Afghanistan all the time these days. They see something in the news and they ask me to explain it. I try to keep up with the news cycle and sometimes I have really intelligent conversations about, I don't know, everything. Geopolitics. Women's rights. Religious politics. Things like that." She stopped and looked over at the two well-dressed, middle-aged couples seated at the opposite end of the restaurant. "But whenever I'm having these conversations, I always feel like I'm giving a lecture."

Robin looked embarrassed. "I'm sure you're sick of people wanting to talk to you about your homeland as if it's this exotic, dangerous place. I suppose for them it's this abstract place that they intellectualize."

"It's not that much of a homeland to me," said Sofi. "I was raised everywhere else but there." Robin and Sofi were leaning toward each other; when the waitress came, they straightened up, making way for the miso soup, chopped salad and water. "Anyway, you're right, though. It's weird for me to talk about a place like I'm a TV pundit, when it's just a country where I played with my cousins and visited my family."

Robin laughed as he mixed his salad together with his chopsticks. He had a short, heavy laugh that was more masculine than Sofi thought it would be.

The sushi came quickly. They ate and continued to talk, a rhythm arising in their conversation. Robin's nervousness dissipated; his words slowed. Sofi began to feel less inhibited around him. She told him stories about growing up abroad, coming to Canada, about her family in Lahore and Karachi, about Khala and Fatima, barely mentioning her parents' separation, and avoiding Sikander and the accident altogether. The more his attention focused on her, the more she noticed things about him: the way his head tilted slightly to his left when he was pensive; the way he always folded his arms on the table; the way his eyes peered into a distant space away from her whenever he was contemplating something she said.

They barely touched their food. Robin paid the bill, even after Sofi insisted on paying her share. As she placed her hand over the small plastic tray containing the receipt, he lightly placed his own over hers.

"It's my treat."

"You don't have to treat me," said Sofi.

"Let this be my way of saying thank you," said Robin.

He gently squeezed her hand before reaching into his coat pocket for his wallet.

♦

Robin asked Sofi what she wanted to do next. She suggested that they go for a walk.

Blasts of wind battered them as they walked in the street. The sidewalks were crowded, and Sofi and Robin glided through crowds of students, occasionally glancing at each other and smiling as the people around them talked and laughed. In an empty stretch of the street, Sofi nuzzled next to him, linking her arm through his, their strides completely in tune, two instruments playing the same song.

A man in a dirty baseball cap came up to them both, asking if they had change. With ease, Robin took out several coins with his free hand and gave them to the man. He smiled and thanked them both kindly.

Sofi looked behind her briefly as the man stumbled toward another couple. The sight of his solitude made her think of Sikander's death. She was struck by the idea that the line separating her and the man was thin, that the loss of all she loved could easily unmoor her from the world she knew. She floated back in time. Mama on the floor crying. The hospital. The kabristan where Sikander's coffin entered the ground, a reverse birth into cold soil, Sofi thought, as she stood back to see the men of the community bury him. And then the expectation of normalcy. As if all was mended. As if she was not a woman without a home.

"Are you okay?" asked Robin.

"He seems so alone," said Sofi.

Robin turned to see the homeless man. "I suppose he does."

"I wonder what happened in his life to get to this stage, with no family or friends."

"Adrift."

"Exactly. Adrift. It scares me."

"What does?" asked Robin, curiously.

"Being disconnected. Having no one you had a history with around you."

"Do you really worry about that?"

"Of course," said Sofi, her voice rising above honking horns close to an intersection.

"I think everyone living is as adrift as that man we just passed. We all have our own minds, our own egos, our own bodies, completely separate from each other."

"That sounds cold."

Robin shrugged. "I actually don't think it is. People put too much value in being together, and treat being alone as if it's a terrible curse that people are condemned to."

"But I'm not just talking about being alone. I'm talking about finding your way after losing everything. How can you live that type of life?"

Robin looked at the sky, taking a thoughtful pause. "I don't have an answer for that question. Maybe, when you've lost everything, you can still find moments when you can discover ways of connecting with people, even if they're brief."

"Small victories through small connections," said Sofi.

"Something to be grateful for, I guess," said Robin. "Like tonight. That panhandler was probably grateful for the change and the ability to just smile at someone. I'm grateful too."

"For getting to smile back?"

"For this," said Robin. They stood at an intersection. "For the night. For getting to be with you."

Light covered everything around them – car headlights, stop signs, the circus-like play of the lights from the large discount store at the corner of the street – and bounced off Robin's pale skin. Without hesitation, Sofi moved forward, tilted her head up and he kissed her.

"I'm grateful too," she said.

6

Sofi's mother and father had fought constantly. They wanted to avoid arguing in front of the children, but the walls were thin and porous. Sofi would close her eyes, pressing her head farther into a pillow, trying to shut out her parents' voices as the intensity of their arguments rose and fell.

Sofi knew a woman was involved in the arguments somehow, not from any words she heard, but from instinct, a noticeable distance between Mama and her father that she assumed – or possibly imagined – was a gap created by a new feminine presence in Babba's life. Her father, unfailingly affectionate with everyone, seemed distant with her mother, the kisses on the cheek he made, even in public – something other Pakistani couples their age frowned on – became emptier, eventually draining into non-existence. Sofi knew something was wrong, although as time edged forward, she realized the domestic unity she'd assumed was real had been only a veneer.

In one of those fights years ago, Sofi remembered her bedroom door opening and Sikander slinking in, crying, trying to choke back his gasps and tears. She turned on her side lamp and he stood in front of her. Tears smeared the dark skin of his cheek, his eyes bleary and red. He looked at Sofi with confusion.

"Come here," said Sofi. She turned back a part of her blanket, and switched off the light after Sikander climbed in.

"Don't cry," said Sofi. She put her arms around his chest. "Just close your eyes."

He lay next to her, a log of sparse flesh, almost entirely bone. She was frightened for him. She wondered how he would feel if Mama and Babba separated. He wouldn't be able to handle it.

His whimpers fell away, and his regular breathing returned. She felt the rise and fall of his chest, her arm draped limply over his body. The shouting wasn't over; it was only quieter, muffled. Sofi was sure her parents went down the corridor, probably realizing how loud they were.

"Are they always going to be like this?" Sikander whispered.

"No," said Sofi. "Everything's going to be fine. They fought before; they'll fight again."

"I wish I could fly away."

"Just stop talking and sleep," she said, her voice exasperated. Her annoyance hurt him, she could tell.

She held him tighter. "Where would you go if you could fly away?" she asked.

"I don't know."

"Would you take me with you?"

He giggled, a snorting laugh, half-amused, possibly; an ever-present sadness there, definitely.

She shook him. "Well, answer me."

"Yes," he said, the word expelled from his body like a long sigh.

"There's one problem. I'm too big to fly. Don't you think?"

Sikander turned his head toward her. In the moonlight seeping through the thin cracks of the blinds she could see him shaking his head.

"You don't think I'm too big?"

He smiled. Moist droplets of tears limned his eyes. "You're too skinny."

"No. I'm big and fat. I have to stay put. And you have to stay with me."

He said nothing.

"Promise you'll stay with me. It's not really fair that you have wings and I don't."

She knew her brother. Precocious at his age, sharp, quiet but incapable of suffering fools, she knew he probably scorned her attempts at making him feel better.

"Okay. I'll stay here with you."

He turned his head away from her. They heard doors slamming shut. Mama and Babba had gone to separate rooms. Sikander and Sofi were the only ones in the house not alone.

Sofi watched Sikander as he fell asleep, the sound of his breathing, his thin chest exhaling. She removed her arm and turned on her side, away from him. "Everything's going to be okay," she whispered. She closed her eyes and tried to sleep, fighting desperately against the thoughts assaulting her: she knew change would besiege her family soon, and she would have to be his protector, the only one with the courage to lie to him.

Sofi often wondered if there were songs that spoke to the times in one's life, times for remembering and forgetting. She was sure that artists and poets and prophets spoke of these things. This seemed like a moment to forget the foul past and focus on good things happening. She did this by spending more time with Robin. It seemed to be the start of something.

One day, Sofi received a message from Fatima, asking if she wanted to get together. They met on a Thursday afternoon outside the library, on the opposite side of the building from where they'd first met. There was a peculiar emptiness on that side of campus, with hardly a student hurrying toward class. Sofi saw Fatima on a lone bench between the library's back entrance and the green, damp lawn ringed with well-cultivated trees. Fatima's eyes gazed peacefully into nothingness before turning to Sofi as she approached.

Sofi said hello, kissed her on the cheek, close to where her hijab met her bare skin, and sat down next to her.

"I never knew this part of the campus existed," said Sofi.

"I love it," said Fatima. "I find myself at peace here."

"It seems like that type of place." Sofi stared at the open lawn with Fatima. After a few moments, she realized she wasn't feeling the same peace Fatima must be feeling; the emptiness of the lawn, the lack of city bustle and of people drained her of stimulation. "It also seems lonely."

"That's not always a bad thing."

Sofi saw Fatima was holding a tasbih in her right hand. "Do you come out here to pray?"

Fatima smiled and shook her head. "Not specifically. It's just something I do whenever I have a spare moment."

Sofi was curious. "What do you feel when you're praying?"

Fatima stared back into the open space, the temples near the border of her hijab pensively strained. "At first I did it to feel calm. I used to get so stressed at school, so Ammi gave me this and said I should recite 'alhamdulillah' thirty-three times and everything would turn out for the best."

"Praising God and hoping for things to work out for the best?" asked Sofi, her smile warm but skeptical.

Fatima continued without a beat, as if ignoring the questioning tone. "Well, I just did it for its own sake. I thought it couldn't hurt. But I really did it because Ammi told me. After a while it became an empty habit."

"Empty?"

"It had no real meaning. I started going to these halaqas, these gatherings for female Muslim students here on campus. We invited this one sister, I think she was doing her PhD in Islamic studies. She was giving a lesson about excellence in worship that really stuck with me."

"What did she say?"

"I think her exact words were 'Every life has Allah as an end goal. Because he should be on your mind at every moment, every act of worship should be God-centred, and you should come to the point where every action you do should be an act of worship in and of itself.'" Fatima looked back at Sofi. "With this," she added, dangling the tasbih, "I can carry him wherever I go. It's stupid. I don't know if you can understand that."

"Yes," said Sofi. "I can."

They walked off campus and had lunch at a café that catered to the college crowd that could afford more than noodles and fast food. They talked about their mothers and everyday school stresses. There was a serenity in her cousin that Sofi found fascinating. Her movements were economical and fluid. She had a reserved nature, a palpably calm and solid inner core that was enviable. Since high school Sofi hadn't been around many religious people, feeling that she had little affinity with them. Part of this, she knew, was a result of her upbringing. Her parents spoke of religion with a quiet dismissal – if they spoke of it at all. Aside from token appreciation of a cultural lineage – an occasional presence by Babba at a mosque for Friday prayers, various Qur'anic invocations made when speaking with family friends or, more importantly, with clients and colleagues who were far more earnest in their religiosity – their household was an unconsciously secular space. Both Mama and Babba cultivated what Sofi knew others considered a relatively Westernized outlook, where left-wing politics, art and literature were far more interesting than traditionalism or pious religious revivalism.

Sofi found herself proud of her newfound friendship with Fatima. That they were kin, yet so obviously different from each other, made the relationship altogether more meaningful to her. She told her cousin she never wanted to lose their relationship.

Fatima nodded in understanding. "Can I ask you a question?"

"Of course."

"Are you interested in coming to one of my study circles?"

Sofi thought about Fatima's offer for a few moments. She wondered what the experience would be like and the reason behind the offer.

"What would I do there?"

"Just come. Be with us."

The circles were held Sunday morning, upstairs in an old house bought by the university and turned into an international student centre. It was the first time Sofi had been there. She met Fatima at the entrance at ten in the morning sharp. Fatima took her on a brief tour of the centre – the Federation of Muslim Students, which Fatima volunteered with on occasion, often booked some of the rooms for functions, meetings and prayers. Most of the rooms on the first floor looked like living rooms transformed into meeting areas or study nooks filled with plain, leather sofas that looked far too contemporary to be placed next to the elegant plasterwork of the walls. They climbed the narrow stairs to the third floor. Sofi was impressed by the floor's neatness: blue carpeting, cubicle table, and furniture packed into miniscule geometric corner rooms, the entire space looking almost bland in its cleanliness.

Fatima led her to an open area meant for prayers. Spare prayer mats were rolled and stacked on top of each other in one corner next to a short, eggshell-white bookcase filled with Qur'anic translations, collections of hadith, sayings of the Prophet and thinner, didactic treatises in English with titles such as "Inheritance Law in Islam," "Women's Rights in Islam" and "Lessons from the Companions." The circle was starting: four women, all wearing hijab, sat cross-legged on the floor. They smiled and quietly made room for them. At once, Sofi felt awkward for not covering her hair, despite her cousin's assurance that it was not required – it was an all-female gathering, and technically they didn't need headscarves. The sensation of otherness, of being somehow inauthentic, a person of marginal, lukewarm faith among knowledgeable and committed believers, assailed her. Sofi's fears were alleviated by their smiles and their unhesitatingly warm salaams. The older woman leading the circle was white, possibly a convert, with greenish eyes, freckles and wide, thin lips. Sofi surmised she was a PhD student, probably in her thirties.

Fatima nudged Sofi to move over. They started with a supplication. Sofi raised her hands with them. They ended their du'a, wiping their faces with their hands to signal its conclusion. The sister at the front of the circle started off by greeting Sofi with an eloquently enunciated "assalamu alaikum" followed by "good to have you here," as if she had been expecting her. Each participant introduced herself briefly to the group: at the head was Halima, followed by Sakina, Ayesha, Farheen, Sofi and Fatima.

The lesson being taught that day was on death and taqwa, God-consciousness. Halima, with a mixture of academic precision and a convert's enthusiasm, peppered her lecture with common, familiar Islamic references to the Qur'an and the Hadith, and even more esoteric Arabic terms that betrayed both her presumed doctoral interests and her immersion in Islamic pedagogy.

At first, the ideas presented to Sofi seemed dense and almost impenetrable. She stopped following the lecture as she began drowning in the words of wisdom she was hearing. Snippets of dialogue attached themselves to her mind:

". . . we always have to remember what the Prophet, sallallahu alayhi wasallam, said, that we must be in this world like a traveller on the road . . ."

". . . It's our responsibility to think about death. When one thinks about death, one really thinks of Allah. And Allah is the end of all things . . ."

The session ended after an hour. Sofi was the last person to stand up, musing on what she had heard. The sisters left, inviting Sofi and Fatima to join them for a meal at a Moroccan place they knew just south of the university. They both politely declined, almost in unison. In a contemplative daze, they walked together to the subway. Fatima asked Sofi if she wanted to stop for a coffee. Sofi nodded and said, "Sure."

In a café beside the subway they ordered two small cappuccinos, sat and looked at each other for less than five seconds before Sofi asked what was on her mind: "Why did you want me to come today?"

"I just wanted to share my interests," she said simply, staring down at her cup. "Isn't that what people do when they want to connect with each other? Are you mad at me?"

Sofi turned away from Fatima. She wasn't angry, but she was upset, not at her cousin, but because of an unknown feeling undermining her sense of calm. "I'm not mad," Sofi said.

Fatima tried to assure her that the sisters there were friendly and well meaning, and that she didn't want Sofi to feel awkward about being there. Sofi assured her that she felt no awkwardness. "But I have to ask," she said. "Did you want me to come here for something specific?"

Fatima looked directly at Sofi, her self-absorption now gone. "This week's lecture was going to be on the life of the grave. I thought it might do you some good to listen."

Sofi's face contorted involuntarily. "Why?"

"Because last time we met you said that you were afraid of losing me. And I felt there was something in that statement that made me think of Sikander."

"So you thought this would make me feel better?"

"I thought it would give you some insight." Fatima's words were soft and clear. At first, Sofi thought she had rehearsed her response, but realized quickly that Fatima's calm serenity communicated a deep sincerity and a desire to help.

Sofi said nothing, a silence that Fatima respected with her own wordless stare. Sofi looked around her. Patrons were lined up for coffee on her left; there was little rush on the weekend. Those who sat down, sat down alone, sipping their coffee pensively, gazing out the window as if gathering repose from the darkening sky.

Slowly Sofi's thoughts on Fatima changed. She realized her cousin was not trying to be a middle-class preacher, the tablighi type, calling her cousin, daughter of a liberal wrongdoer, back into the fold. What started as resentment became an understanding, an acceptance that her cousin was trying to help her – to present the death that had surrounded her as a part of a natural, divine order, therapy by the holy word.

"At Sikander's funeral," Sofi said, "my parents kept their distance from each other. There was a friend of Babba's, Uncle Tayyab, who made a du'a after they finished burying him."

"What was it?"

Sofi waved her hand. "Usual things. Asking Allah mian to protect Sikander, protect his family, protect everyone else's family. After that everybody went their own way, and Babba and Uncle started talking. I walked up to them while Mama was talking to someone, where all the women were. I came up to Babba's side and he put his arm around my shoulder. Uncle Tayyab was still talking and they completely ignored me."

Sofi sighed deeply as she tried to compose her thoughts without tears.

"What happened?" asked Fatima.

"Uncle Tayyab told my father that he needed to recite Surah Yaseen and Surah Mulk as often as he could on Sikander's behalf."

"I've heard that too," Fatima said, sitting back up in her chair.

"And he also said that he should make du'a as much as possible, to grant him the best in the next life, and to protect him from the torments of the grave." Sofi paused. She leaned forward, looked away from Fatima, her arms close to her body as if giving herself comfort and warmth from an invisible, unknowable cold. "The 'torments of the grave,'" repeated Sofi. "That's exactly what he said, in English."

"But that is what we believe in," said Fatima with a pleading gentleness.

"That God tortures us after we die?"

"We need to be protected from our own sins, don't we?"

Sofi sat unmoved, expressionless, trying to suffocate her sullenness.

"I'm sure what that man said to khalu was meant with the best of intentions. If Sikander's innocent, there will be no torment –"

"There's no 'if,'" interrupted Sofi. "No one is as innocent as Sikander." She took a sip of her coffee. "*Was.*"

When they arrived at the subway, they waited on the platform together, Fatima going west, Sofi going east. They stood in the middle of the platform, facing each other. Sofi felt guilty, wondering if perhaps she had been too combative with her cousin, too caught up in the mire of her frustration to have absorbed Fatima's goodwill. As Fatima stood in front of her, hands in her pocket, Sofi struggled to say something beyond "sorry" for her anger. Fatima stepped closer to Sofi and placed her hand on her arm, rubbing it gently.

"You should be angry. There's a lot to be angry about." She took her hand away. "I really hope you didn't think I was trying to preach to you."

"No, you weren't," said Sofi, still unsure whether she meant what she had just said.

"I don't know if I'd ever be good at proselytizing anyway."

"I think you'd be great at it. I've heard there are isolated islands in the Indian Ocean who've never had contact with outsiders.

Maybe you can go there and convert them, you know, teach them how to pray, maybe teach them how to wear the hijab."

Fatima looked stunned, her large black eyes wide and glaring. Sofi smiled, barely containing her laughter. Soon her short giggles bubbled over, infecting Fatima, who covered her mouth as onlookers standing near the yellow marker at the track stared briefly at the noise before turning away.

They hugged each other as the train came, and, for a brief moment, Sofi felt a renewed connection with Fatima as the warmth of her cheek brushed against hers. Fatima promised to call her as Sofi rushed for the train's closing door. She entered and rested her cheek against the clear plastic panel beside her. She closed her eyes and thought of her brother, God and death, realizing this was the first time she had thought about all three things at the same time. Perhaps it was a gift Fatima had given her. Thinking of Sikander was natural, as was death, a spectre she was resigned to have lurking in her mind as long as she could disassociate it from her brother. But God was something separate. She believed in God, but up to this point he had played little part in her life or Sikander's death. For the first time since she was a child she spoke to God, as if he existed in her mind as an invisible accountant that weighed and balanced deeds against each other, and she pleaded with certainty that her brother deserved only peace in the grave and joy in the hereafter, regardless of how his short life was lived, or in what cruelty it had ended.

7

It was Mama who told Sofi that Sikander was gone.

A Sunday afternoon. Sofi was cleaning her room. She loved order in her personal space, even as a child. Every novel and university textbook in her small white bookcase arranged by height, every sweater and shirt folded elicited a sense of control she desperately needed since her parents' divorce. As she finished hanging her last sweater, she heard a long choking sound that pierced into her room from her half-open door. By the time Sofi left the room and turned the corner toward the kitchen, the guttural noise morphed into a deep wail. She found Mama in the kitchen, the phone handset off its cradle next to her, as she sat on the floor behind the dark, oak countertop, her head buried in her thighs, her tiny body sucked into itself. Sofi sat down on the floor and held her mother, cradling her neck like she was her child, drowning in her own fear that something terrible had happened.

She knew it was about Sikander. It had to be.

Tears ran down Sofi's face, trickling into the dark copper-coloured mass of her mother's hair. Sofi's breathing was shallow, her throat constricted. She didn't think of death at first, but of beginnings, the beginning of a new existence, a world suddenly shattered.

The police informed her father about what happened. It was Babba who relayed all they knew to Mama. Sikander told his mother he was visiting a friend of his in Stouffville. Sofi knew those roads – the traffic decreases, the speed limits rise, the suburbs giving way to vast, dark and wooded country stretches. She worried about him, scarcely an adult, still a new driver barely used to the roads.

He ran a hanging traffic light along one of those roads, the type that emerge in lonely roads and are easily missed when distracted. Whatever distracted him, said the police, was enough to cause him to run the light. A truck at the intersection braked in advance, but it was not enough to stop the impact. The force of the collision spun the Toyota around twice.

"Twice around," said Babba. "Like a spinning plate."

It was Babba, exhausted and stoic, who relayed the details to Sofi and her mother as he drove them to the hospital. The lines of her father's face appeared deeper than when she had last seen him. He lived midtown, possibly alone, possibly with the last girlfriend Sofi had seen him with, she wasn't sure. The waiting room they sat in was barren save for a middle-aged couple speaking Cantonese sitting near the door. Their faces were impassive, their conversations muted and, at times, almost monosyllabic. Distress, it seemed to Sofi, assumed a similar pattern with everyone. The couple's calm demeanour was not an acceptance of whatever had befallen them, but fearful resignation, the realization that an event had happened beyond their control, and little could be done to change things.

Her mother sat sniffling and dabbing her tears in the waiting room; she seemed to have expended all her sadness after she had first heard the news, as if the worst-case scenario in her mind had already come true. The physical distance between her parents was palpable. Her father walked in circles, his hands behind his back, barely speaking to his ex-wife. Sofi sat next to her mother, holding her hand.

The doctor who gave them the news was balding but young. When he entered the room, her father stopped still; Mama and

Sofi looked at him. He wore operating room scrubs and had a tender smile that Sofi thought seemed strangely ominous. With soft-spoken directness, he explained that Sikander's injuries were too great: multiple fractures, including his ribs and left arm, a punctured lung and traumatic brain injury. Before he could finish, Sofi and her mother collapsed into each other, their gasping sobs matching each other in a synchronized chorus of grief. When she looked up, Babba was standing still, his wide hand covering his face, his chest heaving in aspirated sobs.

They buried Sikander shortly after. Her mother, usually domineering and lively, became almost serenely cold. Her father called more often, at first directly to the home line – which her mother promptly ignored – then just to Sofi's cell phone. In his conversations with her, he avoided discussing Sikander completely, focusing instead on paternal concerns around school and her life. Mama turned inward. Her friends – middle-aged, elegant, educated ladies, who had laughed at inside jokes, discussed the places they visited, the schools their children were attending – now held her hand and looked into her vacant eyes as they gave afsos, their condolences. Her parents rarely spoke Sikander's name, and then even that rarity stopped altogether, as if Sikander's name was anathema. Sofi found herself shocked at the brevity of their mourning. She knew their pain was a cavernous parental sadness that they kept at bay with their routines: her mother's obsessive-compulsive cleaning and need in knowing Sofi's whereabouts; her father's constant calls, always so needy, always concerned and paternal, asking in his trench-deep baritone if she was studying, if she was going out and meeting people.

Soon Sofi realized, for the first time in her life, there was such a thing as genuine loneliness, a cloak that covered every moment, every experience.

Sofi formed new habits. She fought sleep, often lying in her bed, watching videos on the Internet, studying economic formulae, or sitting in the living room, zoning catatonically into post-midnight talk shows and infomercials. At other times, she gave herself no entertainment or academic escape. Instead, she simply stared at the spaces on her walls or ceiling, giving herself over to its overwhelming whiteness.

Her grief lingered, but her stasis eventually passed. Weeks and months went by, and she found enough inner strength to move beyond her self-enclosed routine. She went out with anyone she knew. She did everything she could to keep her mind occupied, throwing herself into school, throwing herself into anything that could fill the inner silence.

Months later and Sofi still struggled with the emptiness. The week after she met Fatima, Robin asked her out again. Thoughts of Sikander interfered with the enjoyment she wanted to experience. On the phone, she had felt a stinging annoyance when he had asked her, in his soft, boyish voice, to "come back downtown" to where he lived. For a moment she thought there was a selfishness in his request that revealed no place for her own convenience or her desires. She remained silent on the phone, half-expecting that Robin would intuit her feelings and make a magnanimous offer to meet her uptown.

"What's wrong?" Robin asked, breaking the lull in their conversation, his voice bass-heavy and grave.

Sofi was in her room. She peered out her door, staring at the mirror in the hallway. In the mirror, she could see the living room, an image of her mother on the couch embedded in the reflection, curled into the couch like an exhausted child. She heard the murmur of voices from the television. Her mother's eyes were wide and dark, one arm almost touching the floor, remote in hand, her body still and passive as if in a crime scene.

"Nothing's wrong," said Sofi. "I'll come down. I need to be out of here, anyway."

Sofi saw Robin standing outside the subway station exit, pacing back and forth, looking unusually nervous. When he saw her, he stopped and stared, looking strange and worried. Before he could speak, Sofi stepped up to him, grabbed his open coat by his lapels and pulled his face close to hers. She kissed him and, when she pulled back, Sofi saw that his nervousness had dissipated, and a wide, shocked smile emerged in its place.

They went out for dinner. Sofi was growing accustomed to the ease with which Robin spoke about himself, as if the silence between them was a vessel in need of constant filling. Sofi sat listening quietly, paying more attention to her food.

Robin looked at her solemnly. "I feel since I called you've been angry at something."

Sofi stared at her plate. Curry-stained noodles tangled over each other. She rested her chopsticks delicately on the side of the plate.

"Were you mad that I wanted you to come downtown?" Robin's eyes were large and plaintive. "I was thinking maybe you were."

"I'm not mad," Sofi said with a laboured smile.

"You should tell me if something's wrong," Robin said. His face was serious, his eyes narrowed and his lips pursed. Sofi was embarrassed, the strength of her aloofness had vanished, a tinge of guilt bringing colour into her face. She knew she had been powerless over her emotions before, and how bipolar her attraction had been, veering between distance and uninhibited warmth. She wasn't angry with Robin. How she felt had nothing to do with him. She had been sucked into herself, into her memories of Sikander, into her mother's eyes, into the grave.

"Maybe this was a bad idea," she said.

"What are you talking about?" His tone was soft, but drawn and impatient.

"I don't think I wanted to go anywhere tonight. I think I just wanted to be – away."

"From what?"

Sofi crossed her arms and leaned back in her seat. "Everything."

Robin turned his face downward. "You're an enigma to me," he murmured as if talking to the floor.

Clattering noises rang out from the kitchen far at the back, the volume contracting and expanding with every closing and opening of a single swing door. The restaurant was narrow, taking up a thinly sliced portion of the street, and with every ringing of the bell at the door, with every new couple or group of friends who entered, Sofi felt claustrophobic. Thoughts raced through her mind. She felt she had failed herself, failed Robin.

"I'm sorry," she said finally. She felt like leaving.

"There's no need for an apology."

Sofi brought her hands to the table and rubbed them nervously. "Remember the time we saw the homeless man on the street? I wondered how alone he must have felt."

Robin nodded.

She inhaled deeply. "That's the way I feel now. Alone."

"Even with me?" Robin asked.

"Even with you." Sofi shook her head. "But it's not your fault. It's my fault."

Sofi paused, gathering her thoughts. Her eyes were moist. She felt Robin's palm over her clenched hands, his slender fingers rubbing her wrist.

"If there's something you don't want to talk about, you don't have to talk about it now."

From his hand, she felt an avalanche of electricity begin to flow over her, from the back of her own hand, to her wrists, to her body, raising the thin hairs on her skin, like flowers rising toward the sun. The noises of the restaurant faded to a hum. Without saying anything, she felt the comfort of Robin's presence pushing aside the mournful darkness within her.

"Let's go someplace," Robin whispered as he squeezed her hands.

Sofi nodded. "Where?"

"Anywhere."

⁂

They left their meals almost untouched, paid the bill quickly and walked out into the street. They had no idea where they were going, and for minutes they simply walked: past unlit brick churches and construction sites, toward wider avenues, where the city seemed brighter and taxis prowled the streets for fares and pickups.

At a corner, Robin asked Sofi where she wanted to go. "We should decide," he said laughingly. "Otherwise we'll be walking forever."

Sofi looked toward the horizon and pointed east to the park. She wanted to be alone with Robin, filled by a desire for a shared solitude.

As they walked toward the park, passing the museum, the streets turned darker, the streetlamps barely illuminating the autumnal trees. When they entered the park, they were met by an equestrian statue. Robin told her it was a statue of King Edward VII.

"I actually hate this statue. A statue of Churchill should be here instead," he said. "He got things done."

They stood in the faint light staring at King Edward with his hand outstretched.

"There is something about these statues though, isn't there?" said Robin.

"What do you mean?"

He shrugged. "Permanence." He then looked down at Sofi.

"For literally thousands of years, this is what we have done to people. Encase their likeness in metal or marble or ceramic when we want to honour them."

"After they're dead, of course," said Sofi.

"That's the best time to do it." Robin looked back at the statue. "Have you ever seen pictures of Pericles? His bust I mean."

Sofi shook her head.

"Every time you see Pericles," said Robin, "you always see him with blank eyes, a rough curly beard and this helmet on his head. The first time I saw that face I had a sense of" – he hesitated – "regalness. Power. Achievement. My father used to tell me stories of all the great Greek gods and, at first, I thought Pericles was one of them. When I asked my father about him, he said 'He isn't a god.'"

"No," said Sofi, softly. "Just a man."

"Yeah, a man, but not 'just' a man. People can achieve what gods can. If you're honoured enough in this life you may as well be immortal. There's no need for an afterlife, just your name and a list of your good works and," he said, pointing to the statue, "then you become a statue. No more need for flesh."

Sofi recognized that Robin possessed an intellectual austerity, a mind very much attuned to this world and no other. This quality disturbed and attracted her. She found it compelling in its sharpness and brilliance, but alienating in its coldness.

Without noticing, they had been walking in circles around the statue, like pilgrims venerating a sacred object. The temperature had dropped, and Sofi shivered. Robin stopped walking and grabbed her right hand, covering it with both of his, rubbing her hands to warm them up. "Are your hands always this cold? You should wear gloves," Robin teased.

Sofi laughed. "You're the one who's keeping me out here in the cold, showing me monuments to dead kings, boring me about Greek culture," she said, pulling her hand away, and matching Robin's teasing with her flirtatious tone.

Robin threw his arms open. "So," he said, "where do we go from here?"

"Maybe I should go home," Sofi said quietly.

"Don't." His face turned serious. "Why do you need to go home?"

"For my mother."

"Would she mind if you stayed out late?"

Sofi thought about the question. Her mother would mind – but only mildly. There would be a conflict between her protective, maternal hawkishness and her hope and desire for her daughter to live her life.

"No," said Sofi. "She'd be fine with it."

"Do you trust me?" he asked.

"Yes. I do. Of course."

Robin took her by the arm. "Then come with me."

Robin didn't live far, only up the avenue and over to the right. His apartment was large, chic and clearly a residence for someone with money. It was far from the old, worn, dilapidated rentals Sofi's other friends lived in. The entrance and lobby were made of glass, with several leather couches and an off-white marble floor, looking strangely like the new, ultra-modern building the university had built for its business students.

Sofi told Robin she wanted to call her mother before they went upstairs. Mama didn't answer.

"Assalamu alaikum, Mama," she said into the answering machine, her voice nervous. "I'll be late. Please don't wait up." She didn't know what else to say. "I love you," she muttered quickly, before hanging up.

They went up the elevator and exited at the eleventh floor. Robin walked to his door, only steps away from the elevator. Sofi approached slowly, almost dragging her feet, and entered his apartment. Robin stood less than a foot away from her. She could feel his breath and the heat of his presence next to her.

Robin's hand grabbed onto the front of her jacket, tightly, as if he were fearful of her flying away. His other hand moved up to her shoulder, before he reached out and touched her cheek. Robin tilted her chin up and leaned forward. Without a word Sofi felt her mouth open, his tongue meeting hers. She felt completely enveloped by him, consumed, his presence eliminating all thoughts of her past and future.

8

Sofi took her cues from him. Every piece of clothing he dropped first, and she followed. It was the way she wanted it. She wanted his vulnerability on display before hers. Her guard was down, her armour lifted. Robin's eyes were fixed on her, arrested by the same fascination that she had for him. When his hands touched her – his long, pale fingers travelling on her skin – her temperature rose, like a cascading fever overtaking her.

Robin led her to his bed, a low mattress barely lifted from the floor. With a natural ease, she let him between her legs; a brief pain, briefer than she expected, and her arms were around him, one on his back, the other cradling his neck, his head drawn as close to her as she could manage, not wanting to let go. He lay on top of her after it was over, his heavy breathing falling on her neck.

Robin stood up for a moment over her and kissed her on her forehead, her eyes, her lips, before falling back down, his head on her chest, her arms encircling his head once more. She stroked his hair and caressed the lobes of his ear.

An alarm clock next to the bed – the red numbers set to the wrong time – blinked off and on from the bedside table. Sofi felt the weight of Robin's body with every heave of his chest. She fell fast asleep, knowing her world had changed.

Sofi woke up early, wrapped in the blue-black quilt she and Robin shared, and stared at the white stippled ceiling above the bed. He lay beside her, naked and still asleep. She reached down and touched the wooden floor beneath her. It felt organic and alive, and she imagined that she was lying next to Robin in a forest, a fanciful thought that was embarrassing but made her giggle nevertheless.

She knew he had heard her stirring. The mattress springs squeaked as his body shifted itself closer to her and he placed a warm hand on her stomach. The apartment was dry and Sofi delicately moved Robin's hands and rose from the bed, unconsciously taking the quilt with her. It was a studio apartment, one large room, and Sofi saw a glass and a large jug of water on the counter, as if miraculously placed there for her convenience in the kitchenette.

Sofi poured a glass of water and surveyed the apartment, thinking how empty it looked. But it was a barrenness full of possibilities, and her brain began spiralling with visions of rooms, apartments and houses that she and Robin would share in the future, full of foreign movie posters and souvenirs from countries and cities they had visited together. These pictures faded quickly from her mind and she felt immediately silly.

She heard a rustling from the bed. Robin got up and walked, naked and bleary-eyed, toward Sofi in the kitchen. He gave her a soft kiss on the cheek, as if he had spent the night with someone else entirely.

"What're you doing?" he asked.

"Thinking."

"You look funny thinking in *that*," he said, tugging on the quilt. Robin poured himself some water from the tap and walked back to the bed. She placed her glass on the countertop and followed him. He seemed perfectly at ease in the morning chill, his sinewy body curled in a fetal position. He shivered, and she took the quilt and covered them both, embracing Robin from behind.

Sofi closed her eyes, the smell of his sweat rushing up as she inhaled. "Last night, you asked me what was wrong, why I was so quiet."

Robin turned over and looked at her. He placed his hand lightly on her side, his fingers on her rib cage, slightly cold.

"There's something about me I didn't tell you. About my brother."

"You didn't tell me you had a brother," Robin said.

"I have one," said Sofi. "I *had* one."

"What do you mean?"

"He died. In a car crash." Sofi tried to hold back her tears. "It happened before Christmas last year. He was eighteen."

Slowly, with deliberation, Robin pulled her into his chest. Her head faced the window; gauzy light emanated from behind the thin, translucent curtains.

"I didn't want to tell you before," she said hoarsely.

"Why?" he asked.

"I didn't want to think about him when I was with you," she explained. Sofi felt an immense guilt burning within her as the words came out. "If I'm not with you or at school or with my friends, I'm at home with my mother, and he's still there. I look at my mother and I can tell she's dead inside. I get calls from my father and he talks to me as if he needs to protect me, like I'm about to die too."

Her confession came out in a rush. Sofi closed her eyes and felt his hand on her head.

"I'm so afraid of death, I can't think of anything else sometimes."

"Don't think about it," Robin said. "There's no death here."

Sofi lay still in his arms, letting his comfort cascade over her.

Sofi left for home an hour later. When she arrived, she was nervous, and opened the door of the apartment slowly. Her mother was already awake and she could hear the sound of plates clanging in the washing basin and rushing water echoing down the hallway. Sofi entered the kitchen. Mama's back was turned as she hovered over the basin, wearing a jogging suit that was both unusually large and strangely modern and casual for her.

Mama turned off the water and placed a plate in the drying rack.

"I got your message," her mother said, her back still turned to Sofi. "But you didn't tell me where you were."

"With Robin," said Sofi after a pause.

"I thought so. You should have said so last night, anyway." Mama turned around and gripped the edge of the countertop.

"I was safe." Sofi couldn't find the word. "I didn't want you to worry."

"I wasn't that worried," said Mama. "Did you have a good time?"

Sofi hesitated for words. "Yes."

"Good. I want you to be happy. You know that."

Her words, her lack of concern, struck Sofi as strange. She knew her mother wouldn't care that she had slept with Robin, as long as she didn't say it outright. Her mother had no sexual inhibitions, no personal cultural or religious taboos, as long as there was a respectable discreetness to it. Perhaps she was proud of her in some way. But the expression on her face was different, as it switched between openness and sourness.

Sofi came toward her mother. She placed her arms around her with a slow, methodical ease. They were the same height, and for a moment, before they embraced, there was a spark of recognition in Sofi as she looked at Mama: she was a reflection of herself, although one withered by time and circumstance.

Mama let her go. "Protect yourself."

"I know."

"You seem happy now. That's good. You owe that to us."

Sofi's thoughts halted. "What do I owe?" she asked, suppressing with little success the anger speckling her voice.

"Your happiness. Your life."

"I owe it to you and him?"

"I can't live for your bhai," Mama said.

Bhai. Her brother. Sikander. This is what she feared – she had an unresolvable obligation to the dead. And to the living.

"I owe you as well?" asked Sofi, trying to conceal the anger in her voice.

Mama nodded and stepped back from her, as far as the countertop allowed.

"Most of me is with him," said Mama.

Sofi understood her. Every child is a separate dream and a singular hope for a parent. She was the lone leftover, the one to carry on the heartbeat of her mother's lost son. The vitality of the mother she had known – the one who could charm her husband's colleagues over wine and dinner on every topic from Ghalib's poetry to the geopolitics of the oil industry, the one who could sculpt a home out of the marble of whatever country they had landed in – had been sapped. Mama had entered into a half-dead life. The other half could only be lived through Sofi, even if living with the weight of her brother's unfulfilled years would suffocate her.

There were few days of snow, but one could tell it was winter without even looking at the date. Sofi went to school grudgingly. She met with Lily and Andrew for lunch on occasion, and let their conversations whittle down from talk about school and her relationship with Robin to insular chatter about their own relationship, their long working hours at their part-time jobs and when to study for graduate exams and LSATs.

Sofi spent much of her time in her room pondering her life. Her room was unadorned save for an Ikea work desk, a bookshelf and the stacks of textbooks and papers lined up next to her bed. Mama had done her best to create a home after the separation. Sofi knew where her traits and those of her mother met. They had the same drive, the same struggle between a conservative sense of order and a free-spirited need for experience. Sikander's death brought out that conservative side in Mama. Winter was beginning to bring out the opposite in Sofi. She felt a longing and a desire that she could not articulate, even to herself, for something unnamable.

One day, studying in her room for end-of-term exams, she let her mind wander. Usually these mental breaks took the form of thought experiments; that day's experiment was on who would truly miss her if she suddenly died. Her parents came to the top of her mind. Fatima was included; despite their relatively short reunion, Sofi was convinced that their connection was more than just one of blood. Lily and Andrew appeared also; given the length of their friendship it seemed natural, although they would, in time, forget about her, their natural happiness keeping them afloat until she became an archived memory.

Robin also came to mind. The intimacy of their night together stayed with her, but the handful of moments they had spent together since seemed too casual. Their meetings retained the same surface-level warmth they'd had before they'd slept together, but it was an ease without real depth. He voiced his concerns for Sofi, of course, kissing her lovingly whenever they met, caressing her hand whenever they sat down for coffee or lunch or dinner. When he would ask how she was, Sofi kept herself from saying anything more than "I'm doing fine" or "Don't worry about me," with clear, quiet sadness that she found difficult to suppress. Robin would carry on talking, voicing his own academic and professional concerns.

Sofi got up from her seat – a hard, barely comfortable wooden chair – and walked over to the window. Flecks of white snow fell in front of her; she felt as if she was standing inside a giant snow globe, living in a perfectly self-contained universe from where she could watch and admire the world, but never enter.

The next day, Sofi's father called her for the first time in a long time. The conversation started the way it usually did, a guarded hello from both of them, with Babba asking how she was feeling and how her days had been. Sofi's responses were always carefully constructed: on better days, they were full of banal details of her daily routine – friends she was spending time with, exams she was concerned about, post-graduation options she was mulling over in her head. Before Sikander's death, and even after her parents' separation, Babba gave his advice and guidance on almost everything she did. After the accident, his advice – warm even if controlling – all but disappeared.

Sofi was sad and her usual talkative enthusiasm was muted, her responses monosyllabic. She tried to smile on the phone when she spoke to Babba – she had heard from someone that smiling on the phone, though invisible to the person on the other end, still had a calming, placid effect on the listener. It didn't work; Sofi could hear her father's sighs punctuating every one of her responses.

"I want you to come visit me," he said, once the silence had become unbearable.

"When?" she asked.

"Tonight if you can."

Sofi had been to her father's apartment infrequently since the divorce. The first time, shortly after the separation when Sofi was still in high school and Sikander was a precocious preteen, they were invited over to meet Babba's new girlfriend. They had no idea that was why they had been invited to dinner. It was her mother who'd speculated that was the reason. When she'd heard about the invitation, Mama, in an uncharacteristic break of reserve, slammed her coffee cup on the table and said, in cold, clearly enunciated English, "He wants to introduce you to that bitch."

They were allowed to go over anyway. Before Babba picked them up, Sikander asked who the "bitch" was that Mama was talking about. Sofi said she didn't know in a voice that was curt and strained, as if she had been asking this question herself for hours. How her mother had gathered the internal strength to allow her children to go with their father despite her strong feelings was beyond Sofi's comprehension.

They burst out of the front doors of the apartment building as soon as they saw Babba arrive. They embraced him when he got out of the car, throwing themselves at him as if they were toddlers greeting their father after a day at work.

They thought they were going to his new apartment, a two-bedroom investment property on St. Clair West, which he had bought to rent out for extra cash, and which he now used as his own personal, post-separation cave. Instead, Babba took them out for lunch, to a faux-European, self-consciously upscale restaurant west of his apartment. They spoke to each other as if neither Mama nor the divorce existed. Sikander overtook the conversation with bursts of energy, complaining about all the schoolwork he had to do, his fears of not getting the marks he wanted and his random dreams of getting into medical school.

"So why become a doctor?" asked their father teasingly. "Last time we met you said you wanted to go into banking? Get an MBA, yaar, or just go into business for yourself. You're smart enough. That way you won't have to spend fifty years in school before finally starting to make some money."

Sikander leaned forward. "No, Babba, you don't understand. I don't want to be a doctor to make money."

Sofi lovingly held Babba's hand, which was placed on the table. "This is what he's been saying for weeks," she said, with big-sister pride. "Want to know what his life goal is?"

"Can I tell my own life story?" interrupted Sikander.

"So you don't want to be a doctor to make money," said Babba, mouthing every word. "And you have a life plan for yourself. Chalo beta, let us hear this plan of yours."

"I want to complete med school," said Sikander without hesitation, ignoring, it seemed, the mocking tone the conversation was taking, "then I want to go abroad, maybe to Afghanistan."

"Afghanistan," repeated Sofi. Her hand still covered her father's.

"Afghanistan," repeated Sikander, his tone more serious. "Or maybe Pakistan, in the frontier, maybe do some work with Afghani refugees there."

"What type of work would this be?" asked Babba.

"He wants to be a refugee camp doctor," said Sofi. "But what's he going to do after that? You know he's very serious about this. I keep telling him he needs to have a real plan for his life."

"That is a real plan," said Babba, facing Sofi. He turned back to Sikander. "But your sister is right. You need to have a plan to make money. Maybe you can charge those refugees for your medical services." Babba laughed. "I'm joking of course. But we gave you a good name. My father talked about Alexander the Great conquering Persia, Afghanistan and India. Maybe you can conquer Afghanistan as a healer instead of a warrior. 'Sikander the Great,' we'll call you."

Babba stopped talking and looked down. "We gave you a good name," he repeated to himself quietly.

Sofi detected sadness in the air, as if Mama's absence had suddenly become noticeable. Sofi let go of Babba's hand. Sikander looked down at his plate, before glancing out the window. Sofi felt an abstracted dread creeping in, as if the discomfort and silence was the beginning of a new reality for them.

A buzz from Babba's cell phone shook the table. He picked it up solemnly and typed a short message. A waiter asked them if they wanted to order and Babba said they were still waiting for someone. Sikander looked away from the window and back at Sofi, his face wide-eyed, asking Sofi telepathically if she had known they were expecting a fourth person.

Moments later Sofi saw a woman come in. She spoke to the hostess at the front, then walked toward the table. The woman moved quickly in heels, and wore a grey light summer business suit and a white blouse, giving Sofi the impression that she might be a lawyer or a banker frantically looking for her place at a corporate meeting. She approached the table and gave Babba a hug.

"Sorry for being so late," she said. Her voice was husky without being hoarse, a deep, elegant voice. The woman turned and stood facing Sikander and Sofi, smiling.

"Guys," said Babba, his accent changing, like a generic North American accent from television. "I'd like you to meet Diana."

Diana. As Sofi and Sikander shook her extended hand, the name spun around in Sofi's mind. Associations formed like a word game: Diana, the goddess; Diana, like Diane, and how many "Dianes" had she heard of on TV, always the name of some sophisticated and haughty WASP; Diane, sounding a lot like the word "diaphanous," a word she learned studying for the SATs when Babba wanted her to go to an American university, a word meaning "delicate," "translucent." As Diana sat down in the fourth chair, that was the meaning Sofi ascribed to her – she was someone totally devoid of a presence, airy, nearly invisible, the way all foreign objects seem invisible.

Diana ordered a small soup after Babba enthusiastically insisted she eat something. She was tall with heels, but sitting, she seemed diminutive. Her hair was a dull red, shoulder-length, almost completely straight, with a slight bob at the end. Her features were soft: rounded cheekbones, dark eyes, an underrated red shade of lipstick that highlighted the pallid white of her skin. Babba explained that he knew Diana through a friend, his work and squash buddy Simon, a name Sofi had heard before but she had never met him. This did not stop her father from mentioning his name with a certain familiarity, as if he were a desi uncle they had known for years.

"I thought it would be good if she met you both," said Babba with confidence. Diana stayed stuck in her seat, moving little, her fingers interlocked and placed on the table, a closed but wide smile aimed at the children. Sofi glanced at her brother; instead of the distant, sad look he'd had before Diana came, he was remarkably composed, smiling back politely, his eyes fixed on her. She told Sofi and Sikander how nice it was to meet them both, how Babba had spoken about them frequently. Sofi was unsure what was going on – Babba hadn't explained who Diana was – even though there was an obvious answer.

Sofi remembered that she had assumed a woman had been involved in the separation. Diana could have been the one. Or one of several. Or maybe she was unrelated to any of them. Regardless of who she was, Sofi couldn't help the hostility she felt toward her. Sikander, she thought, most likely, felt the same. Diana asked them many questions, about what they studied, where Sofi was thinking of going to university. Their responses were terse, mostly, but both kept smiling. "They're very shy, aren't they," Diana said to Babba.

"These two? Never. You can't get them to stop talking once they're on a roll," said Babba, a nervous laugh underlying his words. Sofi was sure Babba was embarrassed, although it wasn't certain whether he was embarrassed at his children's aloofness or with his complete failure to bring about any concord between them and Diana.

They all left together and, as they stood outside the entrance,

Diana and Babba moved a few paces from Sikander and Sofi, speaking to each other privately on the edge of the curb. Sikander crossed his arms over his chest. Sofi tried to eavesdrop on their conversation. Babba blocked her view of Diana, but Sofi caught a few glimpses of her face and thought she looked sad, the lines on the side of her thin lips straining to form a smile. She hugged Babba, waved goodbye and then walked away toward the parking lot. Babba turned back to his children.

Sofi had the feeling everyone shared her desire to simply end the afternoon and go home. As Babba drove them back to Mama's apartment, he calmly asked them what they thought of Diana.

"She's nice," said Sikander, looking out the window.

"What do you think, Sofi?"

"Yes. She's nice," said Sofi.

"Can you give me something more than 'she's nice'?" Babba said with a raised voice.

Babba sighed and continued driving.

"Who is she?" asked Sofi.

"She's a friend of mine," he said after a long pause, as if collecting his thoughts. "A friend of a friend, actually."

They stopped at a traffic light that seemed to never turn green. "Who is she to you?" asked Sofi.

Sofi saw her father's eyes. They were light-coloured, and even in the mirror she could see anger under his brows. Anger and frustration. She knew the answer, or at least she assumed she knew. Diana was her father's lifeboat, keeping him from sinking in a sea of loneliness and disappointment. She realized for Babba, the question felt more like an accusation than an idle inquiry, a child forcing her father to answer for the happiness he was trying to grab onto when the same happiness was so elusive for his children. She cast down her eyes, steeling herself, so that she wouldn't start crying. When the light turned green, Babba sped down the road without answering her.

Sikander almost leapt out of the car when they got to the apartment, not even saying goodbye to Babba. Sofi stayed in the car for a moment, witnessing an unusual sight: her father, always confident and self-assured, crumpled in his seat, his left elbow leaning against the window, his hand covering his eyes as if trying to shield himself from the world. Any anger and confusion Sofi may have felt during the afternoon vanished, replaced with an overwhelming pity – for herself, for her family, for Babba. She leaned forward and placed her arms around his neck. She closed her eyes and felt Babba touch her face, his fingers rubbing against her cheek. Sunlight came through the car window, and Sofi kept her eyes shut, not wanting to see her father's face. She let go of his neck and got out of the car, saying, "Khuda hafiz," a curt goodbye.

Despite the phone calls, Babba's life was still a mystery to Sofi. She had no idea if Diana was still in his life. Her imagination went through dozens of scenarios about Diana and Babba's possible relationship. Perhaps that time they all had lunch they'd just been friends – a thought Sofi quickly discounted. She was sure their relationship was deeper, and her mind would often fill with narratives that scandalized her: of them living together in a freer, more sexualized relationship than she wanted to imagine her father was capable of, one that made her self-consciously righteous and unapologetically prudish.

She took the subway to Babba's new home, having just moved from his downtown condo to a larger apartment up north. It looked like a housing project from a distance, but had a decidedly upscale atmosphere the moment she entered the lobby – Old World sofas, metal and burnished wood everywhere, a polite but somewhat aloof and preoccupied concierge speaking Polish at the front desk. When she reached the top floor, Babba was at the elevator door.

They hugged each other, and he told her that he had wanted to meet her in the lobby.

"Actually, I should have picked you up at your place," Babba said.

"You didn't need to," she said. She didn't want him to – the thought of him waiting in the lobby with the even remote chance of running into Mama was too awkward a thought to bear.

Babba took her on a tour of his apartment, with his all-white furniture, a wooden dinette set that gave no sign of needing assembling after purchase, and a kitchen with a dark marble island in the centre. The living room had paintings – large prints actually – by Chughtai, beautiful illustrations of large-eyed Mughal women in finery, brown skin contrasting with yellow, red and orange robes, the vibrant colours shining in the light of the table lamps.

For some reason, she expected something less clean or high class. It wasn't out of a sense that Babba couldn't afford it; perhaps she was used to single men in their twenties living with very little, with barely a thought given to decorating their homes with any aesthetic sense. It almost escaped her that Babba was in late middle age, a man formed instead of a man in genesis.

He had cooked for both of them: mutton karahi, daal, rice and a slightly sour eggplant dish she couldn't make out. They ate their meal on the dinette set. Babba had put on some music from a vintage Sony CD player that she was convinced he'd bought in Singapore right before they came to Canada. Someone was playing the sarangi and the apartment reverberated in a high string sound that was both calming and melancholy.

"I needed to see you," said Babba between chews. "You haven't been well."

"How do you know?" asked Sofi.

"The sound of your voice whenever I talk to you on the phone." Babba replied. "I wanted to match the sound with a face."

"I miss him," said Sofi, after much silence.

"You should miss him. You think I don't?"

Sofi was startled by Babba's defensiveness. "I know you do."

"It's hard being a father who's lost a child." Babba thought for a moment. "It's hard being a sister without a brother too," he added.

Sofi wanted to change the subject. "This is a big place for one person to live in. Do you live alone?"

"It feels alone," he said, putting a spoonful of rice in his mouth. "Sometimes. And sometimes you just have to accept that."

"It's not something I would accept."

"I know. That's what worries me about you. It's hard for me to be so far from you. All I hear is your voice on the other end of a line."

Sofi pushed her plate away.

"You know what I hear?" asked Babba.

She shook her head.

"Emptiness," he said.

It was a stark, strange thing her father said; he said it in English, a clipped, formal English. The word was too poetic, too philosophical for someone like Babba, and before she could dwell on it, he continued: "I saw it in your brother too. After your mother and I" – Babba struggled to find the words – "ended. I'm scared for you."

"I'm not him," said Sofi, her reply sounding unintentionally defensive.

Babba shifted in his seat. "I spend most of my time in this apartment. I do my work, then I come back here. I rarely bring people over. I spend most of the time thinking about mistakes I've made, with you, your brother, your mother. I think being alone is my own punishment for these mistakes." His right arm extended across the table, his palm downward as if he wanted to hold Sofi's hand. "But that's just for me."

Sofi wanted to interrupt her father's self-pity. "If you're going to tell me I need to go out and meet people, I do."

"I'm sure you do. But I want you to do something more than that."

"What more could I do?"

"Don't think about your brother. At all. Forget he existed."

Before Sofi could utter a shocked *why*, he continued: "The more you think about him, the further down the hole you will go. It's the only thing you can do for yourself that will help you move on."

"Is that something you would ask of yourself?"

"A parent can't forget." Babba's arms were now extended toward her, palms up this time, pleading. "You have something that your mother and I don't have. You have time. You're young." He was a father determined to give a lesson born of unseen wounds. "Even if we could forget, we can't. There is no use. We have no lives to lead anymore. You can visit his grave, you can keep him buried in your heart, but leave him buried. Otherwise, your soul will die with him."

They finished eating and Sofi felt bereft of words. Her father continued to engage her in small talk with an oblivious good cheer that she at first thought was odd, if not slightly unhinged. She sat in her seat with her forearms on the table, unmoving, affecting a smile in an attempt to approximate normalcy, hiding how strange she found his affectation of happiness. She realized, while helping Babba clear the table and clean the dishes, that this wasn't an attempt to make himself feel better, but to make her feel better. It was his way, a method she knew he had used throughout her life to ease the tension by forgetting there was ever any tension to begin with. She understood why Mama found him so frustrating. A few moments before, he had loaded the conversation with the heaviness of Sikander and his own loneliness. Sofi now watched her father full of domestic vigour, scrubbing CorningWare, dots of liquified lentils buried in the water, his thick forearms flexing as he hummed along with the buzz of the sarangi in the background. She stood next to him, putting plates in the drying tray, staring at her father's impassive face, in awe of the ease with which his mood seemed to change.

Babba walked her down to the lobby when Sofi left. Before they parted, they stood in front of the glass doors of the exit. Two middle-aged women, both dressed in dark fur, came through the doors, letting a chill inside, a howl of wind warning of the winter's cold. Sofi let out a shiver. Babba hugged her, engulfing her in his arms. She put her arms around him, smelling a hint of faded cologne on his shirt. Babba brought her face up gently with his hands, as one would do to a child. "You're my only lifeline to the world these days," he said. "I don't want anything to happen to you." She understood his fear, the fear of a father who drove through the same streets his son did, searching for every dark threat that could have snatched his only remaining child from his grasp. He kissed her on the forehead before Sofi walked out into the cold.

♠

Sofi cried again on the subway ride home. She cried for the family she realized barely existed anymore. She cried for her parents who now shared nothing but a common solitude. She cried for her brother, for his short, fragile life and for his selfishness, for embracing the peace of death while she was still alive. She cried for the unbroken past, the days when her parents walked with interlinked arms in the first snow they saw after coming to Canada, her brother holding her hand as they trudged in the white blanket beneath them, overawed by the purity of the cold. She cried for herself, for her loneliness, for all that lived inside her that trapped her in sadness.

Once she was done crying, she remembered her father's words telling her to forget. To go forward. To be young. She began to realize that he might be right.

A vague memory crept inside her before she slept that night. It was of a park somewhere north of their apartment, months after the family had first come to Toronto. The winter was bracing, but Mama and Babba forced the children to go out as much as possible, almost as a way of acclimatizing them to their new home.

Babba loved the snow and ice more than anyone else. In his fascination with this glacial paradise, he bought Sofi and Sikander a pink snow mat in the hopes they could find ways of enjoying the winter, revealing the mat after taking the children and Mama to the park. He'd heard about the location from a new work colleague. From the top of the park's entrance, it looked like a small valley, with a steep, snow-covered slope reaching down to a line of dead trees and a frozen creek. Across the far end of the slope, a group of children no older than Sofi and Sikander were tobogganing alone on top of a simple wooden sled. Babba gave the mat to Sofi, saying he was taking their mother to see the ice-pond farther down into the park. "Are you okay by yourselves?" he asked.

"You want to leave them here?" Mama asked, seemingly unenthused by the entire outing.

"If those children over there can be by themselves, why can't they?"

"Those white Canadian children have probably been doing this since they could walk."

The tone of the conversation was shifting, coming close to the precipice of a fight Sofi wanted to avoid. She interjected, saying they would be fine, insisting that if the other children could be unaccompanied, there was nothing to worry about. Babba convinced Mama that Sofi was old enough to take care of herself and her brother as they made their way carefully down a series of partially ice-covered steps to their left, signs for "pond" visible on the way down.

She didn't think it odd that they were spending time alone. Since coming to Canada, Sofi had sensed a vague discord between her parents. It was intuition that told her this was an excuse for the two to bond, for Babba to show his wife that he could still present her with beautiful things. Sofi was content to be alone, the sight of the ice-white landscape of the valley looking fresh and lovely, like a playground designed exclusively for her. Without even thinking of Sikander, she took the plastic mat and slid down from the top of the ridge. He cried after her, calling her name, demanding to know what she was doing. Sofi ignored him. With brash confidence she weaved herself in the snow, finding the speed of her descent enlivening as she learned how to shift her weight to avoid any obstacles in her way, and to stop at the exact moment she wanted to.

Sikander stood on the ridge, staring quietly at Sofi as she went up and down the slope. She kept asking him if he wanted to go. His only response was to shake his head and say no. After the third time going down, panting as she climbed up the incline to meet him, she asked him why not.

"I don't want to do it," he said.

"Are you scared?"

"I just don't want to."

Sikander annoyed her. There was something in his timidness that was frustrating, perhaps because the freedom of sliding down the hill was so liberating to her, she couldn't see why he shouldn't experience it either.

"Nothing's going to happen," she said.

Sikander shuffled in the snow. "Are you sure?"

"Yes."

"Come with me?"

"We can't both fit," she said, curtly. He cringed, and she softened her tone, thinking this was an opportunity for him to learn how to let go of his clinging nature. "It's easy to do. You'll have fun. Trust me."

Sofi showed him how to grab hold of the front handles, helping him to lie perfectly flat. She told him to hold fast and not to be nervous before she pushed him down. She realized she pushed him with more force than intended, his body sliding down the slope and accelerating rapidly as she heard Sikander call her name. The sheet, and Sikander, kept on sliding. Sofi rushed down, trying to steady her feet on the decline to prevent herself from slipping. Blind fear overtook her as she saw Sikander narrowly miss a large birch tree as he was ploughing toward the frozen creek. Dire scenarios jumped in her mind: Sikander hitting another tree, or the mat slipping into the chilled water. Her brother's cries for help crystallized her heart-pounding anxiety. She was around twenty feet away from him when the mat veered to the left, hitting a small, withered, denuded bush, spinning Sikander's mat a half-circle until it stopped before a copse of trees bordering the creek.

Sofi ran to Sikander, removing the handful of twigs from the bush on top of him. She held his arm so he could stand in front of her. His eyes were moist as if he were prepared to burst into tears, while his chest, thick with the red winter jacket Mama had given him, heaved rapidly. Sofi gathered him up into her arms. Her panic was assuaged as she sensed her brother's warm breath on her neck. He looked back at her face – with his tears subsiding, she smiled and broke into a nervous laugh. Sikander joined her, his embarrassed chuckles expanding his moon-face even wider. Apart from the electrifying sense of relief, she felt something else: a sense of her own power – not the power of life or death, but the power of comfort, that in her very presence she could smother angst and assuage pain. Their parents, probably hearing Sikander's screams, ran up from the stairs, their worried eyes drifting all over their children. With one arm, Sofi raised her hand to them. It was an adult-like gesture, she'd realize later in life, telling them with confidence that all was well and taken care of and that Sikander was safe, as long as he was embedded in her embrace.

Sofi returned from her memory to the cavernous night, feeling a wretched emptiness as she came to bed, an inner vacuum of failure, of purposelessness. *If only he could be here*, she thought, standing in front of her bed, she would rise and hold him, his shield against death, even if she knew no one was there, nothing to hold or cling close to in the featureless darkness.

9

Sofi began receiving emails from Fatima after she saw her father. Her messages were friendly and apologetic: "Hi, hope you're doing well, hadn't heard from you in some time . . . hope you're still not angry about last time . . . want to get together soon? . . . interested in coming to another study circle?" Sofi didn't respond to the messages at first, still trapped within herself, but as she sat staring at Fatima's last message late one night, she decided to email her back: "Let's meet. I need your help. Love, Sofi."

They saw each other at the same coffee shop where they'd met previously. It was between classes for Sofi. She stayed near the entrance, surveying the crowd. It was busier on a weekday, mostly students wearing backpacks, worn jeans and baseball caps. A group of three girls – Sofi could hardly think of them as women – talking loudly in line at the counter through thick, visible braces. Sofi wasn't old, but she still felt time working against her since Sikander died. She reminded herself of one of Mama's aphorisms: the moment you feel old is the moment you realize how young others are, looking at their youth as a marker you'd long since passed.

She spotted Fatima. She looked at Sofi, clutching her handbag close to her side. Sofi stood up and they gave each other a hug before sitting down. Fatima smiled tentatively, as if she was unsure of what to say or how to act, like someone being careful not to make a mistake or cause unintended offence.

"You've been avoiding me," she said.

"No," said Sofi. "I've just been busy."

Fatima stared at her, her smile worn out. "You said you needed help. I had the feeling something was wrong."

"I don't know how to say what I need to say, and I don't know who to say it to."

"You can say whatever you need to say to me." Fatima took off her coat.

Sofi sighed. "I feel adrift. I can't even explain what I mean by that, but I feel like someone has put me on a raft and pushed me into the ocean. And the winds are carrying me farther and farther away, and I don't know where I am, and I can't tell where I'm going." Sofi pushed her cup of tea slowly away from her.

"Sikander," Fatima said, almost to herself. "I know it must weigh heavily on your mind." Fatima stopped herself and tapped the fingers of her right hand on the table, as if trying to summon what words she should use. "I actually don't know what to say."

"I'm forgetting his face," continued Sofi, her voice sounding defeated. "Is that good? Maybe it's for the best. I had dinner with my father a couple of days ago. He said I should forget about him. For my own good, of course."

"I think he means that he wants you to find a way to move on."

"I think I've already forgotten him."

"What do you mean?"

Sofi sighed. "By living." The thought of living made her think of Robin, how, despite her frustration with him, he had given her something, something beyond pleasure. The moments she had shared with him were a distraction, making her feel out of time, forgetful of the past.

"There's nothing wrong with that," said Fatima, as if not entirely convinced of her own words. "It's natural to go on with one's life."

"What are you supposed to do when someone dies?" asked Sofi.

"You wash the body for the janazah –"

"After that," interrupted Sofi. "I don't mean 'what's the process,' I mean, how are we supposed to think about death?"

Fatima sat back thoughtfully, her face soft, contemplative. "Death is something natural. We're supposed to look at it as an endpoint of one life into another one before the Day of Judgment."

"What does that make the life we live now?"

"A pastime, the Qur'an says."

"So everything we do is meaningless?"

"No," said Fatima, emphatically. "It's the difference between a dream and waking. You can enjoy the dream, or it can become a nightmare, but it's not reality. Only the afterlife is real. It's a clear day after a cold, long night." Fatima paused.

"That doesn't help me. Everything feels wrong. I'm supposed to live my life and forget my brother, and when I do, I feel guilty. And when I think of him, I think of death and nothingness and I feel" – Sofi struggled for words – "like I'm sick."

"I knew someone from one of our study circles," said Fatima. "She was an older sister. One day, she put up her hand like she was in a class and said she wanted to say something. Of course we said yes. It was kind of sweet. Anyway, she mentioned that her mother was dead and she needed some advice. At first she wanted to know if there were any specific prayers she should be saying for her mother. She said she hadn't been that religious before, and she wanted to say something for her. We suggested a few surahs she should be reciting, a couple of du'as she could say. We were all sympathetic and we thought that was all that she wanted. But she still smiled, and she had this look in her eyes, like she wanted something different from us, or that we weren't really solving her problem and she was too polite to say anything about it. She was sitting beside me, and I remember touching her arm and asking her if everything was all right and if she wanted to ask us something else. She thanked us, and then said she wasn't quite sure how to ask her next question. We said that she should just go ahead."

"What did she ask?"

"She wanted to know why people had to die." Fatima stopped talking. "It was so strange, the way she said it," said Fatima, almost under her breath. "It was the way a child would ask a question. I know what she meant, I suppose we all did – she was asking why do people have to die from a religious point of view. Usually that group is full of sisters who can't wait to give their answers to any religious question, but we were all sort of stumped. She wasn't crying, but you could see this blank sadness in her eyes. I guess we wanted to make sure we didn't say anything stupid or simple. Finally this one sister – a friend of mine, Zainab – started telling her a saying that her grandmother had told her: that death is like a marriage. Death is a wedding, where you finally meet your Beloved, except in this case your Beloved is God."

Sofi was intrigued. "Does that mean God takes away what we love and keeps them for himself? That sounds selfish."

"That's actually what the sister said to Zainab. She was trying to be as respectful as possible to her of course, but that awkward smile disappeared and you could tell she was angry." Fatima laughed. "I wish I could have given her a hug then and there, just to make her feel better. Anyway, I didn't have to; Zainab went on. She said that, because Allah is everything, the source of all creation, he has ownership over all things. Everything that we think belongs to us, really belongs to him, even the people we love the most."

"That still seems like a human's possessiveness."

"But isn't there something beautiful in that?" asked Fatima. Her eyes were wide; they seemed illuminated with an enthusiasm Sofi hadn't noticed before. "It isn't like a human hoarding all the things that he thinks belong to him. Because we all originate from him, we're a part of him."

"How is that like a wedding, then?"

"Maybe not a wedding in the traditional sense then," said

Fatima. "But, I don't know, I suppose when you love someone, and when someone loves you, you want to be absorbed into that person. Zainab had a word for it . . ." Fatima looked up, as if searching for the word on the low ceiling above. "A union."

"So what did the sister think about that?"

"She seemed okay. Maybe not okay, but she seemed slightly better. She thanked us, at least. Actually, some of the other sisters didn't like it that much," Fatima said, laughing. "I think all these comparisons between God and a human wedding really made them upset." Fatima smiled. "Everybody thinks about religion as this weight on them. Few people think of how much love can be found in it."

Sofi noticed she was rubbing her hands together and immediately stopped and placed her palms on the table. She was inexplicably nervous as Fatima remained still and serene before her.

"I don't know," Fatima continued, "if that story helps you, or means anything."

"It did," said Sofi. She realized at that moment that Fatima's words shook something inside her, as if the story had revealed an ineffable truth told from a timeless, sacred source. It was a voice that whispered grace and warmth and unbordered love directly inside her heart, a voice that only now she realized she had longed to speak to all her life.

That night Sofi looked out her bedroom window, pondering the bubble of her own solitude. Starbursts of light shone from the streetlamps below. She thought of Fatima's conversation hours before. She thought of God, too, which she found unusual. She was a believer and thought of her faith as both unique and deep, even as it was a faith that was different from those who would consider themselves truly religious. God gave order to life. The lights, the movement of people in the street, in the neighbouring apartments, now all seemed guided by a force that was not merely within her. Fatima's words made her think beyond herself, beyond Sikander, beyond Robin or her parents. Sofi felt a warm sensation, a golden weight inside her she could think of only as love.

When she released the blinds and returned to her bed, Sofi heard the sound of a text message coming in. It was Robin, asking her where she was. She thought of ignoring the message and going to sleep, but she felt guilty for not answering. She texted him back, asking if they could meet soon.

Her heart beat like a metronome, slow, steady and audible. When she closed her eyes, her world went white, a great tender peace slowing her heart, a peace that emerged from caverns inside her she hadn't realized existed.

Sofi told Robin she wanted to go somewhere where she could dance. They met at a bar-lounge on College Street and shared a few drinks together in a booth away from the dance floor. Sofi listened silently and calmly to his concerns about getting into law school and the amount of time it took studying for his LSAT preparation courses. Beneath his gleaming smile, there was worry in his face, frown lines and vacant preoccupied eyes that still shone in the dim light. She sat beside him, and in the moments when his eyes were downcast, she would touch his face, feeling the rough, abrasive stubble on his cheek, and the fine, hard-bone edge of his jaw. The annoyance she had felt for him in the past had dissipated and she felt a newfound compassion for him, wanting to help him feel better, to provide a balm to his worries.

She led him by the hand to the dance floor. Drums synchronized with cheap strobe lights. The dance floor was crowded and small, and Sofi could tell Robin felt as uncomfortable and listless as she was. They left both the floor and the lounge quietly. Sofi went back to his apartment and they undressed each other without saying a word. After his climax, he lay on top of her, and Sofi stroked his hair, holding his head to her chest.

Her senses experienced the semidarkness of the room lit by a lamp on the other side of the bed, the heat of Robin's body, and the smoothness of his hair. Yet it felt different from the last time she lay with him, not an absence of comfort – far from that – but an absence of mystery, of magic.

After some time, Robin turned over with a heavy sigh and faced the wall. Sofi stroked the small of his back.

"Don't get up," she said. "Please."

"What's wrong?"

"I keep worrying about the future. I can't turn it off."

He turned back to face her and held her hand.

"I can't stop thinking about my brother too," she said.

Side by side they lay corpse-like on the bed.

"There is so much sadness in you," he said, coolly, clinically, like a diagnosis.

Sofi turned on her side and looked at him. "I've been trying to distract myself. I've been talking to my cousin. She's a believer. I know her mother's religious. I thought at first she was the same way because of her mother."

"She isn't?" asked Robin, somewhat bored.

"No," said Sofi. "I think she feels something deeper."

"Love, I suppose."

"I think so." She thought about the word "love," letting it ferment in her mind, at the same time unsure whether Robin was taking her seriously. "Yes. Love."

Robin reached out his hand and stroked her arm. "Are you a believer too?"

She thought about the question for a moment, knowing there was a response she wanted to give that wasn't the response she thought Robin wanted to hear. "Yes. I am."

"Does it make you feel better?"

Sofi glared at Robin. "If this means nothing to you, maybe I shouldn't have brought it up."

She got up, but before she could get off the bed, she felt the grip of Robin's hand on her forearm. "I'm not trying to be mean. I'm sorry," he said. "It's just different for me."

The feeling of his hand on her arm, the smell of his sweat, his presence was once again alive, and it felt both reassuring and jarring, as if she had been spending time in an empty room and suddenly realized she was not alone. "It's important to you, isn't it?" he asked.

"It makes sense to me."

"I wish it could make sense to me," Robin said tenderly, as he stroked her hair.

He dropped his hand down to Sofi's back. His fingertips were cold as they passed over her spine, along the vertebral ridges, like a traveller on a new trail, noting every bump, mapping every bone. He stopped, leaving her skin cold. In the silence of the room, a thought saddened her, the realization that Robin's worldview was so different from her own. That thought damaged the evening, making the intimacy between them incomplete and leaving the bed they shared bereft of a spark Sofi desperately longed for.

Sofi didn't stay long at Robin's apartment. When she got home and entered her room, she had an unexpected desire to pray.

Sofi barely remembered how to say her prayers. It was Jamila Khala who had taught her. She had a dim recollection of Khala cajoling her mother to let her teach Sikander, Sofi and Fatima the basics of prayer, Qur'anic recitation and supplication. They would sit cross-legged on a musty, carpeted floor in Khala's living room.

She would cover both Fatima and Sofi's head with one of her spare, white dupattas. Sikander would wear shalwar kameez and a small topi to cover his head. Sofi remembered Sikander taking the lessons to heart at the time, bouncing up on his folded legs whenever he correctly guessed his Arabic letters in order, or when, with impressive ease, he could recite Surah An-Nas and Al-Fatiha by heart. Fatima was a quick study too, as quick as Sofi was, although Sofi's enthusiasm was less divinely inspired and more part of an eagerness to please, a childish earnestness that wanted approval from her aunt in much the same way as she wanted to make an impression with her teachers at school.

Standing in her room, however, she concentrated hard on the movements, the formulas and verses that needed to be said at every bow, every prostration. She had no prayer mat. She had no idea where the qiblah, the direction to pray, was. She found a clean towel and laid it toward the window, for want of any other direction to face. She remembered, from what Khala had told her, when the prayer times were: she guessed it was time for Isha, the night prayer, with four rakat, four cycles. She had a long scarf that she took from her closet to cover her hair. When she raised her left and right hand, palms almost covering her ears, a torrent of words flooded her, and she could remember every movement, every worshipful statement.

When Sofi was done, she turned her head to the right and the left, ending her prayer by saying "assalamu alaikum wa rahmatullah" to the angels who sat on her shoulders – she remembered Jamila Khala had mentioned their presence when she'd taught her how to pray, an idea that, at the time, Sofi thought both ridiculous and fascinating.

She sat on her legs, surveying the stillness of her room. A sharp awareness of everything in it struck her, as if she was in the body of a stranger who was seeing her possessions for the first time – her old, scuffed laptop, an equally ancient but utilitarian printer, an assemble-yourself European designer bed raised only a few inches from the ground, two white lamps sitting on top of white bedside tables and emitting efficient, eco-friendly white light, a red-and-gold carpet Mama had brought back from Pakistan, made in a distinctly Persian design, geometrically perfect lozenges symmetrically locked. For some time, Sofi had thought of her room as functional and sterile; now, with mysterious clarity, each object pulsed as if it were imbued with a secret energy, as if her prayer had unlocked a door to a hidden reality previously unseen.

Sofi realized the mistakes in her prayer. She hadn't even bothered to make wudu, her mandatory ablutions before prayer. She also remembered something she had read somewhere, some offhand research that Khala, for understandable reasons, had never taught her: that after sex a full ritual body bath is needed before any act of worship can be executed. It was a principle of Islamic law that she had known only through her own intellectual curiosity and meant nothing as far as her own life was concerned, but it struck her, in an instant, not just that she had violated a religious protocol, but had committed a sin through fornication. She dropped her head in her palms. The notion of sin had meant little to her, irrelevant to leading a moral life. She didn't think of her moments with Robin as times of sin. She didn't want to debase her intimacy; doing so would feel like a lie.

She opened her palms. They faced upward, heavenward. Impulsively she started to supplicate, her prayer almost silent, a river of words to herself: *I don't know why I do this. I don't know why I do anything. I haven't prayed with sincerity since I was a child. Even then, there were parts of me that may have mocked it. I apologize. I apologize for my life. I apologize for the wrongs I have committed against you. I apologize for those I have wronged. I don't know what I should be saying, or if my words have meaning, or even if they'll be heard by anything besides the walls. I walk the streets, I talk to people, laugh with them, touch them, let them touch me, let them inside me, but I still end my day alone, like every bridge I have with the world is made of mist. I want a connection that will not go away, that won't die, that isn't small, or fickle, that is completely and starkly real. I need to believe that is You.*

Sofi wiped her face with her palms. The night was creeping close to morning. She felt tired but energized with the need to stay awake forever. She wanted to see the dawn and catch a hopeful glimpse of the sun reflected on the glass buildings that surrounded her, to see the holy power she knew in that moment existed in all things.

It was exam season and there was a certain stress that clouded the campus air like a miasma. The various libraries across campus were suffocating with students. Sofi wanted to break free from her hermetic existence at home and spend more time at school. The newfound transcendent energy she felt gave her fuel to engage with the world in a way that she missed. Often she would find a spare seat free in one of the libraries at the south end of campus. She would sit in one of the heavy, chestnut-coloured chairs at one of the long tables placed next to windows overlooking Queen's Park, where mounds of congealed snow from the street formed hilly barriers to her vision. Failing that, she would attempt going north to Bloor Street, to find a nook on the mezzanine in one of the libraries next to the subway, the white glow from the recessed lighting beaming down on her from above. When her mind wandered, she would invariably find someone she knew at any of those locations, who would mercifully disturb her fading concentration. There was Elizabeth "Lizzy" Li, whom she knew from a first-year economics seminar and who had recently broken up with her high school–era boyfriend. She needed some advice as to whether she should respond to the shy "advances" (her word) of some young men she met from the Evangelical youth group run by her church. There was Anthony de Mello, from her political economy seminars: tall, V-shaped, visibly athletic, with an incongruously soft, wispy voice, who confided to Sofi one late evening, as he smoked a cigarette on King's College Circle, that he was gay, that his family didn't know about it, and she was "one of five people living on this planet" that he felt comfortable talking to, a fact that made Sofi weep and quite spontaneously plant a kiss on his cheek. There was Reza Last-Name-Unknown, as short as Anthony was tall, shorter than Sofi, with stubble constantly covering his square jaw, the sides of his mouth always permanently locked back into a joker-grin, whom Sofi had met through Andrew and who initially had left such a small impression that Sofi had trouble recalling anything about him save his first name and smile. She would invariably encounter him not at the library itself, but outside the subway on the way back from the library, where he would eventually tell Sofi, after many meetings on the train, how he hated doing his bachelor of commerce, how he was only doing it to please his widowed mother, and how he really wanted to be a filmmaker, a vocation Sofi said he should pursue with passion.

There were so many more people that she met, people from her past that now seemed drawn to her for reasons she couldn't quite fathom. She was sure something inside her had changed. She had always been amiable enough and people found her agreeable to talk to, as one would a confessor. But Sikander's death had changed all that: Sofi turned into the silent confidante, the sounding board, the sponge for everyone's fears, hopes and tragedies. She felt listless and resentful, angry at being the ear for those around her but not being able to put a voice to her own pain. Now she felt cleansed of that apathy, possessed of a new willingness to engage with people.

Sofi continued to pray. There was no orthodox streak in her personality, but she wanted to do it properly, making it a goal for herself that she would, at the very least, pray Isha every night. She looked on Islamic websites and video-sharing sites online to make sure every word she said was correct, every movement true, that the steps she took to wash her hands, arms, feet and face during her ablutions before prayer were done with as much perfection as she could manage. After the prayer was over, she said her supplications. She asked that Sikander be kept safe, without really knowing from what – she admitted to God and to herself that she was not completely sure what the afterlife was, even if she did believe there was one. She asked for protection for her mother and father and that they be happy. She asked the same for Robin, thinking, in the back of her mind as she looked at her open palms, that Robin would find what she was doing absurd, the idea of prayer a form of false magical thinking that any intelligent person would have grown out of. Most of all she prayed that the light she found inside herself would not be extinguished and that she could remain open to the world.

Sofi thought of Fatima often. She saw her cousin as her lodestar. She knew Fatima took her religiosity seriously, and there was much passion in it, but Sofi had seen little that she found personally compelling before. She called Fatima one day to meet. When they did, outside a library on King's College Circle, Sofi could sense weariness and tension in her cousin as they walked the circumference of the circle. Fatima's eyes were tired; she shuffled rather than strode over the thin, iced puddles. Sofi attributed it to exhaustion and study stress. It wasn't late, but the sky was darkening in preparation for dusk. Sofi told Fatima that she had been praying Isha.

"That's good," Fatima said, surprised.

"I nearly forgot everything," said Sofi with a gentle laugh. "I remembered the times your mother used to teach us."

"Yeah," said Fatima. She put her hands in her jacket pocket. "I remember. You always seemed more interested in learning recitation and saying namaz than I was."

"Really?"

"At the time I just learned because Ammi wanted me to do it."

She looked thoughtfully to her side. "You never really think about spiritual matters when you're young, I suppose. Anyway, I'm happy you're praying."

"I still feel strange doing it, sometimes. Like I'm not sure it's the real me who's praying."

A car slowly lumbered beside them, struggling to find parking in front of the large, grave, Romanesque college building to their right. Fatima was silent and Sofi was unsure if the expression on her face was one of contemplation or annoyance.

"Maybe," said Fatima with hesitation, "you're getting used to the real you. Worship is our natural state. It's how angels live. They don't have the ability to do anything else. Why do you think I started praying?"

The question struck Sofi. She had never questioned her cousin's faith, thinking of it as intrinsic to Fatima's identity without imagining the existence of her life before piety took over. "I don't know," she said.

"Ammi was always religious. You know that. And she made sure I was too. But I never felt any real faith in anything until I was older."

"What changed that?"

Fatima sighed, a long, heavy expiration. "I was a social child, I suppose, but there were all these moments when I felt completely alone. It wasn't that typical high-school loneliness, you know? Kids liked me. Teachers liked me. I never got in trouble, I never had any problems with my parents. But I remember walking to and from school every day through this park that led straight to school. When the snow fell, it was like walking through a white desert. Every single step I took was horrible. The sky was always grey, the land was always white and it was the bleakest thing you ever saw. One Friday, I think it was a PA Day, I went with Ammi and Abbu to jummah. It was Abbu who went there mostly. I remember it was like a warehouse that they had converted into a prayer space. I was sitting at the back with Ammi. The khateeb was giving a sermon on revelation. He said something about how it is no coincidence that prophets receive their revelations from God in the desert. It's a pure place. Because it's empty, you have no distraction leading you away from God. It's in emptiness that you find God."

"Did you find God in that empty field that you used to walk across?" Sofi asked, charmed at the hopefulness of her cousin's faith.

"I did," said Fatima. Her voice was clear and earnest. Perhaps she had noticed Sofi's amusement and interpreted it as mockery. "It wasn't like I had a revelation myself," she continued, her calming smile reappearing. "But I started to think about what he said. From then on, whenever I walked across that field, I saw the world differently. For no real reason I started to recite 'alhamdulillah' to myself every time I crossed, ninety-nine times like Ammi used to tell me after prayers. And whenever I used to do that, the park used to seem less bleak. That whiteness became tolerable, and after a while it stopped being tolerable and became beautiful. In the cold, tramping in the snow, seeing that grey sky, I wasn't alone. Or maybe I was left alone with something more real than I had previously thought existed."

There was a weighty silence between them after Fatima finished talking. They had almost made it full circle and were standing outside the concrete structure of the medical sciences building. "I need to tell you something, but I don't know how to say it," said Sofi.

"You can just say it."

"I have a boyfriend. I've been seeing him for a while now. And I've slept with him a few times." Sofi tried to notice any shock on Fatima's face. Instead her expression was confused, as if she were trying to surmise why she would be told this secret. "I don't completely know why I'm telling you this," she continued. "Maybe I just have no one else to talk to about these things."

"Are you worried about something?" Fatima asked.

"Remember when I said I felt fake? This is what I mean. I pray and then I commit a sin. It is a sin, isn't it?"

"Yes, it is," said Fatima. "A major one. A crime in Islamic law, even."

"I know. It's probably a sin I'll commit again because I don't think it's wrong."

A look of puzzlement came on Fatima's face. "It's not something I can say is *right*. Is that what you wanted me to say?"

"No," said Sofi.

"You can't continue like that."

"A part of me knows that. But another part of me can't ask for forgiveness for it either. You said the last time we met about how everything we do for God is out of love."

"That's true."

"Does that count for people as well?"

"The love you have for God comes first," said Fatima. "You can't betray God by committing a sin and then say you love him."

"How can anything be a sin if it's done out of pure love or pure innocence?"

"Because it isn't pure at all. That's shaitan whispering in your heart."

That's not what I feel when I love someone, Sofi wanted to say. She certainly loved Fatima at that point, despite being wary of her judgment, both attractive in its self-assuredness and alienating in its rigidity. "What am I supposed to do then?" asked Sofi, deliberating every word. "Get rid of my boyfriend? Then repent? Then continue praying?"

Fatima sighed with exasperation. "I don't know exactly what you should be doing. I'm not a scholar. But you asked me a question and I gave you a straightforward answer. In this world, you can do whatever you want. But even if you're not afraid of what happens to you in the next world, you have to know that connection you feel every time you pray is severed when you commit a major sin."

There was an inscrutability in Fatima that made Sofi anxious if not frustrated, that thwarted her attempt to connect with her cousin, to find an answer to the guilt she felt for sleeping with Robin, for even being with Robin, for loving someone now so distant when God – abstract, unseen, unknowable, divine God – seemed more real.

Fatima came close to Sofi and rubbed her arm, trying to placate her. "I'm not trying to be harsh. Really, I'm not." There was sympathy in her eyes. "I can only tell you how things are. I know you want to live your life on your terms. But if you want to take your faith seriously, you have to get rid of that mentality."

Sofi made an excuse and said she had to go back to work. Fatima made a similar excuse, saying she had to go home. They embraced each other with hesitation, as if their relationship had, within minutes, gone in a different direction without either one of them intending it. Sofi went back inside the library. Her mind was clear; she was able to study without distraction. Later that night, when she came home, she ate a silent dinner with her mother. When it was over, she cleared the table and kissed Mama on the forehead as she sat in her chair, her face briefly enlivened by the tenderness of Sofi's affection. Before Sofi went to sleep, she thought of Fatima's admonitions about the need to live a life as she had suggested – as God had suggested. Before she slept she made a realization, that, as wise as her cousin was, she was wrong: she could live life on her own terms as well as God's. Living on those terms was not only a right, but a duty, a duty that she would have to perform far away from home.

10

Sofi developed a routine for herself. She made the night prayer her only obligation, feeling she had no discipline for anything else. She thought, at first, that she needed to talk to someone, an imam, someone to guide her through the process of prayer to make sure that everything she had remembered from Khala and her own reading was accurate. In the solitude of night, she felt a presence as she went through the motions, a reassuring peace inside her that was captivating and unique. Sofi found it indescribable, overpowering, a feeling with the depth of love but without its limits, not centred on one person or object. As it became a habit, the feeling lingered with her beyond the night. The world took on a new colour; even in the shade of winter, the iced streets took on a new luminosity that seemed to have existed forever, beyond her senses, the power of worship opening her awareness of life once more.

When exams were over, school broke off for Christmas and the campus deadened. Many of Sofi's friends and acquaintances left for home, those with means finding random places on the map for vacations, others, like Sofi, remaining in Toronto. The city, like the university, shifted into a slower rhythm. Subways and streetcars ran slower. The hateful winds abated for a while. When it snowed, it came down from the sky languid and unhurried, and the streets became quickly covered in a crystalline beauty.

Sofi met Robin before he left for Kingston for the holidays, and they had dinner near his apartment. He spoke with enthusiastic self-absorption. It didn't annoy her as it had in the past – her sense of love for him was still present, but it was now augmented by her worship, which expanded her love for everyone. She was unsure whether it was a love directed at him specifically or something more general, unfocused.

They went back to his apartment afterward and had sex. Sofi was still caught up in the whirlwind of a desire less cerebral, more purely physical. Sofi felt a saddening emptiness when it was over, like an addict grasping at the narcotic thrill of a first high. Robin lay beside her and asked her if she wanted to go away with him, back home to Kingston. She said she didn't feel like going anywhere.

"You couldn't use a break from school or home?" he asked.

She could. Sofi knew that. "I think I need to be by myself," she said. It was an excuse that was also true.

"You don't want to be with me, then?"

"It's not like that."

"What's it like then?"

She couldn't say, mostly because she was unsure herself. The thought of joining Robin on his vacation, spending time with his family, seemed like a level of intimacy she was unprepared for, greater even than the closeness of lovemaking, which seemed like an act she had complete ownership of.

She felt Robin hovering over her. "Are you running away from me?"

"No. How am I running away?"

Robin lay back and stared at the ceiling with the same unfocused stare Sofi had. "I'm trying to bring you into my life."

"Have you ever tried to be part of my life?" she asked.

"I didn't think you wanted me to be part of your life."

Sofi's impulse to lash out was curbed by the realization that Robin was right. She said nothing; instead she simply turned over and fell asleep. When she woke up the next day, she left the apartment silently, saying nothing to Robin as he lay in the bed barely awake. She left with a sinking realization that the end was beginning, that the limits of their relationship were clear, the date and time before the break the only unknown.

♠

Mama cried that night. She most likely cried every night, thought Sofi. This was the first time she'd noticed.

It wasn't a loud wail, or low moan, the type that cascaded through hallways and bounced against walls. It was a drip of sniffles and choking, as if her sadness were an infection. Sofi was awake, having finished her prayers. She sat on her prayer mat, feet folded beneath her, listening to the sounds. Rather than raise her hands in supplication, she spoke to God directly, a soundless, interior monologue directed to God as if he lived in a chamber inside her. She asked God to protect her brother from any torments in the afterlife. She asked for protection from all harm for her mother. She asked for the strength to ease her mother's pain. Sofi asked all of this, not as a slave begging a king, but as a friend, a lover, sharing her commiseration with her Beloved.

The cries became deeper. Sofi got up and tiptoed down the hallway to Mama's room. She opened the door quietly, the hall lamp casting slivers of light in the dressing-table mirror. Sofi saw her mother's face. Her eyes were closed, the bags underneath them wet, stained with tears. Her body was in the fetal position, facing the dressing table, on top of her quilt. Sofi climbed onto the bed and held Mama from behind. It was only when she pressed her mother close to her that Sofi realized how small, how fragile, she was. Sofi placed her hands on Mama's, feeling the bones in her fingers beneath loose skin. Her throaty sobs grew quiet. This was new. This was the first time since Sikander had died that she felt connected to her mother, two incarcerated inmates who barely spoke of their common imprisonment.

Sofi held her mother close to her as the bedroom hummed in the near dark. She whispered a prayer of gratitude, thanking God for the power that coursed within her, the power that healed and loved.

♦

Sofi applied to grad schools before the Christmas break. She had hardly discussed her choices with either Mama or Babba. Her parents assumed she would carry on in economics and get a decent job in a bank or world-development agency. Sofi applied to very few programs in Toronto, or in Canada, for that matter. Most of her applications were to American or British schools. This would be her escape. She idly imagined that she would gain acceptance abroad, away from the city, a legitimate excuse to be away from Mama, Babba, her pain. Even if that pain hitched itself on her back, she would still have the ability to breathe, albeit burdened by the guilt of leaving Mama by herself.

Of course, there was still Robin. She hadn't heard from him since he'd left for Kingston. His absence confused her. She felt no longing for him, although, for reasons she couldn't fathom, she had expected to miss him more.

Winter gave Sofi a monastic peace. She focused her social energies on Mama, spending more time with her, watching cheap but hilarious Bollywood comedies they bought from a Sri Lankan convenience store in Markham for four dollars each. They even decorated the kitchen's countertop with a miniature Christmas tree, something she remembered Mama doing for them once at Khala's, much to her aunt's disapproval. They talked – never about Sikander, as it seemed to Sofi a topic too raw to be broached – but of other things, mundane things, of classes and final exams, graduate school, jobs, the future. Would other women her age be annoyed at their mother's constant questioning? Perhaps, thought Sofi, although annoyance was out of the question for her. She was, in fact, overjoyed that her mother spoke of the future as if it was an unknown country worthy of exploration.

Sofi prayed more, making it a goal at the start of the winter break to increase the amount of time she spent in worship, eventually moving onto saying her evening, afternoon and midday prayers along with her prayers at night. As dawn was close to her normal waking time, she started making an effort to pray in the morning as well. She studied her religion more, online or by checking out books from the university library – the selection and quality of religious books were always better there than any bookstore she could come across. Sofi wondered whether it was worth getting in touch with Fatima to learn more from her or from her community of religious friends. She felt, however, more determined to learn on her own, partly out of a feeling of alienation, a conviction that she stood apart from them, their lifestyle, their confidence in their own faith and practice. She also felt a personal drive away from everyone, as if her pull toward God was predicated on solitude. The books that attracted her the most were brief biographies of saints, wanderers, mendicants, scholars of the heart rather than of the book. She read about Rabia al-Basri, born poor, turned a slave, who then became the greatest of all female saints when she was freed from bondage. Sofi read how Rabia pleaded with God that she be denied heaven if she worshipped only to enter paradise, and to allow her the grace to see his divine beauty only if she worshipped for His sake and His sake alone. Sofi was fascinated by these ideals of self-sacrifice, immersing oneself in a totality of love. Was this a life for her? Not an ascetic one – that was an extreme few people could manage, she imagined – but to be genuinely pious, a human, natural piety. Even that seemed too far removed from her reality. Fatima could live her life like that; she was, after all, a young woman living under the shield of her mother – the cloak of righteous living, with all its restrictions, had been placed on her shoulders from birth. Sofi didn't have that; her parents' laissez-faire attitude to faith had given her no support in living that type of life, much less a saintly one. She felt the need to live spiritually within the confines of her own reality, not out of a sense of superiority to the religious laws and values that she learned of – if anything, she felt a better understanding and appreciation of that – but out of sense of limitation given her upbringing, her values, her desires.

Sofi thought of Sikander. How futile was her father's request to forget him, the ever-present body next to hers? His presence now occupied her daydreams rather than her nightmares. She pondered the months, weeks and days before the accident, searching for any indication that there was some cause for his passing. It wasn't logical or healthy, she knew; the wisest attitude to have was to simply accept his death as a part of life's unpredictability. Despite that, she continued to search her mind for a cause, a reason.

Sometime before Sikander died, he'd met a girl. She'd forgotten about that; it seemed trivial, a memory whose meaning was lost until she focused her attention on it. She'd never seen this young woman, had only heard about her in second-hand snippets from her brother whenever she could coax it out of him. That was her job: to bring Sikander out of himself. It was a responsibility put on her by Mama and Babba; she was the go-between, the point of contact between him and their parents, the buffer between their concerned intrusiveness and his reactive sensitivity.

He came home smiling from school one day, and walked into the kitchen. She was at the countertop eating an apple and she asked, blithely, barely looking at him, what he was smiling at.

He placed his bag on the floor, opened the fridge to get some milk and mumbled a short "nothing" as a response. He turned from the fridge and went to get a glass, the milk jug held tightly in his other hand. From the side of his face, Sofi saw a hidden happiness encrypted in his slight smile. He looked over at her, pouring milk into the glass with deliberation.

"What?" he asked.

"I miss that smile."

He downed the milk and placed the glass on the countertop. He left the kitchen, his eyes downturned, smile intact, a fire of feeling and thought in his slow walk. An hour later, burning with curiosity, Sofi went to Sikander's room. The door was half open, and she came in without a knock. Sikander was at his desk, typing on his laptop.

"So I don't smile enough, and you think because I'm smiling now something has to be up?"

"That's right."

"Well, it's nothing."

Sofi leaned against the doorjamb, her arms crossed. "I figured it out," she said softly. "That's the smile of a boy who's found a girl."

Sikander turned back to his laptop, shaking his head.

"You have. Now I'm completely convinced." She walked over and sat on the bed. She could see the outline of his face. His smile dissipated; his face turned serious.

"I don't know if I'd say I've *found* anything," he said, emphasizing *found* as if the word were ridiculous and wholly inappropriate for the conversation.

"What do you mean?" asked Sofi. She expected this evasiveness from her brother, the clever male teenager – smart, emotional, but inexplicably incapable of being direct or open.

"I mean, I may have found something. I don't know if I have what I found."

"You're speaking in riddles."

Sikander shuffled in his chair, his normal reaction when anyone – especially his sister – confronted him directly on anything. "I did meet a girl."

"Did you ask her out?" asked Sofi, with enthusiasm and impatience.

"I asked her."

"What's her name? You're not giving me any details."

"Her name doesn't matter."

"Why are you being so secretive?"

Sikander looked at her with soft, calm, thoughtful eyes, and for an instant it struck Sofi that her brother was hardly a boy anymore, and there would come a point when her protective, almost maternal, instinct toward him would be rendered irrelevant by age and time – and that point would be sooner than she expected. "Her name doesn't matter, all right," said Sikander. "Leave me some secrets."

Sofi was disappointed. She wanted a greater openness from Sikander, a way into his life. Her desire was motivated by sisterly curiosity, a need for an unfettered connection between them as siblings. Before she left his bed, her frustration making her presence seem useless, he asked her to wait.

"What is it?"

"I didn't actually want to be alone," said Sikander. Sofi sat back down. "Do you know what I'm thinking about right now?" he continued, as if reciting a monologue to himself. "The future. You're about to say 'I'm too young to think about the future,' right?"

"You are too young. We're both too young." Sofi replied.

"I'm thinking about it anyway."

"Does this girl-without-a-name have anything to do with you thinking about the future?"

Sikander nodded.

"Why are you acting like you have to marry her?"

Sikander was silent.

"What's wrong?" asked Sofi, trying to sound sympathetic.

"I don't know exactly. It's like when I think of her, I can never just think of my life right now. I'm always thinking about what's going to happen next. You say that I don't have to marry her, sure. But lately I've been thinking about it all: dating, marriage, children.

I don't know if that's the life for me."

"Stop being so serious all the time. Just live. Why do you have to think so hard about these things?"

"I don't know," said Sikander. He dropped his head on his chest. "I can't help it."

♠

He always had too much on his mind, thought Sofi. *I should have done more to make him stop thinking. I should have met that girl, should have pushed them together, should have been with him every moment and every day to look out for him.*

Months after she had talked to Sikander, he told Sofi that he and the girl had broken up. As usual, it was information she'd had to pry out of him. He had come home and rushed to his room with almost the same silent ease he always had. This time, however, there was no half-smirk, no hidden teenage joy; his face was impassive, stony without being stoic or even angry, as if he had witnessed an event so traumatic that he struggled to grasp its meaning. Sofi saw his face from the kitchen. He didn't acknowledge her. She followed him to his room, anxiety welling up in her, banishing her calm – she knew something was wrong with him; her instincts detected his emotional states with ease.

He hadn't bothered to close the door. She walked in unnoticed. He was sitting at his desk, his hands placed palm down on each side of his laptop, as he stared into the void of its black screen. Sofi kneeled beside him, took his right hand and held it. He told her that the girl he was seeing, Monica had left him. There was an angry reaction inside Sofi, a protective indignation, and she tried to assuage him, saying he had to forget her, that she had no value in his life.

"How am I supposed to forget?"

"You just do."

"Even with her at my school?"

"Try your best."

"Try your best," repeated Sikander. He stared back at his screen. "You know I talked to Babba about her. A while back, when I first started seeing Monica. Do you know what he said?"

Sofi shook her head.

"He said I should live these days to the fullest because these are the best days of my life. I feel like dying, and these are supposed to be the best days of my life." He raised his hand, palm toward her, a gesture of dismissive exasperation. He buried his face in his hands. No sounds of crying came from him; his entire room, soundless as a tomb.

Weeks later, close to Christmas break of 2003, he would be dead.

◆

Don't overthink it, thought Sofi. *Monica didn't kill him. Sadness didn't kill him. A truck and a dark road killed him, nothing more.*

When the winter break ended, Sofi returned to the routine of school. Before the break, she had booked an appointment with Carol, the therapist, at her office. It was the last appointment allowed under the regulations. After three visits she had the option of being referred to a third-party therapist. Sofi was of two minds regarding the value of her sessions. Her previous visits had given her an outlet rather than a solution to what troubled her. When she arrived, Carol's office was the same, but where sunlight had peered in the last time they met, the sky was now dark in the early afternoon, and snow lined the edge of the window.

Carol sat silently at first, the way she usually did. Instead of it making Sofi feel uncomfortable, this passivity had a strange, soothing effect on her.

"I was thinking of not making another appointment," Sofi said.

"Why? Have you been feeling better?"

"I've been feeling – different."

"Is different necessarily better or worse?"

"I can't say."

Carol shuffled in her chair. "Some change is inherently good." She stared at Sofi. "Have you still been having those dreams about your brother?"

"Dreams, no. He has been on my mind, though."

"He would be, of course," said Carol. "I recall the last meeting we had. I'm not sure you remember me talking about how some people, after a loss likes yours, put a limit on their grief."

"I haven't put any limits on mine," interrupted Sofi, "if you were going to ask me that."

"Fair enough," Carol continued, "but I mean limits in an emotional rather than temporal sense. We all have the ability to curtail our losses and our pains, after a time at least. Do you feel now, as time has gone by, that you feel your brother's death less?"

Sofi thought of her question. Months ago, she would have taken it as a glib and insensitive thing to ask.

"I don't feel his death less, no," said Sofi, with thoughtful deliberation. "But I do feel it differently."

"How so?"

"Before, after he died, I just took it as this great black cloud that covered everything around me." Sofi paused for a moment. "I've started praying," she said. "I never used to do it."

"Religious belief can certainly be a comfort."

Sofi bristled at her words. "Yes, but 'comfort' seems too small a word. I think I turned to God because I thought that it would help me find peace."

"Did you find peace?" asked Carol, after a pause.

"Not peace, no. I found love."

Carol sat up in her seat, surprised by Sofi's response. "That's quite a grand thing to find."

"It's not what I expected either," said Sofi, eyes fixed on nothing. "I don't know what I expected, but I didn't expect that."

"Religious love is something difficult to speak of. It's something deeply personal. I think it's worth examining whether it can serve a purpose."

Sofi's eyes turned to Carol, confused.

"By that," continued Carol, "I mean to ask whether you think it's helped you deal with your brother's death. You yourself said that prayer hasn't given you any peace."

"That doesn't mean it's useless. It's a strange thing to describe," said Sofi as she shifted her weight in her chair. "I feel closer to a God I believed in but had no relationship with before. And the closer I get, the more my world changes, and things seem more pure and more beautiful."

"Does it mask the pain, though?"

"At times," said Sofi. "More so than with my boyfriend."

"Why do you say that?"

"I needed someone to be close to. I thought my closeness with Robin would make me look at life differently. He thinks I'm deliberately distant from him. I think the same of him. I don't want to blame him or make it seem like it's simply his fault. Maybe the truth is I was searching for a peace no one could provide."

Carol's eyes looked thoughtfully to her side. "It's a mature realization. And I think it's perfectly acceptable to reach out to the sacred for solace when the people around us can't give solace to us," she said, her eyes refocusing on Sofi. "It's not for me, however, to judge or analyze faith. I feel ill-equipped to do so. But it seems to me that at least some good has come from prayer and this closeness, as you describe it."

"Not entirely."

"Meaning?"

"I have an idea in me that won't go away. About the way my brother died. I don't know if it was an accident or not."

"The way I recall you describing it when we first met, it seems like it could only have been an accident."

"Unless Sikander purposefully drove too fast, in the dark, on a bad road. Like he was looking for an accident to come and take him away."

"Did he show signs of being suicidal?"

"No. I don't think so."

"Why do you think he purposefully put himself in harm's way?"

"Before he died, he was seeing a girl. He barely talked about her. He barely talked about anything. I know they broke up; he told me that at the very least. I can't say for sure what was going through his mind during those days. He was always a sensitive boy, and he had a gloomy side. Maybe that gloomy side pushed him over an edge that I didn't realize existed at the time."

"There's no way of knowing that for sure."

"It makes sense though," said Sofi, almost under her breath. "Maybe I'm trying to find a cause for it all."

"Does there have to be a reason?" asked Carol.

"No, maybe not," said Sofi. "Having a reason or not isn't all that concerns me. I find myself thinking of the possibility of Sikander killing himself. And I think of the possibility of a God that exists, that I have started to worship in my own flawed way, who hates the idea of suicide so much that he's willing to punish the suicide in hell forever. I want to believe that the God I worship loves my brother enough to forgive him any and every offence."

"Why would you think that God would be that unforgiving?"

Sofi shrugged her shoulders. "Because those are his rules," she said. At that moment, she pondered the many sacred rules she had learned. She accepted the boundaries that God had placed, even if she knew she herself had violated so many of them in the past and may do so again in the future. Sleeping with Robin was one of them, the sin of fornication. Yet she relied on God's forgiveness for all that – she had breath in her, the life force her parents wanted so much for her to use while she had a chance, and in her existence in this world, she knew she had time and opportunity to be penitent. Sikander had none of that. No time. No life above ground where he could learn to look at the sky and cleanse himself with mercy. This is what haunted her the most.

Carol nodded her head and smiled, looking briefly away toward the clock that hung above her office door. The look did not, Sofi thought, signal that she was mindful of the limited time left in the session, but almost as if she were carefully deciding how much she wanted to say before the hour ended. "I'm certainly aware," she said, her words deliberate and thoughtful, "that despite the comfort of religious faith, it can cause a fair amount of guilt. Guilt can be useful, without a doubt. We need it to regulate our actions. But there can be a time when it becomes excessive or inappropriate, even if we cherish the standards and beliefs that create that guilt."

"Who's to say that guilt is excessive if you really have done something wrong?"

"As I said before, I can't judge faith. But there is no way of knowing your brother is being punished for any of his actions. You yourself don't know what was going through his mind when he passed away either."

Sofi lurched forward, wanting to say something, her mind arrested by Carol's words as she understood their fundamental truth.

"There is also a question you need to ask yourself," continued Carol. "How much is the concern about God's relationship with your brother and how much of it is really about your relationship with your brother?"

"I don't understand."

"Do you feel guilty about your brother's death?"

Carol's directness struck Sofi. "Yes. Yes, I do," she said softly. She said it with no tears. Instead, the words were a revelation that had been trapped inside her.

"There is no way you should feel responsible for him dying."

"The dying I don't feel responsible for," interrupted Sofi. "I was sleepwalking beside him as he led his life. I should have been awake to those moments when I knew something would have troubled him, or if there was some danger out there that I could have led him away from. Maybe I could have told him not to see Monica, or not to drive at night, or not to feel things too much. I don't feel responsible for his death, no. But I could have protected him more."

The session ended with anticlimactic haste. Before she left, Carol, with quiet insistence, suggested that it might be advisable to seek a third-party therapist outside the university. "I think it's worth the time and resources to continue with this process. I'm sorry I can't keep on with you," she said, with a regret that felt genuine. She said she would email her some options for therapists, which she did when Sofi got home.

Sofi didn't bother to read the message.

That night, after she said her prayers, Sofi thought of God. She remembered a poem she'd come across in one of the many books on Sufi poetry she'd taken from the library. It had struck her so much, she'd written it down in a journal, coming close to memorizing it after meditating over every translated word:

He heals our nature from within,
Kinder to us than we are to ourselves.
His kindness makes the unworthy worthy;
And in return he is satisfied
With his servants' gratitude and steadfastness.
You have broken faith,
But still he keeps his faith with you;
He is truer to you
Than you are to yourself.

The words comforted her for a moment, the idea of the Divine as incalculably warm. Another idea came to her mind as she prepared for sleep. She lay her head on her pillow, closing her eyes, feeling its softness on her skin, and imagined God as the centre of a circle of unimaginable circumference, a source for all things, who retained an eternal memory of all the things he had created from the beginning until time's end. If this was the God that was to be believed in, then perhaps there was no reason to fear for her brother. The dead existed with him in eternity. Hell or heaven were irrelevant; the only goal was God, and the only action in life was to run toward him as fast as one could.

There was, of course, one other thought: that this hope she had – for her brother, for her family, herself, the world – may be a false one. The punitive God and the God of love existed in her mind; she had to prepare to choose which one would now take ownership of her heart.

11

Winter became harder, colder. The edges of the sidewalk were lined with snow, their blanched beauty tainted with the dirt and sediment of the street. Wind tunnelled between buildings of the city. Sofi's classes were at night, and when she walked to and from the subway on streets and passageways through the grey concrete buildings of the university, she felt overwhelmed at the length of winter, its indifferent ceaselessness. She thought of that not in despair but in wonder, of how much her mind changed during shifts of months and seasons, of how her desire for warmth dominated her needs. Winter was for her now what spring or summer was for others, the season for sensuality, desire and rebirth.

Robin had come back from Kingston. He called Sofi once he was in Toronto, asking if he could see her. She suggested meeting at the Starbucks on the south end of campus. "I need to talk to you," she said.

There was a chilled silence on the other side of the line. "About what?" he asked.

"Everything."

⬥

They met the next day after one of Sofi's late afternoon classes. She came early to the Starbucks, buying a drink and sitting with expectation at one of the tables that lined the window overlooking the street. She was nervous. She said she wanted to speak about "everything," but the "everything" she wanted to speak of was too expansive: their relationship, Sikander, her sadness, God. How to channel the cyclone of emotions left her with an unshakeable disquiet.

In her periphery, she saw Robin come in, wearing a dark overcoat too thin for winter. He walked over and stood at the table for a moment's hesitation. Before Sofi could rise to embrace him, he leaned over and kissed her while she sat. "How have you been?" he asked.

"I've been okay," said Sofi.

They talked about how they had spent Christmas. Robin had spent most of his holiday time with his parents or studying for the LSAT. Sofi felt weary as he talked, the spill of his words exhausting her already anxious state.

Robin stopped speaking. "You're miles away from me right now," he said, annoyed.

"You're right," said Sofi. "I'm sorry."

"So what's going through your mind? You said you wanted to talk about something."

"I don't know," said Sofi. "I can't say there's one thing."

"Life. Home. What?" he asked. He spoke directly and firmly. If there was kindness intended, it was buried under a sense of impatience. "You always seem to have something going on inside you," Robin said. "More of the same, is it? You don't talk as much as you used to. I wish you would, to me at least."

A sense of remorse and guilt welled in Sofi, remorse for the words she now realized she had to say. "I don't know how we can continue on."

Robin's face – usually locked in a subdued smile – fell into a bitter frown. She avoided his eyes and looked through the window to her left, ignoring the view of the students and the passing streetcar under the faint winter sun gleaming between greying clouds. "I guess I should have expected this. You've been distant," he said.

"We've been distant from each other."

"I guess that's true. We've both been feeling that, I know. It's funny – if you hadn't said we needed to talk, I would have probably said it myself."

"Somebody had to mention it," said Sofi, with resignation.

"What made you realize that things had changed between us?" asked Robin with a questioning calm, as if backtracking through time, searching for moments in his memory that Sofi was sure to remember with greater lucidity.

"When I knew how differently we saw the world," Sofi said, her voice strong with a clarity she only now realized. She looked back at Robin. "But it isn't your fault. Maybe a part of me wanted to be healed by you, and I wasn't. That's my fault. I was expecting too much. Maybe I needed something that was impossible for you to give."

"What did you want from me that you couldn't get?" he said, barely able to conceal the anger veiled beneath the softness of his voice.

"I need people around me who can respect where I'm coming from, and what I believe in."

Robin looked at her with a mixture of bewilderment and hurt. "You're talking about God?"

Sofi nodded. "You're not a believer."

"Not in the slightest." Robin said. "That's not something I can apologize for. But I never looked down on you if you believed in all that, especially with your brother and everything that's happened."

"Everything that's happened?" repeated Sofi.

"I didn't mean it like that." Robin's face looked exasperated. "What do you want, Sofi?" he asked her. "What do you need that you don't have?"

Perhaps Robin couldn't sense the magnitude of the question,

she thought. Her needs felt powerful, deeply felt but barely visible, like the constant shifting of the Earth before a quake. "I can't even count all the things I need. But whatever they are, I can't see them being here, in this city."

"So what would happen to us if you'd want to move away?"

They stared at each other, him looking for an answer, her hesitating to give the only answer she had.

"I don't know."

"There probably wouldn't be an 'us,' would there?"

He was right, of course. When they'd first met, she once thought of the potential life their relationship would have brought her, a hope that seemed so powerful back then.

"I doubt it," she said.

A slow, caustic feeling of guilt welled inside her. How much did they love each other, if ever at all, she asked herself. The finality of the moment lingered uncomfortably between them. "I'm sorry I can't be the one who fills those gaps inside you," said Robin. Sofi shook her head, holding back tears, wanting to reassure Robin that there was no deficiency within him. He continued before she could speak. "But whatever it is you really need, I hope you get it. And if you never get it in this life, I hope you can still find some way of being happy."

Robin remained in his seat, his face bearing the look of someone suddenly encountering the precipice of loneliness, with no ability to move across the impasse. He turned his head away from Sofi as she picked up her bag and rose from the table. Before she walked through the door, she thought of turning to see him one last time. She stopped herself, afraid that glimpse would immobilize her, nullifying the decision to move on from the promise of a better life with Robin that she had once assumed was fated to her.

Sofi expected the tears, although she didn't expect how soon they would dry, how quickly she would become accustomed to the thought of being alone again. She cried for a few days, intermittent bouts that stretched for minutes between classes, in silent, empty staircases or when she was alone, sitting on benches in front of the many libraries scattered on campus. She made it a point to cry alone. With a steely strength of will, she made sure she spent time with others, chatting with friends like Lily or other acquaintances after class. Robin became a memory with a speed that seemed shocking to Sofi, almost as if her sense of time passing was somehow impaired. The thought of it was terrifying: how strong feelings can dissipate with ease, a passion transformed into an embarrassing memory, the suddenness almost invalidating the entire experience.

Would it be like that with her? When she died, would her loved ones be told to move on? Did Robin have a similar conversation with his own friends, about how fickle and unworthy Sofi was? She wondered this for weeks. She wondered if this was why people worshipped God, why she herself was attracted to that devotion. God the eternal, keeper of an immutable love, with no limits of intensity or of time.

Spiritual love. The only kind with meaning, the only love not ephemeral.

It was crunch time at school and, as exams approached, the weight of stress on everyone was palpable. Sofi was sick of studying. The weather was improving, at first merely an increase in temperature, turning the banks of sullied snow on every corner into melting glaciers, flooding the pavement and the gutters. After a few days, the bloom of spring arrived, and the thought of renewal seeped into Sofi's mind. After studying, she would take long walks east toward the park, sometimes gazing at the statue of King Edward. There was something feminine in the spring change, as if the air around her made the trees and grass more fecund, and the cast-metal statue all the more cold and lifeless.

Admissions for graduate school had come to Sofi's friends and acquaintances. For some they considered marks for previous years, with conditional acceptances based on their performance in the final year. Sofi received periodic calls from her father, asking what her academic intentions were. She said she would weigh her options soon. She had applied to graduate schools in Toronto; New York; Washington, DC; and London, England, although she had no intention of going to any school but the one in London. Her father made it clear to her that he would pay for everything, regardless of location. Babba spoke to her, however, as if he expected that she would stick close to Toronto, partly because Mama needed her only child to be close by and partly because he had his own fear of being too far from his daughter. Her conversations with him were clipped and muted; underlying her terseness was her guilt at the abandonment she was planning and her awareness that moving across the Atlantic for school would put more financial pressure on her father.

She received letters of admission from every school except the university in London. The chance of escape seemed unreachable; the stress of not being able to grasp it added to her exam pressure. After exams were done, she received an oversized letter, large and slightly battered, bearing Royal Mail stamps, a memento from an exotic land. It was Mama who delivered it to her room, silently, with a solemnity that indicated her fears of Sofi leaving her. The letter was plain save for the red-and-white logo of the university that marked the top-left side of the envelope. The letter inside congratulated her on her unconditional admission to the university, gave her information on visa applications, frequently asked questions and options for residences, among other sundry details. She read the words without fully absorbing their content, almost as if she were entering a fugue state, aware of the reality of a new place with new ways of living. Reflexively, she thanked God – not a formal du'a, but a sincere statement of gratitude that echoed inside her.

The next morning was Saturday and Sofi hadn't told anyone about the acceptance. As she sat with Mama at the table eating breakfast, Mama was unusually talkative. She spoke of work gossip, passive-aggressive senior managers in the bank, the lines on her face still visible, crevice deep, but her face stretched out in a smile. "Some of them are so rude, these managers," said Mama, buttering her toast. "But I never let them get the best of me. Your grandfather told me fools never have any manners or sharafat, and there are no fools in our family, correct?" She looked at Sofi with a love that she hadn't seen in months. It was deeply maternal, but contained a sense of longing, a look already used to loss.

Sofi told her about the contents of the letter. She said she wanted to take the London offer.

"Accha, you will?" blurted Mama quickly. She stared at Sofi for a moment. "How long is the program? You never tell me these things."

"Just one year."

A pause. Mama continued to stare at her in disbelief.

"It's a specialized international development program," said Sofi, almost as if to placate her mother for an unseen and unknowable offence. "They offer an international relations and economics specialty too."

"And of course you'll be back after a year."

"Of course."

"Do you know Samreen Auntie?"

Sofi shook her head, confused at the seeming non sequitur.

"You've met her, a long time back," said Mama, waving her hand backward. "She had a daughter, older than you, who took an international development or international relations master's degree, I don't know which one." Mama grabbed the mug of tea in front of her. "She found a job in London. Not for any developmental organization, but a bank, mind you." She took a long sip from her mug. "She started to hate it. She left after a year."

Sofi remained silent.

"Are you thinking of staying put there, finding a job?"

"Mama, I haven't thought that far," said Sofi.

"You can do it, but you'll be back," said Mama, as if Sofi had already answered the question in the affirmative. She took another sip of her tea, placed her mug down abruptly, got up and started washing the dishes. Water rushed loudly through the taps, putting a full stop to the point Mama seemed to be making.

Sofi turned around in her chair. "Maybe I'll give it a try anyway," she said.

"Try at what?" asked Mama over the water, the clanging of plates in the metal basin adding to the noise. "Leaving here?"

For a few moments, Mama continued to wash the dishes. Her hand pressed on the lever of the tap; the gush of water, the stream of it, stopped. She turned around, drying her hands with a small hand towel that had been placed near the sink, and looked at her daughter. There was that usual stony face, a hard beauty that would have retained its form if Sikander had lived, a face that would not have been aged through sadness. Her expression changed, the sides of her lips dropped, her eyes were cast down to an undisclosed, unfocused spot on the floor. "Do you need a change from me?"

"No. Nothing like that," said Sofi softly.

Mama gave Sofi a look of resignation and loss, then walked over to her and stroked her cheek. "Work hard. Get your degree. Have fun. You'll come back and find a job."

Sofi smiled at Mama and touched her hand gently, feeling the warmth of her mother's skin, the sensation of her callused fingers sliding along the fine edge of her cheekbone. For an instant, Sofi felt that leaving Mama, leaving Babba, was an abandonment.

Mama turned back toward the basin and continued to wash the dishes as if the conversation with her daughter had simply not taken place.

Sofi looked over at her mother before returning to her room. *Perhaps abandonment was needed*, she thought. Her mother would remain in this apartment, cocooned inside. That wouldn't change. Looking out the window, Sofi glimpsed the buildings across from her room and for an instant the city seemed like a necropolis, her apartment one of many slots for the dead. Life was a force, but for Sofi, a current that she wanted to swim in, toward any destination away from home.

12

Sofi's parents both attended her graduation ceremony in the summer. A cold civility allowed them both to enjoy this important milestone with their only child. They stood on either side of Sofi as her friend Althea, who was also graduating, took their picture. Lily and Andrew were there too and wished Sofi well, flashes of sunlight blinding her as she hugged them both. Babba took pictures of Sofi and her friends on the large green lawn in front of the college with enthusiasm. Mama stood close to him, teary-eyed and proud. Sofi knew she was their anchor, and worried that they would be unmoored when she left for London. She walked over and embraced each of her parents. She held both their hands, trying to forge a connection between all three of them. *Sole survivors*, thought Sofi. *We should be so close, especially after everything that's happened*. Instead, they were like lighthouses on the same island, each looking outward, shining away from each other.

Babba offered to drive them both back to the apartment, but Mama smiled and politely declined, saying they would take the subway home. As they walked together, they passed a tent in the middle of the lawn selling frames, T-shirts and other university memorabilia, lined with graduates and their parents, diplomas and mementoes in hand.

Sofi looked up and saw Fatima, her head covered in her hijab as she walked in front of the visitor's centre. She had a sense she'd be there, having told her about the acceptance. Fatima smiled when she saw Sofi, Mama and Babba. Sofi stepped forward and hugged her and when she turned around, she caught Mama's eye. She was staring at Fatima with stunned but warm recognition, as if the years no longer mattered, as if the distance between her and Fatima's mother meant nothing. Mama came forward and pulled Fatima to her, holding her, touching her cheeks as she let her go. Babba looked equally stunned, his hand touching Fatima on her shoulder in a way that was both paternal and distant.

Sofi looked at all three of them with joy and satisfaction. In that moment, it felt like her damaged world had been unexpectedly repaired. Fatima spoke to Mama and Babba in enthusiastic yet soft tones, her hands clasped together in front of her. She nodded politely at Babba's questions, which were mostly about school, her courses and when she expected to graduate. There was no mention of Jamila Khala in those questions. It was Mama who brought up the subject by asking Fatima how her mother was.

"She's absolutely fine, Khala," said Fatima in Urdu, smiling.

"So she's keeping well? Healthwise?"

"Absolutely," said Fatima.

"God, how you've grown," said Mama, almost to herself. She grasped Fatima's forearm lightly, not wanting to let her go, as if worried that her niece would disappear if she released her grip.

"Chalo, it was good seeing you," interrupted Babba. He looked at Fatima and Sofi. "I have a feeling these two wanted to see each other and not us."

"No, no, it's not that," said Fatima with a polite, reassuring laugh.

"Jaan, no need to make us feel better," he said. "I know at your age there's no value in talking with old people like us."

Fatima laughed again. "I did want to congratulate Sofi, but I also wanted a chance to see you both again."

"Thank you so much, jaano," said Mama. Sofi couldn't

remember the last time her mother was so enthusiastic. "I'm so happy I got to see you."

"Let me have a moment to speak with her," Sofi said.

"Okay," said Mama, lovingly patting Fatima on the back of her covered head.

Sofi and Fatima found an empty bench only a few feet away and sat down. Fatima set down her handbag on the bench between them and took out an envelope, which she handed to Sofi with two hands.

"A present?" asked Sofi coyly.

"Of course," said Fatima. "But don't open it now."

"Why not?"

"Open it before you leave for London."

Sofi agreed as she clutched the card close to her. They apologized to each other, for being so busy lately, for barely being in touch. Sofi had told Fatima that she would be leaving for London in September when she emailed to ask about Sofi's convocation date. "I'll still be here in the summer," said Sofi reassuringly. "I want to spend more time with you."

"I know, I wish I could spend more time with you too, but I'll be in Pakistan this summer. Two of my cousins on Abbu's side are getting married. I don't know why they decided to have the shaadi in that heat, but whatever, I'll manage."

They both laughed in unison. "I'm going to miss you," said Sofi.

"I'm going to miss you too," Fatima replied. She reached out and took Sofi's hand.

Sofi looked over Fatima's shoulder. The sun's light reflected on the leaves of the tall trees that lined the circle, swaying when brushed by the wind. "I don't want to lose you," she said, looking back at Fatima.

"You won't lose me," said Fatima.

"Nothing's permanent, right?" said Sofi, her voice weakened. "Life, love, relationships. They invited this business tycoon to give the commencement speech today. Every other sentence was some cliché about using this time as an opportunity to evaluate where you're going in life, how you need to make the most of your time now that you've graduated. It just seems so easy for some people to plan ahead, to have everything in place. I'm sure half the people graduating today have it all figured out. The tracks of their lives all mapped out. The second I start thinking about laying out my tracks, I feel like something's going to derail."

Sofi stopped talking, suddenly embarrassed.

"I'm sure," said Fatima with halting, clearly enunciated precision, "that with Sikander gone, it's easy to see nothingness as the result of anything you do. But I think you're still obliged to go on and live a life without counting the days, and without despairing that everything you have may disappear."

"I have no right to complain. I'm lucky," Sofi said after a pause.

"You are," said Fatima. "You're going off to England to study."

They both laughed. "Yeah," said Sofi. "Hopefully I'll make the most of it."

Fatima put her hand on Sofi's shoulder and told her she needed to leave. They hugged each other. Sofi whispered in her ear, "I love you." Fatima said the same. They walked back to Mama and Babba, who were speaking to each other in hushed tones, the sort of half-whispering that always alarmed Sofi when her parents were still together, unsure of whether, in the quietness of their voices, there was a discord they wanted to shield from their children. When Sofi and Fatima approached them, they stopped speaking, and turned to the girls with beaming faces.

Mama changed her mind and accepted Babba's offer of a ride home. She sat in the front seat. During the drive, Mama and Babba seemed to speak with a renewed familiarity, without acrimony or anger. "I can't believe she's done," said Mama to Babba, looking back at her daughter with amazement. "You've made it, beti," said her father. "You can go anywhere from here." For a moment, all things seemed at ease, the graduation, this marker in their daughter's life, having woven a thread between Sofi and her parents. They discussed the past, about Khala and Fatima, with a nostalgia typical of couples still together.

Sofi clutched Fatima's note in her hand as if it were her real diploma. She still needed to make plans, many of the logistics of travel and study still needed unravelling, but, for the moment, Sofi felt as if she had all the time in the world ahead of her.

A few days after graduation, Sofi drove herself to the cemetery. She had been there twice before, once with Babba, once with Mama. This time she felt the need to be by herself at Sikander's grave. The day before, she'd emailed Fatima, asking what she should do at a gravesite, and Fatima recommended reciting Surah Yaseen from the Qur'an. In a dusty top corner of the large bookshelf in her apartment's living room was a small booklet containing the surah in Arabic accompanied by a Roman phonetic transliteration in English. She took that along with her to the multi-faith cemetery, a large verdant expanse of grass and graves and narrow, labyrinthine paths. The day was blessedly bright, she thought to herself, as she walked toward Sikander's grave, light blanketing the cemetery. Did the developers choose a location that was uniquely at rest, one of those patches of untamed, forgotten land that seemed to stand apart from time? Or was it arbitrary, a simple matter of resources and convenience that led them to drop a city of the dead in this place? Was the serenity she felt merely a random confluence of the loveliness of the day, the sun skimming lightly on far-off trees and expertly cut grass, the wind brushing against her in brief, warm gusts?

Sikander's tombstone was made of dark marble. His name, written in Arabic script and English, was inscribed beneath the words "la ilaha illallah" – there is no god but Allah. She recited Surah Yaseen from the booklet, her eyes at first focused on the transliteration, then moving to the Arabic, finding herself increasingly comfortable reciting from the original, just as she remembered Jamila Khala teaching her. The words flowed from her mouth, the verses taking on a fluent, liquid quality.

When she was done, she felt a bewildering blankness inside her. Fear and anxiety were non-existent, as was the calm that she had been feeling. Before she left for the car, she looked around her, surveying the panorama of graves standing like stone menhirs immovable under the sun.

She drove back home slowly along main roads, just below the speed limit, cars and trucks signalling and overtaking her. She drove down Yonge Street, where the road rose and then dipped on a hill. As she coasted down, her car seemingly propelled by its own weight, the city appeared on the horizon. She would be in London in a few weeks. *God is the Opener, the gatekeeper of the future*, she thought. He will cleanse me of the past, and I will carry nothing with me when I cross this threshold.

On the day of her departure, Sofi said goodbye to Mama, who held her tightly before letting her go, her eyes filled with tears Sofi knew she did not want her to see. Her father was waiting for her outside and placed her luggage in the car. As they drove toward the airport, Babba asked Sofi repeatedly whether she wanted him to join her in London to help her settle down.

Sofi declined. "I think it's best I do it myself," she said softly.

At the airport, she hugged Babba before going through security, waving at him one last time through the frame of the metal detector. She waited at the departure gate silently, surveying her fellow passengers, some families, some business travellers, cranky toddlers climbing over exasperated mothers, couples and students in cargo pants looking as if London was but one stop toward the rest of Europe.

Minutes before the boarding announcement, Sofi decided it was a good enough moment to read Fatima's letter. She took the envelope out of her handbag and removed the card slowly. It was thick, handcrafted and covered in a geometric North African pattern, red and gold lines crisscrossing each other against a black backdrop. Fatima's words, rounded cursive, were inside:

> *Sofi, My Dearest Cousin, My Lost Sister,*
>
> *My Abbu went on a business trip a long time back (somewhere in Europe). He brought back a prism – just a small bit of crystal or glass that refracted light whenever I held it up to a window. I was fascinated by it. Abbu used to make a religious lesson out of showing us the prism. He used to tell us that people are a lot like the light we see. There is always one light, Allah, and the colours we see are his creation, including all this. It was a beautiful idea, although I don't think I thought about it for some time. It's come back to my mind more and more thinking about you and Sikander and everything you've gone through. I know there are moments when you might feel disconnected and saddened. It's easy to feel adrift. But I believe we're all different shades of a spectrum, all coming from the same light. The only things that separate all of us are time and the grave, and even those things have their limits. God alone connects us all.*
>
> *I didn't want this letter to be heavy and serious. I didn't want to preach. This may be a new beginning for you, the start of a new path. Whether it is or it isn't, I know you'll reach those places you want to go, and you'll find what you need to be happy.*
>
> *We'll be in touch soon.*
>
> *Love, Fatima*

She closed the card and heard the boarding announcement. The passengers rose and dutifully formed a line like schoolchildren.

Sofi looked at the line, at the pale and dark faces, their points of origin and destination unknown. She would now join them, one more shade of the spectrum, moving toward the plane.

PART 3
MURAD AND SOFI

On one of my journeys, I met a woman and asked her what is the end of love. "Thou fool!" she cried. "Love hath no end!" I asked "Why is that?" She answered, "Because the Beloved is without end."
– Dhul-Nun al-Misri, quoted in *Aphorisms of the Mohammedan Saints*

1

We invent the ones we love. We project our image of them on a reality we would sooner ignore. It is a pull so strong even knowledge of that process wouldn't stop us from doing so.

I don't think I really knew you, Sofi. I wanted to. I wanted to know the history of your life, every rhythm of your days. I knew only what you told me and what I inferred to be true. The rest, my imagination created. Because you existed only in my memory after that day at the station. My mind created an image of you in the void, no matter how much I didn't want you there.

◆

It was only back in Toronto after grad school that Murad realized how much Sofi had changed him. His medication ran out shortly after leaving London. He worried that he would relapse, living life in an emotional free fall without a parachute. Instead, he found himself feeling relatively calm, afloat but not drowning. At first he thought it could have been a simple result of the pills, a pharmaceutical cleansing of the soul. He eventually convinced himself it was Sofi. He left London with no sense that love had cured him; if anything he felt diseased by it. But it was an illness that had meaning, direction and power, the injuries of a real life at a time when life could scarcely be experienced at all.

He returned to the family's empty suburban home outside the city. He received calls every other day from Ammi and Abbu in Pakistan, asking him to perform a variety of household tasks, unsure, it seemed, if he could handle taking care of things while they were in Lahore. He handled every request with zeal. The house – split-level, with wooden floors, full of some of the same mementoes from Asia that the family had kept in their Lahore home – was his to manage, and he felt all at once thrust into responsible adulthood without ever having truly lived an adult life.

Murad spoke to few people. Hardly any of his friends knew he was back. He had two choices now that he was home: do nothing or find a job, any job. Starting his master's degree, he had visions of studying international relations so he could escape, joining the United Nations or another global body that would take him out of Canada entirely. Now with the degree done, back in the very place he wanted to leave, escape seemed futile. It was the desire of inmates looking for an opportunity to break out of prison, and for too long he kept his own mind as his cell. Now all he wanted was to run toward life, any life, even a less-than-ideal one.

A connection of Abbu's directed Murad to a contact he had in a bank downtown. Abbu insisted he meet him. "You need to start thinking of your future," he said over the phone in mid-October. "Banking, I know, isn't your ideal, but you have to consider stability –"

"I know, I'll talk to him," said Murad, interrupting him.

There was a brief silence, as if his father was taken aback by the acquiescence. "Good," he said. "You must."

"I know. I should."

His name was Javed Imran. He was the son of the cousin of one of Abbu's employees, part of the extensive network Abbu had seemed to build miraculously among Pakistanis working in the financial industry in almost every major English-speaking city in the world. He had agreed to meet weeks after he arrived back in Canada from London.

Murad sat across the table in his claustrophobic yet immaculately maintained office downtown, near King and Bay. Javed was in his late thirties, in human resources, partially balding, with a paunch as prominent as his overconfidence, secure in the power given to him in whatever hierarchy he happened to find himself. Aside from a brief greeting, he spent the first few minutes carefully perusing Murad's resumé, breaking his false concentration to glance at him from over his glasses. Murad expected Javed to tell him, with cold politeness, that he couldn't possibly see a fit for him anywhere at the bank, ending the meeting with a handshake and little else.

He finished reading the resumé, dropping the sheets of paper on his desk. "It seems you know how to write," said Javed.

"I believe I can."

"You did well on your master's thesis?"

"I received a distinction," said Murad, feeling more at ease now than he had when he'd come in.

"I saw a position open up in corporate communications. They're looking for someone with writing skills. You'd be surprised. In the financial industry we get a lot of people with business backgrounds who can't write properly. They're actually looking for people with experience in the humanities and the social sciences."

"Really?" he asked, genuinely intrigued.

"Yes, I mean compared to the BBA or MBA types, you can at least write a proper English sentence."

They both laughed comfortably. His judgment of Javed had been premature. Behind his seriousness and ego, he seemed friendly and gregarious. Murad realized, for the first time in very recent memory, he felt connected to someone, a brief moment of ease felt with a stranger.

Javed mentioned an opening for a junior communications specialist that he wanted Murad to interview for. "It's an entry-level position, but worth looking into," he said. He interviewed twice for the position, once with a slightly bored, nearly middle-aged HR consultant named Brenda, once with the hiring manager, a bespectacled, goateed and unusually chipper man in his late thirties named Anthony DeMarco.

Murad waited for the interview results for weeks without fear of rejection or hope of acceptance. His spare time was spent consciously applying a monastic approach to life. Instead of going inward to find God, or to wallow in a void, he went inside himself to clear the remaining mist in his head. He frequented the gym. He read all that he could, everything except the book Khala had gifted him in London. It sat with its red cover in his corner bookshelf, its presence a vestige of a time not quite forgotten. He tried to maintain an emotional equilibrium, letting the softness of Sofi's face glide into his thoughts without letting the pain of her image drag him down.

Finally, in late November, he received a call from Anthony saying he'd been accepted for the position. Murad was to begin in December, an ideal time to start, he claimed. "You'll get to meet the team right as people are taking off for Christmas," said Anthony.

"I look forward to it."

"I'm sure you'll have fun in this role," he said with more earnestness, making Murad think the job wasn't quite as enjoyable as he was trying to suggest.

Adulthood, real adulthood, began the moment Murad started work. He felt as if he had just come back from a war, realizing that the world had moved on, encountering people uninterested in the places he had travelled, the battles he had lost. A week after his phone call with Anthony, he met the team: Sapna, the project leader, Margaret and Paula. Sapna and Murad worked on the text for the quarterly and annual reports, gathering information from each line of business, like journalists in need of a story. Margaret and Paula did their own work, mostly online marketing, very little of which he understood. Anthony seemed to be in constant battle with his senior directors and executives, his down-to-earth effervescence noticeably on hold whenever a nasty email was received, or an impossible demand arrived.

Routine quickly constructed a web around Murad. He rose early, took the bus to Finch, rode on the subway to the very heart of downtown, accepted train delays with humour, got home, ate, read for a bit, then went to bed early. He accepted the heartless boredom of everyday, quotidian life. He didn't long for a vacation, even as others took their own; when he was forced to use up his vacation time, he stayed at home. He spent time with Ammi and Abbu when they came from Pakistan to Toronto every few months. When they asked him to come to Pakistan for some distant family wedding, Murad simply concocted work-related excuses about why he had to stay put in Canada.

He returned home one evening from work, thinking about Sofi. He had an urge to write to her. Without eating, barely stopping to take off his shoes or change his clothes, he went straight to the basement to turn on his computer. After some hesitation, he began writing. The first sentences were tepid and formal greetings, asking Sofi how she was, describing in flat, perfunctory detail his life of work and banal office politics. He looked at his sentences and deleted the email in its entirety. Like an artist inspired, he wrote a completely different message. Raw, honest, he laid out his sense of hurt and his desire to know why she had abandoned him at the Underground.

Murad stopped writing, fearing he was trying to bolster bridges that should have been burnt down some time ago. Contacting her was out of the question. He deleted the message and turned off the computer, letting the ghost of Sofi live in the past.

⁂

Murad was the only member of the team younger than thirty. Sapna, who married a few months before he had come on board, was close to her thirty-first birthday. Along with Sapna, Margaret, Paula and Anthony had, between them, four partners and five children by the time Murad had joined the bank. Among them, their conversations were limited in range: children and parenting, mortgages, career gossip, restaurants frequented. He took part in these conversations as a way of fitting in and engaging in the new professional life he led. Cerebral discussions on the need for troop de-escalation in Afghanistan or the value of the European Union for its member states had no place. Their interactions as individuals were warm yet functional, the deliberate superficiality that workmates imposed on their relationships with each other.

Sapna and Murad became much friendlier as the months passed. Although happily married, she was wary of having marriage limit her life in any way. "You're not one of those people who like rushing back home after work?" he asked, one Friday night sharing a sushi dinner.

"Being a family person is one thing, but I have no time for living in the penitentiary of wife-life, Murad," she said, deadpan.

It was a phrase that made him laugh out loud, bestowing on Sapna a witty mystique he had noticed only months after beginning to work with her. Her reserve had been carefully cultivated, it seemed, and they began talking as friends rather than as co-workers. They had common interests in literature, film and politics, their intellectual lives not limited to finding ways to advance their careers. They liked each other at a basic, human level. She had a network of friends who lived downtown, and she often invited Murad along whenever she met up with them.

Saskia was one of those friends. They met in late September almost a year after Murad had begun working. He joined Sapna early one Sunday afternoon for brunch at a small restaurant off Bloor Street that sold only sweet and savoury crepes. Summer was dying, chill winds rolled through the streets, but the skies were still clear. Sapna and Murad arrived early; Saskia, who was to join them, came late, rushing into the restaurant impatiently and apologizing profusely for her tardiness. She was dressed casually for the weekend yet carried herself with a professional formality. She was petite, her hips rounded in parenthetical curves. Her hair was a deep yellow, a silky blond. Murad found it difficult to look at anything but her.

She hugged Sapna and shook his hand. Saskia was Sapna's friend from university, a fellow English graduate from Western, with some business skills honed by doing a certificate in corporate public relations. She worked at a large insurance firm uptown, the name of which was unfamiliar to Murad. After they exchanged news, Saskia quickly apologized for talking about herself. She asked him about his job, about school. He told her about his experience living and studying in London, not mentioning, of course, Sofi or his depression. Saskia listened to him speak with a mesmerizing attentiveness, her conversation devoid of empty speech, acting with a reserve that seemed more typical of the Europeans he met in London in comparison with the easy openness he found with the other North American students.

Their brunch together went by quickly. They parted ways almost as soon as they finished eating. Saskia hugged Murad with the same intensity as her embrace with Sapna. "It was so nice meeting you," she said in a low voice, her warm cheek flattened against his.

The next week, he received an email in his work inbox from Saskia, addressed, strangely, not to him and Sapna but to him alone. She wrote that she was glad to have met him, saying, "hopefully we can get together again . . . sooner rather than later." Murad drafted a short reply: "Hi Saskia, Thanks for your email. It was great meeting you as well. We should do something with Sapna sometime soon. All the best, Murad."

He looked at his draft for a few moments and deleted it. He wrote Saskia a new message, asking her if she wanted to meet for dinner on Friday. Within fifteen minutes, she wrote back and said yes.

Abbu and Ammi had always discouraged dating. They were proud of their traditionalism, wanting Murad's life to have a trajectory that was straightforward, dignified and respectable. Life was segmented into three parts: school, job and marriage. There was no courtship, and at his age it was also expected to do the rounds, meeting young women suggested to his parents by colleagues, friends and members of the community. "You should look for compatibility," his father was fond of saying. The women's khandan, their family and accompanying value system, was what his mother emphasized. Among her own friends, she scoffed when she heard of the sons and daughters of acquaintances going out behind their parents' back. It was a sign of poor behaviour, if not poor upbringing, innocent or not.

Murad started seeing Saskia a week after Ammi and Abbu returned to Pakistan. They had come home to avoid the summer heat. Now Abbu had work to attend to that couldn't justify him being away from the country any longer, and Ammi wanted to be back in Lahore for the wedding of the daughter of one of her childhood classmates from Sacred Heart Convent. He was alone and free. His time spent with Saskia was guilt-free, rarely thinking of the values his parents had instilled in him. It would be wrong to say they were his parents' values alone. He embraced them as his own as well. Meeting Sofi had changed his allegiance to those values. Going out with Saskia was a continuation of that change, the start of a new way of living.

Saskia and Murad went out for sushi close to her apartment on

Eglinton Avenue when they met for dinner that Friday. Her company was warm, familiar. They spoke to each other with genuine curiosity, barely hiding their mutual fascination. She told him of her parents: they lived in Ottawa, although her father was from Toronto. "My mother's Dutch. It's where I get my name from. It was actually my grandmother's. I know, everybody thinks it's a weird name," she explained with a slight giggle. Her mother was a painter who sold her artistic skills over to the commercial world of graphic design. Her father was a lawyer and amateur poet. The way Saskia described them, her parents seemed to live dual lives: professionals at work and artists at home.

"They didn't want stick to their art full time?" asked Murad.

"No," said Saskia, elongating the "o" as if he said something ridiculous. "They're too middle class. But they miss their art too much to give it up completely."

"A world apart from my parents," he said, almost to himself, playing at a piece of maki with his chopsticks haphazardly.

"Well, how would you describe them?"

He laughed. "Middle class too. But that's probably a simple way of describing them. They don't need artistry. They have their sense of order – work, family, God, duty, obligation – and that suffices. I never felt they missed anything. I don't know if they had imagination for much else." He paused and thought of what he'd said, if his assessment of his parents was too uncharitable. "No, that's not true. That's too easy to say. I can't even guess the things they lost over the years." He stopped playing with his food, gazing over Saskia's face to the window, as if he could envision Abbu and Ammi through their years in the darkness of the Toronto night, every friend or family member lost, every path in their lives taken or forsaken, a catalogue of hopes and absences.

"Maybe that's generational. Maybe they learned to accept the past better."

He came back to Saskia. "Could be true. And even if I was

right, and they don't long for anything, they probably live with an advantage. It doesn't always do you any good."

Saskia tilted her head. "But don't you long for anything?"

Murad hesitated. "No."

"I don't believe that. Didn't you tell me that you went all the way to London for your master's degree? Weren't you looking for something?"

He was afraid of revealing too much, of Sofi, of that entire moment of his life. "London was an island."

"An island to run away to, or an island to be marooned in?"

"Both," said Murad. "Maybe 'marooned' isn't the word. But you're right. I thought London was someplace to find something. And if you ask me what that 'something' was, I couldn't tell you."

"Did you find that 'something'?"

More than he ever wanted, he thought. "No. But the experience gave me a lesson. Between running away to London and running back from London, I realized once I came back here that I had to live my life like finding it wasn't that important. I had to *pretend* it wasn't that important. I needed to be" – he struggled to find the exact word – "still."

They both fell silent. Saskia stared at him, wearing a slight, gentle smile as she excavated his life with blue eyes that bore into him, making him realize for the first time since London that he had bared a part of himself to anyone.

◆

As fall turned to winter, they began to see each other more. Chaste embraces gave way to European cheek-kisses. Kisses on her cheek, the smoothness of which surprised Murad, gave way to kisses on the lips and lingering gazes whenever they left each other. Spending time with Saskia was novel, different from Marjan, certainly different from anything he had experienced with Sofi. With

Marjan, his conservative shyness had prevented him from engaging in the closeness she wanted when they were together. His time with Saskia had no such inhibitions – religion, culture and family tradition were compartmentalized in favour of the physical joy his upbringing had long prevented him from experiencing.

One Saturday in late January, they went to see a movie, a British film about a bank robbery in London. Ten minutes into the film, Saskia put her head on Murad's shoulder. Her hair had the clean, refreshing scent of apple shampoo. Saskia kept her eyes on the screen, unaware that his attention was fixated on the proximity of her body to his. When the film was over, she lifted her head and looked at him, holding his gaze for a brief and tranquil moment.

They left the theatre and walked around aimlessly, trudging over pockets of refrozen ice with Saskia holding onto Murad's arm, laughing together when they slipped. He thought of leaving. His desire to spend more time with her was stronger than his desire to return home.

He walked her to her building, a small, four-story complex. As they stood outside, he said

"It's freezing," largely at a loss of thinking of anything else to say.

"I know," she said. "I kind of like the cold, though."

"How come?" he asked. "I've been in this city for a long time, and I'm still not used to it. It's not even about the temperature or the ice or the snow. In the winter people seem different. Everyone goes inward."

"I don't think that at all."

"No?"

"I see winter as a time of warmth, togetherness. People clinging onto each other." She came close to Murad. "You don't have to go, you know."

"I know. I wasn't planning on going anywhere."

♦

She led Murad by the hand into her apartment, which was bare, save for a few sundry semi-impressionist paintings of lakes and forest scenes. It was a studio; her bed was on the floor illuminated by a side lamp. It had been left on while Saskia was away, as if in preparation for their return.

Her body was small compared to his own, but she controlled everything, every step to her bed, every motion afterward. When they finished, he laid his head down, exhausted.

Adrift in her softness, Murad felt the night rush away until the happiness he experienced became clouded by concern, the anxiety that he had just passed through a door closing behind him, with no point of return available. He held Saskia in his arms. She placed her head on his chest, eyes closed. He marvelled at her calm as he looked at her. She had none of his misgivings. She didn't come from a world where this was a sin, he thought. There was no worldly punishment for this, or a reckoning in the afterlife. No religious law was trampled on, no cardinal violation against the sacred committed, only skin, only contentment, only a momentary connection.

It was nearly one in the morning. The light of the hallway outside etched a glowing bar at the bottom of the apartment's door. Murad got up. He took his clothes from the reclining chair near Saskia's bed and started dressing quietly, thinking, perhaps oddly, that he could slip out into the street without her noticing. As he buttoned his shirt and put on his sweater, he saw her staring at him. She lifted her torso from the bed, bringing her quilt close to her to protect her from the room's chill.

"Where are you going?"

Murad took his coat from the chair and slowly pulled up the zipper, thinking of what to tell her. "I think I should go home."

"Did I do something wrong?"

"No," he said, trying to reassure her.

"Why are you looking so sad?"

"There's no sadness here," he said, realizing he truly meant it.

"Why leave then?"

In the faint light, Murad meditated on the gentleness of Saskia's face. It was almost maternal in its concern. He sat back down on her bed, reflexively putting his hand on her pale, rounded right cheek. She placed her hand over his, her fingers thin and warm. She gave an understanding look and kissed him.

He left her apartment, stepping into the wind-frozen streets, walking to the subway in a strange daze. He had lied to her; they had done something wrong, or, at the very least, he had done something wrong. He had sinned, wilfully – yet the act of sinning seemed to hold little weight in that moment. The religious laws that Murad used to believe, that carried meaning and set moral boundaries, should have made him feel, at the very least, guilty and ashamed, and yet he felt nothing. He couldn't muster any regret or remorse for the night. The punishments for and prohibitions against everything he had with Saskia, which would have drowned his soul before London, existed only as strictures from a past life.

When Murad went to bed he reflected on the night. He understood the sadness he had felt when leaving Saskia's apartment. In her company he found the warmth and comfort of a refuge, a way station rather than a home. Did other young men think like this? Ruminating over the future when the present was the only objective needing pursuing? His curse, perhaps. A flaw, definitely, because he thought only of permanency, realizing, even after weeks and months of knowing Saskia, that no inkling of longevity existed, that what they had was a fling, an experience only. Could his parents accept her and how their relationship had come about? For that matter, could he?

Sofi could have given something different. It was a childish thought, imagining a happiness that always existed in a place other than where he was. That's how it worked, thought Murad. Comparing your loves, past and present, to your first love – the first woman who could create an alternate future and let you act out stories of a life lived with thousands of permutations.

He closed his eyes. In his imagination he held Saskia close to his body. As he thought of her more, Saskia changed shape. Her skin became burnished, her lashes thickened, her eyes grew black, like dusk turning into night. It was Sofi he held in his arms before the darkness of sleep.

2

Sofi counted the days and weeks: it had been seven months since she had left London.

It was Ian who made Sofi leave the city. She'd had no desire to date anyone when she first came to London. She left Canada with the original intention of finding and healing herself in solitude, a sentiment amplified by the end of her relationship with Robin. Her desire for solitude wore off quickly when faced with the loneliness of being in a new city by herself. She had made friends in class and at her residence with ease, as she was always able to do. Sofi realized, however, that she was not yet at the stage where her connection with the Divine was sufficient enough to satiate her heart.

Ian had changed all that. He was a friend of an acquaintance from her residence. Sofi was drawn to him quickly. He had an aura of glamour that surrounded him, along with an ease in adding charm and worldliness to those people in his life: dinner and drinks, everyone in London so finely dressed compared to Toronto; friends coming in from Europe, the Middle East and beyond. London was the great commuter city for a shrunken world. Ian had a liveliness that made life shimmer. Next to Robin – her only point of comparison – he was less cerebral, more grounded in the realities of everyday life, and had the charisma of someone who could talk about high or low culture, depending on the company.

Sofi asked Ian once, walking one night at the university on

a lone cobblestone path, if he believed in God. He said he did. "I'm probably one of the few people I know who still do. I think it's something I get from my parents. My mother was the granddaughter of a vicar. She always said belief in God was a mark of civilization. I suppose that's still carried with me."

The thought of God bringing civilization and refinement to his children touched Sofi. More importantly for her, the thought that Ian held fast to a belief in God as part of a familial tradition deepened the connection she wanted from him, the connection she had failed to have with Robin.

They rented a flat together shortly after classes ended officially in September, near Shepherd's Bush. Her parents accepted her living with Ian. Mama simply said nothing, acquiescing to her life choice without commentary. Babba seemed strangely upbeat, without justifying her living as an unmarried couple. "Just live your life," he said one day over the phone. "Don't worry about your mother or myself." It was the same message he'd told her in Canada, to move on, to forget.

The flat was small and expensive, like everything else in London. She warmed to its coziness, its intimacy, and the fact that Ian could afford it. He interviewed for a job at an investment firm during the summer at the university; by October the job was his. Sofi tried to find work with little success. She took a series of contract jobs with a few NGOs, none of which developed into anything permanent. The stagnation of her career was an acceptable frustration; for her, life was a series of balances that needed to be maintained.

Sofi and Ian spent their life outdoors, in pubs with mates, in restaurants dressed as if every evening were its own celebration. With each other, things changed as the months went on. They shared a life that was close but not intimate. Eventually, their conversations became shallow and light. Silence filled their apartment when they were alone together, like an elemental spirit. In company, he spoke about her with pride, as if constantly grateful for her presence. Alone, he spoke hurriedly of his own stresses, his own professional worries. "I should go back and do a law degree, then at least I'd be more marketable," he said one Sunday morning over breakfast. "Maybe we should go to Canada, the job market's fucking dead here." She soothed his concerns, gave balm to his anxieties with her words, her touch, yet she began to feel exhausted and empty, realizing how much her relationship with Ian mimicked that with Robin, the feeling of giving so much of her spirit with so little in return.

Nevertheless, she continued to pray for Ian. Sofi's prayers in London were informal, with no prostrations, no hands upturned to heaven, but they were no less sincere. She prayed for the strength to be compassionate, to be a vehicle of mercy to him and to the rest of the world. Even still, she drifted from him, and thoughts of God carried her when her life in London began to weigh on her. The city, this supposed centre of the world, started to seem less of an escape and more of a place of exile from all those things and people she valued.

Murad was one of them. She longed to speak to him, thinking of him often, the frequency of her thoughts increasing as the lustre of her life in London dulled. She knew he had a quiet thoughtfulness that she needed. Underneath his sadness, she saw gentleness, a purity she thought could assuage her loneliness. Whenever she felt the urge to email him, she stopped herself. It was the same dilemma she had faced when she received that last call from Murad asking her to meet him, a struggle between the desire to see him and be in the presence of a real friend, and the idea that her own presence was harmful to him. She knew she was an object of his longing, an unreachable desire that would only cause Murad more pain. Such a strange thing life is, she used to think, where none of our affections fit properly with each other, a puzzle of emotions constructed without any care. She pondered the possibility of seeing him differently, wondering if the love she had for him could change and bloom into something else, something that would satisfy part of her own loneliness as well as his. Perhaps he could have been more than a kindred spirit. Had she not left him at the Tube, could there have been an opportunity to continue their friendship, a friendship that could have turned into love? Did she already love Murad in those moments they saw each other – a secret, esoteric love? If that were true, why could her mind not fully register the signals her soul transmitted in those days?

All meaningless questions, of course, ones she posed when she despaired of her relationship with Ian the most. Nevertheless, Murad haunted her. She wondered whether he still thought of her, whether those thoughts were bitter ones, full of resentment. If only he knew, she often thought, what portion of her being she kept in reserve just for him. She wanted to apologize for any hurt she caused Murad, for any opportunity to heal the lacerations in his heart.

Those weren't the only opportunities she considered. Sofi often thought of how the image of him had shifted in her mind. First, the sad-eyed young man she had known peripherally from class, sitting alone in the blistering wind in front of the library. Then the friend, the new entry in her life, whose kindness resonated loudly within her. Then there was Murad the brother, a mirror of Sikander and her brother's sensitivity. *A unique soul.* So unique she realized only later that it blinded her to thinking of him as anything more than someone whose sadness mirrored her own, and who could be a companion to a spiritual journey she had only recently begun. It was a dangerous love for him, she felt, the type of love that could only damage him further if she didn't separate herself from him.

This was at least how she assuaged her guilt, even if the regret of the damage done to Murad pressed upon her. There were other regrets as well, thoughts that she tried to cut down as soon as they sprouted. In the moments when her connection to Ian seemed to wane, when his eyes seemed to look at her with more distance, when her dislocation was at its most painful, she forced herself to suppress that corner within her that pondered every scenario where, had Ian had not been in her life, Murad could have been in hers, not as a unique soul or fellow traveller, but as a deeper connection, with a worldly love that could have given her all that she needed but couldn't find.

A few months before she left to return to Canada, Sofi and Ian went to a party near Portobello Road. Charlie, a friend of Ian's, was house-sitting for a friend of the family. The home was two stories tall, with an all-white interior. Charlie was a mate from Ian's school days at an impossibly posh public school in Essex. He was short, blond, bespectacled and loud for a Brit, thought Sofi, a universal loudness that signalled both insecurity and domineering arrogance. By her estimation, most of the people at the party had gone to that school. There was a strange insularity in the way they spoke to each other. Even Ian's manner changed when he drank and spoke to his old chums: he became more crass, quick to judge and snide about old friends.

The night was tiresome for Sofi and her friendliness faded quickly. Ian, Charlie and a few of their friends whose names she didn't bother to remember huddled together in the living room. Drinks were passed and an earthy, weed scent wafted from the side room behind them. Sofi got up from the sofa, needing a break from the gossip about former boyfriends and girlfriends, about who'd slept with whom. There was a balcony on the second floor, and Sofi wanted to head outside, her need for solitude never more urgent. She climbed the stairs, but before she could open the door to the balcony, she felt a hand touch her arm. A young woman stood beneath the archway of the door. She looked tipsy, a dark glass held delicately in her left hand. Bright, exquisite red hair fell over her right shoulder.

"Hello," she said to Sofi, warmly.

"Hello."

The woman inched out of the doorway. Her lips were full and deep red. She was beautiful, an intimidating beauty, that Sofi thought would magnify and not diminish with time. "You're Ian's girlfriend, aren't you? Sofi, yeah?"

"Yes."

"I'm Katherine," she said, extending her hand to Sofi. Her fingers were thin, her palms cold. "I was hoping to get to meet you."

For the first time that night, Sofi felt genuinely pleased to talk to someone. "I'm really flattered. I'm sorry I didn't get to meet you before. How do you know Charlie and Ian?"

"School," she said, somewhat curtly. "You could say, from childhood, really."

"A long time –"

"Like I said," broke in Katherine, interrupting her as if wanting to stifle any other line of conversation, "I wanted to make sure I got to meet you." She looked Sofi up and down. "You really are a prize," she said.

"I'm sorry?"

"I never thought Ian would be into Asian girls," Katherine said. Her eyes were wide, partly mocking, partly amazed.

A deep anger grew in Sofi, a fury so quick it stopped her from saying anything or to retaliate in any way.

"Ian wasn't a bloke who was into exotic types," continued Katherine. "He really wasn't. But with you I can understand. Sofi the Trophy." She brought her drink to her lips quickly, as if realizing she had said too much.

Beyond Katherine two women were talking, both fresh-faced and blond, so identical they could have been sisters. They broke off their conversation and pulled Katherine gently away from the doorway. "No wait," said Katherine. "I'm sorry." Katherine's friend apologized too, the contrition of genuine embarrassment.

Sofi stood outside the door and closed her eyes, hearing only the sound of Katherine and her friends whispering to each other in terse, angry tones. For the first time since coming to London, she felt she existed in another world, her otherness brought to the fore.

By the time Sofi and Ian left the party, the Underground had already closed down, so they shared a cab with a couple that lived near them. After they had dropped off the couple and walked to their flat, Sofi told Ian the story of Katherine. "Katherine was such a spaz in school," he said in a low, frustrated voice. "She never could keep her mouth shut. You know she was in love with half the boys in every class she was ever in?"

"So what, this was just jealousy?"

"Yeah," said Ian, as if the answer was self-evident.

Sofi couldn't sleep that night. She went to the bathroom and stared into the mirror as if it were a portal to wisdom she desperately needed. Her dark eyes gleamed in the artificial light. Her face, when looked at directly, had a doe-eyed symmetry. She looked at herself without narcissism or pride. Sofi the Trophy. An exotic prize, her clear brown skin a currency that could be exchanged for status.

She shut off the bathroom lights and went back to bed, easing into sleep, her insomnia defeated by the thought of creating an ending for this chapter of her life.

Sofi's breakup with Ian was slow and natural. He seemed to understand its necessity, even as he bore a sullen resentment that Sofi felt was due to the fact that she had initiated the parting. He read or did work on their small, bare wooden table as she packed her belongings to return to Canada, his silence a form of punishment that both saddened and strangely empowered her.

Going back to Toronto was her only option. Her contracts had finished. She had friends in London, but she had stayed only for Ian, her love an anchor that no longer existed. Living with Mama again would feel dreadful, but she was caught up in an inner conviction that the only ones who loved her, who truly loved her, shared her blood. Family exerted an inescapable pull even when it exhausted her.

Mama had hardly changed the apartment. When she walked back into her room in March 2008, it seemed no different from when she left for grad school all those years ago. The familiarity of her room disturbed Sofi, as it looked like she had just fallen into a crevice in time. The window that overlooked Yonge Street and the neighbouring condos was clean and polished, giving clarity to a view she had looked out on frequently over the years. It remained an inert portal to the world; she had found no insight into her life then, and it offered no trail out of the labyrinth in the life she lived now.

Sofi's first days back home were spent with Mama and Babba separately, both parents overjoyed at her return. Their enthusiasm softened as the unease of her homecoming became more visible on her face, in her body language and an increased passivity when around her parents. Mama and Babba went on with their lives, leaving Sofi alone in a haunted world.

The longer she spent alone and without work, the more trapped she felt. Aside from exchanging emails with Lily, who now lived in Montreal with Andrew, within the first month of coming back she barely spoke to anyone. Throughout her time in London, she had been in contact with Fatima, though her emails became less regular and more formal over time. Despite her love for her cousin, Sofi didn't bother to get in touch with her when she returned. She was away from the city anyway and contact on the phone or over the Internet felt insufficient. There was something else that worried Sofi about Fatima: a renewed fear of judgment. It would feel strange talking to her cousin after almost two years in London and living with Ian – it was a life completely alien to Fatima's value system.

Sofi prayed in her room in Toronto as she had before. In her supplications, her prayers roamed toward Murad. She asked for God's succour, to give him peace. Since her brother, there was no one she had prayed for with such sincerity. These prayers were reserved for her family. Through each du'a she realized what a force God's love was, how it pulled Murad deeper into her heart.

Mama oscillated between her usual stoic melancholy and something altogether more vibrant. Sofi was certain her presence back in her home made her mother happy. While she had no evidence of it – Mama wasn't given to sharing her judgments – Sofi was sure living with Ian was an arrangement her mother hadn't approved of. Whatever her mother's true feelings, she came back from work some days energized just to see her daughter's face. Other days, there was a weariness that Mama carried into the apartment like a chill air from the street.

One day, in one of her more serene moods, Mama told her about a wedding she wanted Sofi to attend with her. It was her friend Uzma's daughter, Zareen, who was getting married. Mama seemed genuinely enthusiastic about attending, an excitement that animated Sofi. She agreed to go with Mama, the thought of being at a wedding, feeling the joy of being around people, seemed a way to get herself out of the lonely gyre she found herself circling in.

Sofi and Mama skipped the mehndi, coming only to the walima being held at a hotel downtown. They wore shalwar kameez and draped themselves lightly in jewellery. Sofi was proud of the way they both looked, especially her mother, who, despite the confines of her own solitude, still maintained a sense of natural elegance.

It was a dry wedding, which disappointed Mama. After a reception on the mezzanine, the guests were marshalled upstairs to the fourteenth floor for food. Sofi and Mama sat at the same table, making small talk with the other guests. The crowd was a mix of hijabis and their bearded husbands and what Mama called a "modern bunch" of desi women with bare arms, wearing skirts; and slick young men in designer jackets. What seemed to bind them all together was money, the aura of middle-class comfort. Half the guests came from Mississauga or North York, some from farther north than that. Many of the young couples that Sofi met, who were her age, seemed to live downtown, enjoying young professional urban life. They were conscious that soon their lives would follow a common blueprint as they transitioned north, with children coming soon and mortgages in need of payment.

While Sofi knew no one at the wedding, Mama was in her element. She gossiped with the few aunties she knew, and then continued that gossip with other aunties she had only recently befriended. She introduced Sofi to these women, a confetti of "N" names like Nighat, Nusrat, Nasreen, Nargis and Neelum. They were middle-aged, with rounded faces and equally rounded bodies. Uzma Auntie came by as they were seated and hugged Mama. She was taller than Sofi expected, with chocolate-brown skin, wearing a magenta shalwar kameez, a tennis bracelet and a diamond choker around her neck. Mama introduced Sofi to her, but before she could stand, Uzma Auntie hugged her, stroking her cheek. "You're a beauty," said Auntie. Sofi laughed and thanked her. Auntie's compliment put Sofi at ease.

In the front of the hall stood a lectern. Zareen's sister Anum – rail thin, dark-complexioned, looking as if she had barely escaped the awkwardness of her teenage years – stood nervously as she announced that dinner was served. It was a sit-down meal, different from the buffet setup so common to most Pakistani weddings Sofi had attended, but the menu was standard fare: butter chicken, lamb korma, palak paneer, vegetable pulao, naan, mixed vegetables and vegetarian kofteh served in the middle of each table for all to share.

A woman in hijab asked one of the servers if the meat was halal, and the server confirmed unenthusiastically that it was.

Sofi's eyes wandered over each table, in the idle thought that she might see a familiar face. Near the lectern, at the farthest end of the hall, she saw a middle-aged couple, the woman light-skinned, her husband slightly darker, a broad smile fixed on his face beneath a trim moustache. Next to him was someone Sofi took to be the couple's son. His face was turned away, as if looking for a waiter. One came, bringing a glass of what looked like ginger ale for the young man. He turned his face back to his parents. Sofi's heartbeat accelerated like a careening train.

It was Murad. He had his mother's fair skin. His face looked lean and angular, more distinctly aged than it had been in London, yet it seemed to have a healthy glow she hadn't seen there. He continued eating, looking at the couple his parents were speaking to, smiling between chews as if trying to be attentive and polite. Sofi stared, unblinking, as if wanting to make sure that the image of him was somehow possible. After a moment, Sofi realized she had never even thought that Murad might be back in Toronto. It seemed dreamlike, and yet he was here, all too real.

Zareen and her new husband, Kamran, gave a speech midway through dinner. Aside from the snide criticism by one of the uncles seated at the table behind her (complaining that no one gave speeches at weddings in Pakistan), Sofi remembered nothing that had been said. The rustle of the room fell away as she looked at Murad, his head turned back to listen to the newly married couple. Tears of joy rolled down Zareen's face as she spoke of her happiness with Kamran. Murad's face looked pensive and melancholic. The speech concluded quickly, and the room burst out in applause. Murad clapped too, his contemplative frown morphing into a sincere smile.

When it was time for dessert, Sofi was brought back to the discussion at the table, interrupting her study of Murad. A couple, both doctors in their thirties, were asking Sofi how she would compare rental prices in London versus Toronto. She tried to converse with them, even as she remained distracted by Murad's presence.

From the corner of her eye, she noticed Murad's chair was empty. Sofi excused herself from the table. She went out to the hallway, hoping to see him. There was idiocy in this, she thought, standing near the elevators outside the dining room. It had been too long. She wondered if she should simply ignore him? She was the one who had stood him up at the Underground. She was the one who couldn't give him what he wanted. Who was she to upset his life? Yet it had been two years already, enough time, she felt, for both their lives to have begun again. Their past together in London was of no value to the present. That place and time, where she could only see him as a friend, seemed far from the island where her soul now landed itself. Since then, her heart had grown in a different direction. She always knew within Murad was a kindness, a lapidary light that was familiar and warm. But in the moment she saw him, a different feeling emerged. It was as if, in her isolation since coming back to Canada, he evoked a feeling of home, of comfort and safety.

If they had met at a different time, if the world had thrown them together before she met Ian, could it have been different? Could she have loved Murad the way he wanted to be loved? Could she have filled all those empty pockets within her? The questions flashed in her mind, and then dissipated. Perhaps they could start again. Sofi became buoyed by the opportunity of starting a new history with Murad, this time, she hoped, with the potential of forging the connection she knew they both needed, a deeper love without mistakes and misjudgments.

Around the corner, beneath the bronzed bathroom sign, she saw Murad. He was walking slowly, looking down at a random spot on the ground. His suit was elegant, a light grey, with a crisp white shirt beneath a thick grey, white and black tie. He seemed larger to Sofi, as if his frame had expanded with an inner confidence and poise she hadn't noticed before. When he looked up, the contemplation on his face withered, his eyes narrowed, a quizzical expression forming on his face, as if he were unsure of the reality of Sofi's presence.

Murad stopped in front of Sofi, speechless. She thought momentarily of holding back from embracing him, but ignoring any possible awkwardness, she lunged forward, wrapping her arms around his chest. He hesitated at first, but then she felt his chest heaving with a sigh and his arms rising up to press her farther into him. When they let each other go, Sofi looked into Murad's face. Gone was the quizzical confusion; he was stunned, yet seemed quietly elated. "I saw you inside," said Sofi. "I wasn't sure whether I should say hello or not."

"I'm glad you did."

"How are you?" asked Sofi.

"I'm fine," said Murad. He stared at her. "I'm doing well."

They stood in the hallway talking about the wedding: how they each knew Zareen ("Her mother's the friend of a friend of my mother," said Murad), who they were with (his parents had dragged him along), what they each thought of the wedding (fun for Sofi, tedious for Murad). They walked slowly back inside together, talking about the evening as if the past was inconsequential. Inside the dining hall, Murad's parents were up from their seats, saying their goodbyes to Uzma Auntie. Sofi realized how late it must be. Murad stared at his parents knowing he needed to join them. Sofi asked if he was leaving.

"It looks like it," he said. "Ammi and Abbu like going to bed early these days. I should take them home."

"Do I get to see you again?" asked Sofi.

The question seemed to take Murad aback. "Yes, of course."

"It would be good to talk," she said.

Murad seemed momentarily distant. "Yeah. It would be good. Let's meet."

Sofi said she'd email him the next morning. Without an embrace, or a handshake, Murad smiled, said goodbye and joined his parents. Sofi walked over to her table. Mama was huddled with two women, talking quietly and laughing loudly, almost as if conspiring over a plan that was necessarily secret yet sadistically funny. As the tables emptied, as guests left the wedding, family by family, couple by couple, Sofi sat down staring at Murad as he left the room without turning back to look at her.

3

It was only after Murad left the wedding that he fully understood Sofi's power to unnerve him. Abbu and Ammi had been back from Pakistan since March. He should have expected her to be in Toronto at some point. He should have realized the world would throw them together. He was so willing to forget her, eager almost, despite the difficulty of that effort. Yet the moment he saw her, she had taken hold of him. Did anyone else in that wedding see her the way he did, he thought? It was the Sofi that he remembered manifested in flesh, the Sofi who walked in loveliness, in a glory only he could see.

Ammi asked Murad who he had been speaking to when they arrived home. He told her it was a friend from London.

"Mashallah, such a pretty girl," she said, as they took off their shoes near the back door. "I should ask Uzma who her mother is."

"Quite pretty, actually," said Abbu. "Forget about Samra; that's the type of girl you should marry." He laughed quietly, as if telling himself a private joke.

Ammi made an annoyed, clicking sound. "Samra's pretty too. And she has substance."

"That's true," said Abbu.

"Besides," Ammi continued, "It's the ones who are too pretty you have to worry about most of all, Murad. Looks mean nothing if you're shameless, and believe me, half the pretty girls you'll meet have no sense of shame."

Abbu laughed again, wearily this time, and told her to relax. Murad cringed at everything they said. He feigned exhaustion and went to his room, Sofi's presence at the wedding weighing on him as much as the thought of his own marriage.

Murad had met Samra a few months before he saw Sofi, and a few months after his relationship with Saskia had ended. In the weeks after he slept with Saskia, they had become more distant. They had seen each other several times afterward, dates that felt more like mere encounters. Their time together was superficial. They enjoyed the laughter, the banter, the embrace of friends. The pace of Saskia's conversation was quick when Murad wanted it slow. They made excuses to leave each other frequently. A wall erected itself, at first unseen, then increasingly visible to both of them. Eventually there was no bypassing the barrier. A breakup was unnecessary. They just stopped seeing each other.

It was his fault, ultimately. Murad readily admitted that to himself. The normality of modern relationships was unsustainable for him, as he'd never been brought up in a culture where Western dating norms existed to be sustained. In the days after he last saw Saskia, he realized he was the one who pulled away from her, realizing that to continue with her would circumvent his upbringing: the love of God and faith, the acknowledgement of the superior judgment of family, the self-restraint that would be rewarded through marriage. Even as he silently resented all those things, he knew those codes were markers of a tradition stamped into the foundation of his soul.

Maybe it was Sofi that cursed it all. Murad thought of her more as Saskia's presence withered away in his life. He had never loved Saskia as he did Sofi. She was an unsinkable island whose shores shone light on the surface of the waters. Yet as ever-present as she was in his mind in the days before his parents' return from Pakistan, Murad found in himself a strength he hadn't observed before, the ability to suck in his frustrations and loneliness as if they were a source of an energy needed to live, rather than a force that enervated it.

It was that state that Ammi and Abbu encountered when they arrived in Canada. Murad had changed, in their estimation, for the better. "You seem reinvented, beta," said Abbu one Sunday at breakfast. They sat at their small, white kitchenette near the door to the lawn's wooden deck.

"You do, jaano," said Ammi. "You look happier. I think it's because you're working."

"I'm too busy to think about being happy or sad," Murad said, jokingly.

At the time, there was truth in that. He lived what he thought a true adult life was: not quiet desperation as much as an acknowledgement that time was fleeting, and he had to hoard experiences as if they were gold. Whether those experiences were good or bad, pleasurable or not, made little difference.

There was another motive behind his parents' interest in his well-being. One Sunday, weeks after his parents arrived, Abbu came to him as Murad sat at the dining table working on a template for the bank's upcoming annual report. He sat down next to him, frowning and hesitant. Abbu's silence disturbed Murad's work more than his presence. Murad asked him what the matter was.

"How ready are you to start settling down?" he asked.

It took a few seconds for him to understand exactly what Abbu meant. "You mean marriage?"

"There're a few families we want to see with you. Contacts of some of my contacts in Pakistan. People I know from the bank, a friend of your mother's cousin. I need to know you're ready to start meeting people."

Abbu spoke with a mixture of concern and authority. Murad struggled to think of excuses to give to avoid the awkward encounters with random families and unknown women he knew would be in store. Before he could speak, Abbu continued. "Your mother and I know how difficult it's been for you in the past few years. We also don't believe in delaying these processes for too long."

"What if I said I wasn't sure I was ready? It still hasn't been that long since I've started working. I barely feel settled in my job for me to commit to anything."

"I know. And you're probably telling me you're still too young. I would say that I was only a bit younger than you when I got married, and I'd barely started a career myself. There's never a good or bad time to begin looking."

Murad sank into his chair and sighed. "What if I said I didn't want to meet anyone?"

"You could say it, of course – I could do nothing about that. But consider how long you want to wait. This is a way of starting a new life, and you have to start looking for that new life at some point."

He understood then what his father was saying and doing. This was his lure: marriage as the continuation of Murad's personal renewal. He had no ammunition with which to fight him, no energy for an argument. Abbu made him think that perhaps this was an opportunity to move forward and cleanse his past.

The first woman he met was in April. Her name was Asra Mirza. She was the daughter of one of his mother's cousin's friend from her days as a student at Government College in Lahore. Her family had settled in Mississauga by the time Asra was three. Murad and his parents had tea at Asra's parents' house on a Saturday afternoon. It was Asra who first greeted them at the door. She was tall, only two inches shorter than Murad, with dark brown skin and a slightly curved nose. Her bearing struck him as quietly sophisticated, polite without indicating effusive interest in anything. She directed them to her living room where her parents, sitting on their chestnut-coloured sofa, rose to say their salaams, an ornate tea trolley already present next to their coffee table bearing tea, mithai and several large samosas. Ammi became quickly engaged by Asra's mother as tea was served, who regaled her with stories of her cousin in school, their speech darting between formal Urdu and very colloquial Punjabi. Abbu's attempt to engage Asra's father, a former Army major, was noticeably less successful. Moustached, with deep, sagging bags underneath his eyes, the major had the face of someone used to stern command, with every question posed by Abbu answered with terse economy. Murad's conversation with Asra was equally awkward. Their fifteen-minute exchange of basic information on schooling ("I have a BCom") and employment ("I've been working for an insurance company since I graduated") gave way to a halting back and forth on interests ("I'm not really into books, and I don't have time for movies or TV") and places visited ("Besides Pakistan and visiting my cousins in New York, I really haven't travelled much. I'd like to go to Cuba one day"). Their respective parents posed questions of their own, largely covering the same job-interview background Asra and Murad had gone through, albeit with more enthusiasm from both of them, as if those parental interruptions were small mercies from a dialogue that ebbed more than it flowed.

On the way back home, Ammi asked him what he thought of "the girl." He hesitated for a moment, feeling mentally exhausted by even that brief meeting. Before he could say anything, Abbu, sitting in the driver's side seat, turned around to answer Ammi's question: "She's not for him."

Humaira Bhatt was the second woman his parents wanted him to meet. Abbu told Murad she was the daughter of one of his colleague's brother, who'd sent her to school in Canada upon her insistence not to do her university studies in Pakistan. Humaira was in Toronto alone, working for a research lab at one of the university hospitals. He was given her local number to arrange a one-on-one meeting with her to, in Abbu's words, "see what type of person she's like" as "I know her chachu well, but her father, I have no idea." Ammi voiced her reservations, finding the idea of Murad meeting Humaira by himself improper. "Look, if her father is like her chachu I know she's brought up in a proper khandan," countered Abbu. "We have nothing to worry about. Let them meet."

He met Humaira after work on a Friday, at a Starbucks between his office and the hospital she worked in. He was running late when he saw her, recognizable from the photo shared by Abbu, seated in one of the soft single-seat couches in the back. She was fair-skinned, with straight black hair and a face that seemed in perpetual focus. That was, at least, his initial impression as he came closer and saw her preoccupied by a text message she was aggressively punching into her phone. She greeted him with an abrupt hello as he sat in front of her, ignoring his profuse apologies for being late. Humaira leapt into conversation the moment he settled into his seat, speaking in cultivated English with a hint of an accent, peppering Murad with questions on where he worked ("a bank"), where he saw himself in five years ("It's a good question. I feel I'm too new to figure out if I want to stay in the banking industry forever"), whether he saw himself living with his parents after being married ("I can't say I've thought about that much"). He tried to respond as honestly and politely as possible, his initial nervousness at being late giving way to a generalized sense of annoyance as he felt their interaction had turned rapidly into a one-sided interview rather than a starting point for a possible rishta, a marriage proposal.

Slightly more than half an hour into the meeting, Humaira excused herself and left. Coming back home, Murad debated whether it was worth even sending a message of thanks for her taking the time to meet with him. He texted her anyway, not wanting to seem rude. He even asked her if she was interested in seeing him again, an impulse motivated less by an actual desire to speak to her further and more out of duty. After Asra, he felt the need to prove to himself that he was willing to give the women he'd meet through his parents a chance, that he had to climb over the barrier in his mind that made solitude more attractive than companionship. Ten minutes later he received a message back: "It was nice meeting you, Murad. I don't think another meeting is necessary. I'm not sure we're compatible and seeing each other wouldn't be valuable for both of us. Take care."

Murad laughed the moment he received the text. That evening at dinner, Ammi and Abbu asked about his meeting with Humaira. He told them everything, including the message. Abbu was taken aback. "I can't believe she'd be that rude and curt. Coming from that family, with those values? Complete nonsense, I tell you."

Ammi was less bewildered. "I had a feeling she'd be like that. I'm sure she's found herself a boyfriend since she came to Canada, and she was just meeting you because her father wanted her to settle down with someone decent like you."

Someone "decent." As spring turned into summer, Murad thought often of his mother's estimation of his son's "decency." Since Saskia, there were moments when he felt he'd lost his sense of respectability, and that such a loss was irretrievable. Chastity was an invaluable quality – the pure marry the pure, the impure marry the impure, according to the Qur'an, at least according to what he was taught. He wanted to bury the taint of sinfulness within him, to never admit it to anyone, especially as he was led along the path of seeing women to marry he assumed were imbued with greater moral strength than himself.

It was with that mindset that he finally met Samra Aftab early that summer. His mood was clouded the week he'd first met her. He'd been offered a slightly higher position at a different unit in the communications department, an offer he took, largely as a way of avoiding the increasing boredom he felt as a junior staffer in his existing unit, and partially to avoid Sapna, who had become uncomfortably distant in the weeks following his breakup with her friend Saskia. The challenge of learning a new job that proved far more demanding than he'd imagined strained his spirit, creating cracks that let other demons swim to the surface. Thoughts of Saskia made acute both his sense of shame and his annoyance that he should still feel ashamed of what he'd had with her. More than Saskia, Sofi dominated his soul's condition. As his parents raised the spectre of marriage again, he longed for a world where Sofi and he were together. In this fantasy, he could avoid every sit-down meeting, every awkward conversation with random women and be happy. That such a world was fundamentally absurd didn't stop Murad from longing for it.

That fantasy didn't stop Abbu from coming to his room again in July mentioning another woman he wanted him to meet. This was another connection of a connection from his father's seemingly endless professional network. The Aftab family was originally from Karachi. Samra's father worked with one of Abbu's underlings at a bank in the city years past, eventually finding a job in Kuwait at a different bank. Not wanting to go back to Pakistan, and unable to stay in the Gulf due to visa restrictions, the family had decided to settle in Canada. Samra's father contacted his friend looking for possible rishtas in the Toronto area for his eldest child, a daughter. His criteria was simple: the boy should be from a good family, traditional, a "moderate" practising Sunni Muslim (meaning, from a family that took Islam seriously without being rigidly obsessed by dogma), a non-smoker and non-drinker. Given the criteria and the connection to his father through his colleague, Murad's name rose to the front of the potential groom list. "They've invited us for tea next weekend," said Abbu. "Your mother and I can meet them first. We can make an excuse and say you're too busy."

"No," he said. "I'll come with you."

He was in no real state of mind to go. He could have said no and let his parents see the Aftab family alone. They would have come around, eventually, to have him see Samra. Out of a desire to not prolong the inevitable, he accompanied them. They lived close, no more than fifteen minutes east of their house. Hasan, Samra's younger brother, greeted them. Samra's parents, Rehan Uncle and Maha Auntie, stood behind him as if waiting endlessly for their arrival. Samra was conspicuously absent, although neither his parents nor Murad made mention of that fact as they were invited to sit in the drawing room. Hasan engaged him in polite small talk. It was only moments later that Samra entered the room. She was petite, with an olive complexion and curly hair that came down to her shoulders in ringlets. Her face widened into a broad smile when she said her salaams to everyone. Samra kept her smile when Murad instinctually rose from his seat as she came closer and sat down next to her brother. Hasan excused himself – a typical, preplanned action to allow Samra and him more time to talk and be alone. She had a soft voice and spoke with gentle, inquisitive enthusiasm as she asked him about work, school, his travels as a child and his time in London. The ease with which he could talk to her was unexpected. They were so involved in their back and forth that Murad hardly noticed Hasan coming back to sit on a chair next to the sofa where Samra sat. They still talked as Abbu and Ammi rose to leave for home, about life in the Gulf, about her childhood in Karachi and the inevitable comparisons of that city to Lahore.

His parents didn't speak about Samra until dinner the next day. Ammi asked Murad if he felt comfortable with her. He said he did. "Her mother called me," said Ammi. "They're wondering what the next steps were." He took that to mean whether he wanted to talk to Samra further. He said yes with the condition that he wanted to speak to her again, alone, without family or a brotherly chaperone to accompany us. "They may not allow that, beta," said Abbu.

"Can you insist on my behalf?"

"Why?" asked Ammi, her tone both impatient and curious.

"We already know they're from a good family. I want to know if she's a good person."

Auntie and Uncle, according to Ammi, had no objections to their daughter meeting Murad by herself. He got Samra's number through them via his mother. She seemed friendly and open to seeing him when he messaged her. They met the next weekend at a restaurant in North York. Murad came early, his nervousness elevating as the minutes came close to their meeting. She came five minutes late, walking hurriedly into the restaurant. He rose instinctively and said his salaams as she took off her jacket, sat down and apologized for her tardiness.

"Please don't worry about it," said Murad, softly, with a wave of his hand as if dismissing Samra's concern.

The gesture seemed to instantly calm her. "Thank you," she said, her voice light and airy. "I really appreciate it." She folded her jacket in half while she looked down at the floor pensively, as if thinking of the exact sequence of words to say. "I had this strange fear that if I came late, you'd leave."

He was amused. "Why did you think that?"

Her gaze rose up to see Murad. "Anxiety, I guess. I didn't want to mess up so soon."

There was a mystifying mix of vulnerability and candour that charmed Murad, even if it seemed a bit strange, as if she had taken for granted that they had already known each other for weeks.

She put her jacket on an empty side chair to her right. She wore a red blouse and business casual trousers. Samra's manner had an aura of formality and familiarity. They ordered coffee and started to chat in the gentle interrogatory style of two people attempting to gauge each other in too short a time. The conversation wasn't simply a continuation of the perfunctory, job interview-style dialogue they'd had at Samra's parents' house. She leaned forward, legs crossed, attentive to everything Murad said when they spoke of their family histories, their fathers' mutual origin in pre-Partition Uttar Pradesh, or their own mutual dislocation living in Canada since coming from abroad. "We lived in a small apartment in Kuwait," she said. "No matter how limited that life seemed – just school and that flat – I still felt freer there than I do here, sometimes." Samra spoke with deliberation, every word slow, clearly articulated. Murad could sense an ungraspable inner loneliness in Samra. Her frankness was liberating. The solitude she spoke of resonated with him. For a moment, he was taken back to London. To Sofi. He shook off the gravity of the past, leaning forward in his seat, mimicking Samra.

They spoke of the world, what they longed to see, what activities occupied their lives, their friendships. Talking to her was unexpectedly easy, and the conversation was natural, with silences free of awkwardness. In the pauses, Samra would wrap her slender fingers around her cup while her eyes wandered across the restaurant, more out of thoughtfulness than boredom. Yet despite this comfort, Murad felt weary, as if he needed to go further, trying to think of a question that would truly allow him to understand her.

"What's most important to you?" he asked.

The question, unexpected as it was, seemed not to have taken her aback. "Family and deen," she said. "Actually, faith's probably the most important thing to me, if I had to give an answer."

It felt like a standard response. "What about deen is so important to you, personally?"

Samra pondered the question. "Because it binds everything else in my life together."

Murad was struck by the answer. It was unexpected in its elegant simplicity. Samra asked him if faith was important to him as well. "Not as much as it used to be."

"How come?"

He realized he'd set himself onto a path of self-revelation he was unprepared for. "I don't think my heart feels it as much as it used to."

"Okay," said Samra, with curiosity. "But you can always feel it again. You know what the Qur'an says, that God is closer to men than their own jugular veins."

"I remember the saying."

"And the jugular vein leads to the heart, right?"

Murad laughed. "I guess that's true as well."

"The path that leads to God leads to the heart. Think about it," she said, a broad smile opening in her face.

"I'll be sure to do that."

He felt at peace when he came home. He wasn't quite sure what Samra thought of him, an uncertainty that was broken when she sent a text message, thanking him for coffee. With ease, they continued communicating by text and on the phone in the following weeks. There was rarely a sense that talking was simply an exercise in getting to know each other solely for matrimonial purposes. There were occasional questions posed by Samra that seemed slipped in from her parents, questions on whether Murad wanted to stay in banking (he said he wasn't sure) or whether he'd been in a previous relationship (he lied and said no).

At first, there were no questions raised by their parents about the aim of Murad and Samra communicating. After a few weeks, he noticed a growing impatience in Abbu and Ammi, asking him constantly whether he was still talking to Samra, if she seemed interested in him, or vice versa. He'd pushed back against those questions, saying they still needed time to know each other. There was nothing wrong with Samra – she would be anyone's ideal, he often thought. His parents were certainly enamoured of her, giving hints of their fondness. Ammi was keen to comment on her politeness and her parents' piety. Abbu noted her prettiness and gentle demeanour. Perhaps their partiality toward Samra was largely a result of their increasing closeness to her parents. Conversations between their mothers became frequent over that summer, long talks punctuated with more laughter emanating from Ammi than

Murad had ever noticed previously. Abbu talked to Rehan Uncle with less frequency, although his own observations of him were always laudatory, praising his dignified demeanour and old-fashioned khandani values.

Everything about the situation should have been ideal, but it was a shallow idealism, devoid of the emotional fever Murad realized he needed. Sofi's memory paralyzed any capability to make a decision that he knew Samra's parents – or his parents – were to pose at any minute. Perhaps his time with her in London was different, unique and incapable of being replicated. He wondered if he had never met Sofi, would it be easier to propose to Samra?

The morning of the day they were supposed to go to Zareen's wedding, Abbu and Ammi told Murad they were invited to the Aftab family's house for dinner in two weeks. "I don't think they're looking for a rishta right there," said Abbu. "But they'll be asking where this is leading."

"They might wonder if their daughter's been led on if there hasn't been a proposal," said Ammi.

Abbu made an annoyed clicking sound. "For God's sake, they're not that type of family."

"I'm not scaring him, I'm being realistic. It's different with daughters than with sons. They might not say those things to us, but they have to consider their daughter's reputation."

Abbu sighed. "Look, don't worry. But your mother has a point. This has gone on for some time. If we want to end it, let's end it. But after that dinner we should make a decision."

He thought about that decision for the rest of the day. The Aftab family would be expecting an answer. There were moments when it seemed their families had said yes on their children's behalf, and it was Murad's only job to affirm their collective hopes. And what of his hope? Sofi had been that hope – once. It seemed, as he pondered in his room alone, that she'd changed in his mind, an obstacle blocking his future rather than the future he had wanted to grasp.

One hour before they left for the wedding, before his parents started to iron their clothes and his mother brought out her jewellery, Murad came to their room. He stood in the frame of their door and said, calmly, as if announcing the completion of a chore, that he wanted to say yes to Samra and the Aftab family. He didn't want to wait for the dinner. He would give them an answer as soon as possible. His father beckoned with his hands to come inside the room. Abbu and Ammi embraced him. His mother said she would give the formal proposal over the phone to Samra's mother tomorrow.

That decision, to move forward and propose to Samra before coming to the wedding, and even thinking that Sofi could be in the same city as him, haunted Murad's thoughts throughout the function. The minute Sofi entered his sight, those thoughts vanished, as if his mind were cleansed of everything except her. She emitted an indescribable radiance: there was a joy in being close to her, in speaking with her, as if talking to his dual self. In the middle of that reverie, as he entered the dining hall, he realized how ludicrous his happiness was. This was still a woman who had rejected him, who had left him alone to wander at a Tube station years ago without even saying goodbye.

He harboured anger as much as longing, a bitterness that needed to be assuaged. That's why he needed to meet her again, even if time had slipped forward, decisions had been made and commitments needed to be honoured.

Sofi emailed the next day as promised, saying, in a slightly formal tone, how happy she was to run into Murad yesterday, asking if he still wanted to meet. He sent an email back, saying that he wanted to see her, suggesting a place near Lawrence Station the next weekend. Her next message confirming the time and place was more enthusiastic ("I can't wait to see you!!!").

He had some idea of what it would be like seeing her again. There would be questions only partially answered and past disappointments not quite healed. With all that in mind, he waited for the day, anticipating the riot of emotions he would feel.

♦

The midtown café Murad asked Sofi to meet at specialized in tea. Saskia had mentioned it once. He imagined it would be an ideal place to meet: quiet, but not too gloomy or solitary, midway between home and downtown, away from where he might run into Saskia or even Samra. He needed to be with Sofi on neutral ground, as if their meeting marked a peace accord.

It was late afternoon, windy, the streets strangely desolate. From the outside, the café had a quaint, homespun look, as if someone had lifted the facade off a small-town bed-and-breakfast and placed it in the middle of one of Toronto's more urban, decidedly chic, locations. From the inside, it looked no different than the other coffee shops and restaurants in the area: modern, with wood and plastic chairs, abstract art pieces on the walls, the entire geometry of the place limited to squares and rectangles.

Sofi was already there, sitting at a small table at the edge of the café window. A thin, bespectacled barista said hello as Murad walked past the front counter. The sun shone in patches through the window. A sharp ray of light struck him as he approached the table. His eyes shut reflexively in the same moment he heard a chair screeching and felt Sofi's arms wrap around his neck.

There was already a teapot, cups and saucers laid out on the table. "I knew you'd come exactly on time," she said, pouring a cup of tea for him with care. "So I came early and got us both a pot."

They sat, talked and drank their tea, an odd yet comfortable domesticity surrounding them. Sofi asked Murad about his life after London. He told her briefly about his job, his day-to-day life, living with his parents, and the acquaintances he had met and taken as nominal friends. He said nothing of Saskia or Samra, even as he felt behind Sofi's constant prodding a desire to see if he had a woman in his life.

Without prompting, she gave an account of her life in London. Sofi's words flowed in torrents. She was voluble and enthusiastic, as if she had been counting the days to speak to someone with this level of openness. She told him about her apartment near Shepherd's Bush, her many contracts and the stress that comes without the security of stable work, of life in the glorious yet monstrous city of London, the urban whirlpool that sucks people in, the noise, the glamour and the filth of that world. She didn't mention Ian. Her boyfriend. His face and name, blotted out of Murad's memory, surfaced in his mind as Sofi spoke. It was a subject he didn't want to broach, afraid of being overtaken by envy, despite his best efforts.

He realized he had forgotten the main reason why he had wanted to meet. Sofi's chattiness briefly subsided, and, in that pause, he told her he needed to ask her something.

"Sure," she said. "Of course. Anything."

"The night we were supposed to meet at the Tube station. In September, right before I left London. Why didn't you show up?"

Steam whispered out of the teapot. They sat in silence, Sofi stared out the window.

"I thought of not bringing it up," said Murad.

Sofi continued to stare out the window. When she didn't reply, he asked if she had forgotten about that night.

"I didn't forget," she said quietly, as if wanting no ambiguities in what she wanted to convey. "I just thought it was time to let it go." She spoke with confidence, as if laying out a logic she knew was bewildering to Murad but wholly sensible to her.

"It's not so easy for me to let go," he said. He leaned forward in his seat and continued. "I needed to see you one last time. One glimpse of you to talk, not to say how much I was hurt but just to say" – he struggled to find the words – "to say I was glad I had known you, and the time we had was like gold. That was an end to the story I could never get."

Murad felt strangely calm, staring at Sofi with the same unwavering certainty with which she now looked at him. "So you want us to let all that go?" asked Murad. "How is this a story I can just forget and leave behind?" The steam from the teapot shrank to a small thread of translucent mist. One of the young women from behind the counter passed by the table, asking if they enjoyed the tea and if they wanted something else. Sofi said nothing. He told the server they were fine for the moment, and that the tea was outstanding. A sharp pain gripped him, the pain of knowing he had hurt her mingled with the satisfaction of his unfiltered honesty.

"But that's your story, you realize?" she asked. "I have my own. I had a brother once. I loved him and cared for him almost as if I was a second mother. He died in a car accident." She stopped speaking, wiping a tear from her right eye while continuing to look directly at Murad. "When he died, he took a lot of pain with him. The type of pain that weighs down your soul. I was convinced he didn't feel the world was for him anymore. I felt that loving anybody or anything had no purpose if it all ended in nothing. But eventually I learned to love again. I learned that you don't need flesh and bones and a body to truly love, because that's how we love God. I felt that love, and that feeling was more powerful than anything that I had ever felt before."

She continued: "But when I came to London I hadn't escaped from the things I was running from. I found someone to love, or at least I thought I did. I was studying, I was in the world. And I met you. A friend, a wonderful, beautiful friend. The closer I felt to you, the closer I saw things that reminded me of my brother. That same connection between your mind and your heart. When I realized how you felt about me, once you knew I was with someone else, I wanted to protect you. The only thing I could think to do was to separate myself from you completely. I hated doing it. But I thought it was the best thing for you because it was the only way for you to forget about me."

A silence stood between them like a wall.

"That's why you didn't show up to the station," he said, more to himself than to Sofi. "To protect me."

"Yes," said Sofi.

Murad felt a labyrinthine confusion. "I don't know what to do now," he said. "I'm not sure what you want from me."

"To understand me. To forgive me. And to start over."

Gone was the sadness. Her face was full of a tenderness that paralyzed Murad in its sincerity. The days and months and years of his existence became meaningless. Suddenly, he found himself caught back up in his need for her, the power of his desire undiminished since he had left London.

♠

They paid and left the café, walking along the sidewalk as an early summer wind barrelled down the street. A recreated London, Murad thought: a different city, a different time, yet there he was again, an aimless stroll next to Sofi, with little discussion between them as they witnessed the world together. Boutiques and chain coffee shops lined each side of the street. There were few tall buildings to obstruct their view of the clear, soft-blue sky. It was always the same sky, he thought, the same in London, in Lahore and anywhere else they lived and would live.

Sofi asked him what he was thinking.

"Time," said Murad. "It's evaporating. It's slipping away from me."

"From both of us."

"I got an email," he said, "from someone I knew from high

school. He's getting married a year from now. I'm sure I'll be getting more of those messages in the next few years."

"That's the process of life," said Sofi. He looked at her and felt torn between the warmth of her face and his own bitter irritability at her optimism. "I came back to Toronto feeling everything would be different for me," she continued. "Like London cleansed me."

"It didn't?"

She shook her head. "No. My mother's doing better. So is Babba. He seems to be happy at work. That's all he does, really," said Sofi wearily. "But me? The second I came back home, I felt like time here had gone by without me, and I could smell death where nobody else could. Sometimes I feel so trapped. It's as if nothing has changed." She stopped talking for a moment. "I deserved that, maybe. I left because I wanted to forget about my brother and my family. I think God forced me back here as a kind of lesson."

She stared at Murad and asked if he was happy. "You *seem* happier," she said, observing him closely.

His parents had said the same thing when they had come back to Canada. Perhaps it was true, that he had found a measure of happiness since leaving London that was noticeable to everyone but himself. In the moment, with Sofi near him, happiness seemed irrelevant. "It's not something I think about," he said.

"I'm really glad I got to see you," she said. Her face glowed. "I needed to see you."

They were next to the subway entrance. Murad told Sofi he should be heading home. She said she felt like walking a bit more. "Do you have to go back so soon?"

"I do."

"I wanted to spend more time with you."

"Sofi," he said, trying to collect his words, "I don't know how to move on from here."

She looked at him with a strange aura of hesitancy. "I never appreciated how much you loved me in London."

"You didn't want it."

"I know. Maybe I couldn't feel it or appreciate it the way I should have. Not at the time. I can now. I made so many mistakes when I tried to love people, or when people tried to love me. It was only long after that I thought – that I realized – that maybe the world turned for us to meet in London. You were a sign I couldn't see properly."

"A sign," he said. He couldn't help but smile, despite his confusion as to what the word truly meant for both of them. "I don't think about signs anymore. I don't think about fate. I thought we were supposed to be together. I thought all the signs were there in London, and I was wrong. Because there are no signs, only choices made."

"What choice could you make now," asked Sofi, an impatient eagerness visible on her face, "if right now, you could keep walking with me?"

"None. You're giving me a choice I can't make."

"What do you mean?"

Murad told her about Samra. He didn't want to. He had wanted to avoid mentioning her, this new woman whose existence was delivered into his life in Sofi's absence. Yet he told her anyway, of having been introduced to her by his parents, of the closeness growing between their families and the pressure put on him to marry her.

Sofi looked at him with a deflated expression. "Do you love her?"

"Not now," he said. "But I could. Possibly."

"Do you still love me?"

Murad forced himself to ignore the question, pretending, to himself as much to her, that his soul had petrified in her presence.

"Could you say no to the family?" asked Sofi, pushing beyond his mute response.

He shook his head. "Next weekend, I'm going to the family's house for the engagement."

In London, in the days before he'd left the country, he had wondered if, had he known Sofi earlier, before her heart could have been given to anyone else, would they have loved each other? Could he have ended that time in their lives without feeling as if he had missed an opportunity for happiness? Time had braided a new pattern now – was it Sofi who now thought time, in its absurdity, had made her lose a similar moment? Moments ago, he dismissed Sofi's idea of destiny – but how could he admit to her that the freedom he had to say no to Samra and her family was bound by his parents' reputation and honour, along with his own?

The wind picked up. Passersby brushed against them. As they stood on the sidewalk like two twinned islands, Murad's whole being drowned in resentment. Was this part of God's destiny, that she could stand before him possessed by a love that he had forced himself to forget? Had she come back to Toronto a year or even six months earlier, would he have pushed the world away for her? Destiny was sadistic, a misaligned matrix of human lives.

"You don't want to say no," said Sofi, "even if you don't know for sure if you could love her and be happy?"

"It's a chance to be happy," he said. "There've been times since London that I've done everything I possibly could to push back against that time. Other times, I longed to be back. Because you were always there, where I could find you."

Sofi reached out and held Murad's hand.

"But I can't go back to the past."

She nodded her head as turgid tears slipped from her eyes. She let go of his hand and put her arms around his chest. He held her as she pressed her head to him. They said nothing when they let each other go. Murad walked toward the subway entrance, dazed, effervesced by the thought of being close to her, fearful of what that closeness would do to him. Nothing needed saying between them, not even a farewell, it seemed. It was only when he opened the doorway leading underground that he heard Sofi's voice calling to him, saying his name as if calling from a dream. He turned around and saw her again. "I prayed for you when I was in London," she said. "If I had all God's powers, I would give anything in the world to make you happy. I know you will be."

Before he could muster anything to say, she turned around and walked away as he stood watching her, the sound of an ambulance effacing the noise of the street. Murad closed his eyes, letting the oscillating siren noise drown the world from his mind, shuttering away the unbearable sight of losing Sofi again as he had lost her before in London, across that desiccated ocean of time that could never be reclaimed.

Murad took a few days of vacation time. He stayed at home with Abbu and Ammi, who continued with their daily routine. Abbu often fielded phone calls from Pakistan on some business matter. Ammi was largely engaged in lengthy gossip sessions with various aunties on how she saw Friend X's daughter wearing skimpy clothes at the mall the day before, or how Friend Y's daughter had recently got engaged without Friend Y telling anybody. The thought of his marriage lightened her mood in those days, her smiles and shared laughter with his father becoming more regular and sustained.

Images scrolled in his mind as the days went by, images of impossible moments never to be experienced. Sofi's hand in his own. A stroke of her cheek. A kiss on her shoulders. Skin against skin. An embrace that spanned the night and remained locked until morning. It was the same ache from the same love born amid the grey wilderness of central London.

The night after he met up with Sofi, he went to his room and stared at the walls and his book-lined shelves. On one of those shelves, he had placed the book Khala had given him in London. He took it out and randomly picked a page toward the end:

We see, in many of these poems, an outpouring of sentimentality not altogether different from the rather abject suffering often ascribed by the Roman Church to its pantheon of illustrious saints, of which St. Theresa of Avila and St. John of the Cross come to mind. As this author argues, there is a touch of the luxurious and the opulent in these works without equivalency in the writings of these or similar saints. It is quite easy to explain this effusive language as the natural sensuality essential to the character of most Mohammedan cultures. An argument needs to be made, however, that the longing of these so-called "friends of God" that these Mohammedan masters describe is of a universal quality, an Eastern version of a human yearning to be bound to the majesty of God's love. That this is a sentiment that should be held dear by devoted Christians in civilized lands should come as no great shock, as it should be of no great shock to those individuals of our own civilization who increasingly show disdain for religious truths. Even the European non-believer blessed by the bounties offered by an all-too-human romantic love can see the parallel between his own expanded heart and the emotional intensity of these saints whose lives and experiences exist in realms far different from his own.

He flipped through the pages again, picking another poem at random:

Let sad longing live in your heart,
Never give up, never abandon hope.
The Beloved says, "The broken are My dear ones."
Smash your heart and be broken.
– Abu-Saeed Abil-Kheir

Murad closed the book and placed it on his bedside table with great care, treating the fraying yellowed pages with reverence. In the past, such poems would have left him enraptured, speaking a language that whispered straight into his core self. He looked around at the walls of his room, the room he slept in, the room he used to worship in, where he stood outside of time in every moment of prostration while the world spun around him. *God the Beloved loves the broken-hearted*, he thought, *maybe as a way of bringing his worshippers closer to Him*. Perhaps this longing worked between people as well. Perhaps the love he had – the love he may always have – was better felt at a distance.

❖

The next morning, before breakfast, Murad went to the back lawn, opening the door from the kitchen that led to the deck. He sat on a metal chair that was already showing signs of rust. The grass was clipped. Winds shook the trees that bordered the house. The day was clear and unblemished save for a few lone clouds gliding across the sea-blue sky.

The door creaked. Abbu ambled outside wearing a crisply ironed, all-white shalwar kameez. They said their salaams. He came to Murad and placed his arm around his neck playfully, kissing the top of his head. "What are you going to do with your final vacation days, young man?" he asked, patting Murad's arm before sitting in the chair beside him.

"I'm not sure."

"Ya rabbil 'alamin," he said, an exhalation as much as it was an appeal to the Lord of all Worlds. "Just rest, beta," he said. His eyes lingered on his son's face, looking him up and down with a combination of love and pity. "With work and Samra, I know you have a lot to think about."

The door to the kitchen opened again. Ammi came out to the deck. She was dressed in a light-coloured shalwar kameez, her translucent dupatta properly draped around her neck, looking strangely formal for such a lazy morning. Her hands were clasped together; as she walked closer to Murad, he could hear her reciting

Surah An-Nas above the sound of chirping sparrows. She approached him and finished her recitation, blowing on the side of his face three times.

"Aray, are you worried that a jinn spoiled his plan today?" asked Abbu with a laugh. "No," said Ammi. "I just want my son protected." She kissed the top of his head and placed her hand on his shoulder. He held her hand there, feeling its softness. What she wanted to protect him against she didn't say. Life, Murad supposed.

Ammi had cooked a late breakfast inside. Aloo ki bhujia and scrambled eggs. Abbu joked that he had to judge between his cooking and his mother's. They laughed, even Ammi. Abbu rose slowly, and he and Ammi went back inside. When they noticed Murad was still seated, Ammi called to him. He turned his head and saw his parents standing on each side of the door, waiting for him to join them.

"I'll be there in a few minutes," he said.

Abbu placed his right foot across the threshold. "Let him be," he said to Ammi. "He'll be in when he's ready."

It was warmer than he expected for this time of the year. Perhaps the world had changed, and global weather patterns had been irreparably altered. Murad perceived the heat differently as a child. The summers in Pakistan were unbearable when they used to visit, but so was late June in Canada. Before the liberation of the last day of school, he would spend recess with the other children caught in the languor of the sun. Between the mindless joy of baseball and water pistols sprayed at each other and the knowledge that part of the summer would be spent in boredom while the heat bore down on them, he secretly wished for a quick return to the routine of school. Now there was no need to desire routine, as routine grabbed one the moment that adulthood landed. Time flows quicker with each year, a widening funnel that allows more minutes, hours and years to pour out.

His summers in Pakistan had been solitary. Often in spare

moments, when there were few cousins to play with, and adult discussions turned to the politics of the day or gossip around weddings, he was allowed to run off by himself in one of his grandfather's five gardens. He would walk along the perimeter of the smallest garden, surrounded by the rose bushes that outlined its circumference. Monsoon rains heightened the smell of the soil and made the sun even more intense and dizzying. He imagined a world where the sun was somehow different than that which hung over his school friends back in Canada, as if they all lived on alien planets orbiting their own unique stars.

It was the same sun, of course, then as it was now. It shone on him as he sat on his deck as it would shine on Sofi in whatever city she found herself. His mother blessed him that morning, and he felt the need to do the same for Sofi – no, not *for* her but rather *to* her, a blessing born of gratitude. *Thank you for your existence, Sofi*, he thought. *For your beauty, for the devotion I could see in you only too late. Forgive me for the hurt I created, the injuries I caused. Grant me the ability to love you from afar, as that is the only way I can possibly love you now. That love is stronger anyway, the love that distance creates, like the love saints have looking up toward Heaven.*

The mangni, the engagement ceremony, would happen in only days. He would come with his parents, sweets in hand, to their house before the celebrations would start with the sounds of women beating a dholki on the floor of their living room. This would be the start of the future destined from birth, the future he convinced himself would bring a happiness never to wane.

He rose from his chair and walked to the kitchen door. Inside would be food and family. Before he entered the house, he took one last look upward. More clouds floated past the still-blue sky, a sign, perhaps, that the world still turned in unknowable directions. And of what use was it to know the direction? He asked himself this as he went inside, accepting the mystery of this spinning life.

PART 4
SOFI

All lovers are now alone with their beloved, and now I am alone with thee.
– Rabia al-Basri, quoted in *Aphorisms of the Mohammedan Saints*

1

The boy looked at Sofi with teary exhaustion. He was called "Meedo," a play on Hamid, a name his parents had chosen after months of mutual negotiation. The day in Meedo's mind must have been wearying and tortuously long, Sofi thought. She understood his tears and the crankiness that exasperated his mother, Fatima. When he cried to Fatima that he wanted to go home, it was Sofi who agreed to take him across to the Square to get him the junior-sized cone from the ice cream man. She knelt down and wiped Meedo's tears as the man delivered the cone directly to his hand. He squeezed her hand as they walked back across the bottlenecked intersection to a tired but grateful Fatima, who thanked her cousin for sparing her a few minutes of tantrum-time. Sofi didn't mind, of course. She loved the time spent with her cousin and nephew. It was those small acts of love that energized her, that gave colour to her time with her family.

They were downtown together to shop for a birthday present for Fatima's husband, Parvez. He was a doctor, bearded and older than Fatima, with a kindness and spiritual modesty that displayed itself by his soft voice and retiring manner when speaking with women other than his wife, Sofi included. She was fond of Parvez regardless – it was Fatima and Parvez's wedding that had brought her mother and aunt together again, where the discomfort of their previous rupture was slowly overcome. During the shaadi, Sofi would circle around them periodically to observe their interaction. Holding hands; brief, trumpeting peals of laughter. Perhaps it was time that had moved them to bridge over their past rifts, or out of the sense that age made discord and stubbornness tiring that Sofi felt they had reached a turning point in their relationship, a tacit understanding made at the wedding that they would restart their sisterhood in whatever small ways they could.

She returned to her apartment in the evening. She received a text from Fatima saying she had invited both their mothers to Parvez's birthday party. The thought pleased her – she wanted as many opportunities for Mama to be with Khala as possible. An idea flashed within her to ask Fatima to invite her father. She thought better of it: her parents had been good lately, talking with some regularity while maintaining a distance. Babba was coming closer to retirement, and with the slow end of his professional life, Sofi noticed him withdrawing deeper into himself, losing interest in the world. Memory took the place that work once did, memories of his past, of his divorce, of Sikander. Sofi did her own part to alleviate the cocoon of sadness her father had placed himself in. She had dinner with him whenever the opportunity arose, meals passed in tender wordlessness, evenings ending with Babba listening to his ghazals on his now-archaic CD player. When his eyes wandered in the space of his apartment, she'd hold his hand as they sat together on the sofa, the warmth of her palm bridging him into the present world.

Sofi never felt lonely herself. Fatima had asked her once, months ago, whether she'd considered getting married. She would shrug off the question, avoiding the subject as if she had been asked to excavate a past best left buried. In truth, she wasn't sure why she hadn't. In those spare moments when she reflected on it, it seemed that being by herself was a comfortable destiny to which her heart had acquiesced. Opportunities for companionship presented themselves to her on occasion. Fatima once suggested she could help set her up to meet men from her "community," a suggestion Sofi dismissed, good-natured as it was. She knew she wasn't meant for those men, men like Parvez, reserved and pious. At a certain point, she was unsure whether she was meant for any men. She was aware that male admiration, the spotlight that followed her throughout her younger years, dimmed only slightly as life passed on. Those subtle cues of desire and attraction became less lustrous for reasons that took long for her to discover. Some men stood out. Talal, a Palestinian lawyer years older than her, was the first man after Murad who drew her out of herself. Dynamic, handsome, he also suffered from a gentle melancholy that came across as self-absorption to others. Sofi felt she had the ability to know him in a way others couldn't, a way of appreciating his capacity for abstraction as thoughtfulness and intelligence. It was only months into their relationship that his egocentrism was made plain – his control over her time, his casual dismissals of her wishes – that she knew she had to end it.

Dylan was the second, a fellow teacher, a few years younger than her, a colleague of a colleague who taught intermediate children at a North York elementary school. He pursued Sofi with shy tentativeness. She was touched by that quality in Dylan, a trait that came across as sincere and almost innocent. Their relationship was warm but chaste. He touched her face one night after they'd seen a movie. His hand lingered on her cheek, the look in his eyes warm and full of needfulness. Sofi realized in her heart that she couldn't reciprocate that need. She placed her hand on his, drawing it down gently. They mutually agreed to stop seeing each other, a decision that was logical but still painful for her. She wept in a way that shocked her in its intensity, not for the loss of Dylan so much but at the perception that her heart had frozen over, that she was no longer capable of love. Within days, however, she let go of her attachment for Dylan, devoid of any will to move onto someone else to fill the void of his absence. The lack of desire shook her until she realized that desire was unnecessary. She soon realized that the ease with which she got over Dylan and Talal and everyone else was due to the acknowledgement of solitude's liberation. The saints, the friends of God, she knew, were solitary creatures too. What better way to get closer to God than to shut her eyes to the yearnings of this world as they did?

♠

She worked a streetcar hop and a ten-minute subway ride to school where she taught second graders in the east end. Sofi had tried various jobs after she'd come back to Canada – after she'd last seen Murad. She worked briefly for the government and in various non-profits, seeking, with some frustration, a fully contained life. All these occupations wasted her energy, she felt, being so far removed from the vague longing for purpose she found difficult to articulate. Beneficence, a direct relationship with human wounds, was what she needed. She contemplated working internationally as her intention had always been, but it was home, the warm trap of Mama and Babba and family that drew her to remain in Toronto. Where once she sought assiduously to run away from family, she was now its preserver, the one responsible for solidifying the connection between her relations' disparate segments.

Becoming a teacher seemed like a logical vocational step. Years ago, she came across a quote that to trust in God is to be like a child who knows his mother is always aware of his condition even if he never calls for her. God the parent, God the maternal, God the protective veil. It was children she knew needed protecting the most. She had been Sikander's protector when he was alive – it was therefore only natural that she should once again go to school, get her education degree and find her calling close to home.

The first Friday of the new school year was enervating. The summer heat still lingered, and students and teachers alike adjusted to their new schedule poorly. Sofi went to the mailroom before she left for home. Among several memos and a letter from a parent of a former bullied student thanking her for her kindness the previous school year was a small package. Thick and heavy, it had an unknown return address without the sender's name. Her initial wariness faded after realizing quickly from its shape that it was likely a book. Curiosity overtook her; she dropped the package in her handbag. She opened it as soon as she came into her apartment, a dull red cover emerging, the title *Aphorisms of the Mohammedan Saints* written in gold lettering. The inside cover bore an inscription:

> *Sofi – my prayers are few. My supplications are weak. In those seldom moments I spend my time praying, for all those who have come into my life, know that your name always comes to the surface, wishing you all the happiness in the world, just as you wanted for me all those years past.*
> *Murad*
>
> *P.S. Page 54.*

Stunned, Sofi turned to the page. A poem, highlighted and partially underlined in pencil shone from the text:

> *O God,*
> *How can I remember, when I am entirely remembrance?*
> *I have thrown in the wind the reaping of my own signs,*
> *How can I remember the One I could never forget?*
> *– Anṣārī*

♦

She did her chores before she said her evening prayer, thinking of Murad, thinking of how and why this artifact of her soul's history had been excavated. She'd been careful not to put too many personal details online. Perhaps somewhere in the reaches of cyberspace, her name had emerged, some association with a former student, teacher or volunteer organization easily made for Murad to have sleuthed an address with which to send the book.

The "why" of his sending the book she soon tired of. There was no "why" beyond the fate that none of God's creation knew. Perhaps the memory of her had been rekindled somehow in Murad's mind, a random glimpse of Sofi caught from afar without her knowing. There were too many possibilities, too many opportunities for chance encounters. She only knew now, somewhere in the city, that he lived and breathed, that her image was still embedded within him, even as the flood of years uprooted so many other memories.

The week would begin on Monday, the routine of lesson plans and children let loose in the burning days of late summer. The pinkish blush of the sky gave way to darkness. In the dim lamplight of her living room, she skimmed through the book. Sofi felt tired, her eyes glancing over words. She placed the book on the table, staring at the cover, thinking of its provenance, the last hands bending its now weary spine belonging to Murad. It was her only reminder of him – she had no pictures, no other memento of their connection. Only words, words ancient but vibrant, that spoke to his past yearnings. Did he yearn for her still? She wondered that as she went to her room and prepared for sleep, remembering the last moments they had seen each other. The hurt of her own unfulfilled hopes for Murad lingered too long in the weeks and months after that day. Sofi learned to accept what fate had plainly decreed for them both. On her bed, warmed only by the torpor of the day that seeped into the night, she longed for Murad, not for his love or presence but for his heart's peace, that he would find comfort in that same night, cloaked in both his wife's warmth and God's shade.

Sofi's classroom was a bright mess of pastel construction paper affixed to bare white walls. Her children's sense of disquiet in their seats became palpable as the hours trudged on. They had enough awareness of time as seven- and eight-year-olds to know the tragedy of their entrapment indoors, and the joys to be held under the sun. Sofi understood their predicament, more amused than frustrated when they laughed uncontrollably at another student's jokes, or when her simple math questions were met by silence. Even when she scolded any of her brood, it was never out of impatience – her chiding always took the form of disappointment, that of a mother expecting more from her children than a tyrant demanding obedience. The little ones' drooped faces touched her with both guilt for making them feel ashamed, and a deep affection for the bond she was convinced she had created with them.

During recess, she ran into two of the senior teachers in the East Wing hallway, Mr. King, who taught grade five, and Ms. Ng, who taught the joint seven and eight intermediate students. Ms. Ng asked Sofi if she was ready to quit the day already. "Or quit for good," laughed Mr. King.

"Not at all," she replied with more earnestness than the question likely warranted. "I'll miss them too much." She pointed to a group of Mrs. Kraft's grade three children being fiercely persuaded by their teacher to go outside to play. Both Ng and King teased her supposed youth, and lack of jadedness, jokes Sofi was familiar with as most of the staff assumed her vigour in teaching was the result of her being five years younger than she actually was.

They left her indoors as they exited through the twin push-bar doors outside to monitor the children. Sofi walked to the end of the hallway. She was drawn to the main foyer, where the sun dripped off the greenness of the ferns guarding the main entrance. Thoughts flittered within her, gaining traction with the emptiness of the foyer, thoughts of children, of her brother Sikander, a child of her own, of sorts. As she walked aimlessly with crossed arms, she recalled the quote she had reread in Murad's red book the previous night, thoughts that had led to Murad himself. For years she had been weighed down by the tragedies of her life, of her parents divorcing, of Sikander passing, of Murad slipping away. With Murad, she no longer saw any tragedy in their relationship, how quickly they had accelerated away from each other like two vehicles speeding along the same avenue.

Minutes passed. Recess would end soon. Sofi walked back to her classroom, still caught in the reverie of her thoughts. Between the teacher's lounge and her room, she heard whimpers from the passageway leading to the intermediate section. Sitting with his back to the wall was a boy, a kindergartener or slightly older, sandy-blond hair, head buried in his knees. Sofi knew him – she knew many of the children outside her own homeroom. His name was Ivan. She remembered seeing him around school, mostly in the morning, speaking to his young, slim, nervous-looking mother in Russian around the first bell. He struck Sofi as fundamentally solitary, a sensitive boy who'd grow to be a sensitive old soul.

Sofi crouched down next to Ivan. He raised his head to look at her. She pulled him gently toward her, placing her arm around his shoulder and her cheek on his head. The bell would ring soon, and she would have to let him go to class. In that final minute, before the hallways would be flooded with children, before Ivan lifted himself to the harrowing, lonely day, he would stay safe with Sofi. This was her calling, she would think at that moment. A spiritual calling, God's own vocation, the protective veil over His children both small and aged. She marvelled at how far she had come in accepting all that had occurred, how much the pieces of her past had wounded and softened her heart. Of all those shards from her memory, the glint of Murad shone brightly that moment as the bell rang, its metal woodpecker sound rattling along the walls. Sofi whispered in Ivan's ear, telling him to go to class as they both lifted themselves from the cold floor. She walked back to her classroom, thinking of the gifts of her past, gifts like Murad that allowed her to expand her heart. She would continue her prayers for Murad, she promised herself, praying that the mercies of existence would illuminate his every step, as she wished for everyone who passed through this life and this world.

ACKNOWLEDGEMENTS

Bismillahir Rahmanir Raheem

Writers never work in complete solitude. It would be difficult for a novelist to document everyone who made their novel possible and, with that caveat, I ask for advanced forgiveness should I have omitted the names of anyone who I owe my gratitude.

I would like to thank the staff of Buckrider Books/Wolsak & Wynn (Paul Vermeersch, Noelle Allen, Mahak Jain, Ashley Hisson and Jen Rawlinson) for quite literally making this publication possible. In the course of writing *Drinking the Ocean*, I have had the pleasure of working with many writers, editors and mentors in the development of the manuscript. These include Ibi Kaslik, Dennis Bock, Janice Zawerbny, Pat Kennedy, Alexandra Leggat, Aeman Ansari, Ann Y. K. Choi and many others. Some of the first readers of my manuscript were students at the University of Toronto's School of Continuing Studies' Creative Writing program. These include many of my "Friends on the Eleventh Floor," who never failed to pick me up in the moments when my enthusiasm for the writing process faltered. I would be remiss if I did not recognize Lee Gowan's directorship of the program for helping provide such a warm and supportive environment for aspiring authors. A special note of thanks must also go to Tali Voron-Leiderman, whose personal championship of my writing has been invaluable.

While the book *Aphorisms of the Mohammedan Saints* is fictional, the mystics quoted in it are real. Those sages who have given the world the beauty of their words deserve the utmost praise. Minor literary license has been made in the rendering of their poetry in this manuscript. If I have committed any spiritual error in the representation of this sacred art, those mistakes are mine and mine alone. At an artistic and emotional level, I am also forever indebted to the many academics, old and contemporary, who have translated these sages for the English-speaking world. These include R.A. Nicholson (particularly his book *Translations of Eastern Poetry and Prose*, published in 1922), A.G. Ravân Farhâdi (with reference to his translation of Abdullāh Anṣārī's work in *Abdullāh Anṣārī of Herāt (1006–1089 CE): An Early Ṣūfi Master)*, Vraje Abramian (specifically his translation of Shaikh Abil-Kheir's poems in *Nobody, Son of Nobody)*, William Chittick and countless other august scholars whose names have been locked inside my memory through years of voracious reading. Their scholarship has had a direct inspiration in the genesis of this novel. In my own small way, I hope I have honoured their efforts.

Drinking the Ocean is, among other things, my attempt to examine the many varieties of love we as humans can experience. In my darker days, where the world seemed bleak and less than loving, I have had to remind myself of the many family members and friends who have demonstrated their love for me in ways I will always be grateful for. I hope I can be given the opportunity to repay that affection in the fullness of time. Ultimately, my greatest worldly thanks must go to my siblings (Aisha Khan and Emad Khan) and my parents (Omar Khan and Fauzia Khan) for teaching me in word and in action what love and devotion truly is. Life is too limited in the years I would need to reciprocate what gifts of the heart you have bestowed.

Allah ta'ala aap ko apni hifazat mai rakhe.

SAAD OMAR KHAN was born in the United Arab Emirates to Pakistani parents and lived in the Philippines, Hong Kong and South Korea before immigrating to Canada. He is a graduate of the University of Toronto and the London School of Economics and has completed a certificate in Creative Writing from the School of Continuing Studies (University of Toronto) where he was a finalist for the Random House Creative Writing Award (2010 and 2011) and for the Marina Nemat Award (2012). In 2019, he was longlisted for the Guernica Prize for Literary Fiction. His short fiction has appeared in *Best Canadian Stories 2025* and other publications.